PRAISE FOR "BROKEN HOPE"

"Rubin's revenge thriller is fast-paced and full of plenty of unexpected twists and turns…a true page-turner"

— *KIRKUS REVIEWS*

"This brilliantly clever, thought-provoking plot will keep the reader engaged from start to finish."

— *READERS' FAVORITE*

"clever cat-and-mouse games…highly recommended"

— D. DONOVAN, SENIOR REVIEWER, *MIDWEST BOOK REVIEW*

PRAISE FOR "FATAL ROUNDS"

"Rubin makes the most out of an uber-creepy premise in this superior medical thriller"

— *Publishers Weekly* (starred review)

"A knockout that's just what the doctor ordered for thriller enthusiasts."

— *Kirkus Reviews*

"A brisk, page-turning read."

— Rachel Howzell Hall, *New York Times* bestselling author

PRAISE FOR "FRACTURED OAK" (PEN NAME DANNIE BOYD)

"Uniquely original and a fascinating read from cover to cover...deftly blends mystery, suspense, and magical realism."

— *Midwest Book Review*

"a lyrical, inventive detective novel"

— *Akron Beacon Journal*

"Two remarkable heroes enliven this absorbing crime story."

— *Kirkus Reviews*

BROKEN HOPE

BROKEN HOPE

CARRIE RUBIN

INDIGO DOT PRESS

Indigo Dot Press
indigodotpress@gmail.com

First edition, 2024

Library of Congress Control Number: 2024906427

FIC031080 FICTION / Thrillers / Psychological
FIC031040 FICTION / Thrillers / Medical
FIC030000 FICTION / Thrillers / Suspense

ISBN 978-1-958160-07-7 (trade paperback)
ISBN 978-1-958160-08-4 (ebook)
ISBN 978-1-958160-09-1 (audiobook)

Cover design by Tea Jagodic (www.teajagodic.com)

To humanity. We've got this. Right?...

PROLOGUE
TWENTY MONTHS AGO

The old woman hobbled into her Boston row house and hurried to her husband in the living room. Although the threat was gone, her body still trembled. She hugged her purse to her chest and eased herself onto the sofa, struggling to find the words.

Noting her distress, her spouse of fifty-nine years floundered for the TV remote and silenced the Seinfeld rerun. Had his Parkinson's allowed, he would have leaped from his recliner and rushed to her.

"What is it, my dear?"

"Our doctor," she managed to say. "Dr. Hope Sullivan. She saved my life today."

Her husband relaxed. Hyperbole, that was all. "She saves our lives every day. Or at least the medicines she prescribes do."

"No. She truly saved my life. I was mugged."

This time the husband did rise—stiffly, tremulously. "My God, are you all right?" He shuffled to the couch and lowered himself down.

The wife unclenched her vise-like grip on her purse. "The

fellow didn't get anything. Tried to. Grabbed my bag right off my arm and ran."

"I don't understand. You have your purse."

"I was in the alley behind Hal's Bakery when he snatched it."

Her husband frowned. "I've told you not to go there. Shortcut or not, it's too deserted."

"That's when Dr. Sullivan made an appearance. Our very own doctor, jogging by at the moment he ripped my handbag away. At first, she and I just stared at each other. She was as shocked to see me as I was her. I thought I was hallucinating."

"Did she call the police? Is that how you got your purse back?"

His wife uttered a strangled laugh and shook her head. "After Dr. Sullivan's surprise wore off, she got mad, really mad. I've never seen such a fierce look on her face. She sprinted off after the man."

The husband's mouth dropped open. "No, our Dr. Sullivan? That woman is the gentlest creature I've ever met."

The wife sank deeper into the sofa. The act of telling the story and knowing she was safe at home dissolved some of her anxiety. "Gentle she is, but not today. She rammed right into the man—he wasn't much bigger than her—and tussled him for my handbag."

"No!" the husband repeated.

"Yes. I could hardly believe my eyes. My doctor, wrestling with a purse thief on the ground. I worried she would get killed, or at the very least, end up in the hospital. I yelled for help, but no one was around. My phone was in my bag."

The husband rested a shaky hand on his wife's. "But she got your purse back."

"She got my purse back. That awful man got away, though."

The couple stared at the family photographs on the wall, each lost in their own thoughts.

Finally, the wife said, "We called the police. Told them what happened, described the fellow. I doubt they'll find him. Besides, I have my handbag, so is there even a crime?"

"Of course there's a crime. He can't go around stealing purses."

The wife shrugged. "Dr. Sullivan was really kind. Handled the police for me, ran back to the bakery to get me some water. I was too rattled to do much of anything."

"That's our Dr. Sullivan. The same woman who checked in on me every day when I was laid up with influenza."

"After the police left, she walked me home. She changed, though."

"Changed? What do you mean *changed?*"

"She got nervous. No, not nervous. Restless. Agitated, even."

"Well, I should think I would be too after a purse-snatching."

"It was more than that. I've always said she has a sadness to her. Those grieving eyes."

"Maybe," the husband replied, "but you're better at picking up on those things than I am."

"To be honest, her behavior concerned me. She kept muttering about all the terrible people in the world. That it wasn't right so many of them got away with it. That someone should do something."

"She's not wrong."

"Well, sure, but I told her we can't have a bunch of vigilantes running around."

"Not unless they're Liam Neeson. He has a very particular set of skills."

The wife chuckled but then sobered again. "After I made the remark about vigilantes, Dr. Sullivan got quiet. The rest of the way home she ruminated on something."

"You should have invited her in. That was a brave thing she did for you."

"I did. I mentioned you'd want to thank her too, but she said she had to leave. She had a look in her eye."

"What kind of look?"

"A determined look. A fiery look. In fact, there was more life in those sad eyes than I've seen since we started going to her as patients."

"Probably just the excitement of the ordeal."

The wife hesitated. "Yes, probably so."

She remained bothered, though, and not at all convinced.

Those fiery eyes had worried her.

1

PRESENT DAY

As a doctor, I don't enjoy deliberately inflicting pain. My stomach twists, and my body stiffens as if trying to tell me, *This isn't who you are.* But during my thirty-five years of life as Hope Sullivan in this human cesspool of a world, I have come to believe, strongly, that sometimes the brutes, the bullies, the assholes out there need a little mental reshaping. A cognitive tune-up, if you will.

Tonight, the bare-chested wife beater tethered to a chair in the middle of my barn is in particular need of a tune-up, his wrists cinched behind his back with duct tape, ankles bound to the wooden legs, forehead strapped against the high seat back. His gray eyes shoot bullets at me, and his neck veins bulge, but he's nothing but an oppressive abuser, one who hides behind an Armani suit and a Bvlgari briefcase and stinks of an after-work Scotch.

Slowly, I approach him. A pair of pliers rests in my palm, the steel cool against my hot flesh. My hands shake, and sweat beads on my temples, but despite eighteen months of this macabre pastime, I can't shut these physiologic responses down.

The wife beater stares at the pliers and falls silent. His

muteness won't last, I'm sure, but I'll savor it while I can because ever since the sedative wore off, he's been cursing and yammering as if he's the one who has been abused every day for the past several years. First it was all, "Look, lady, you've made a mistake. I don't know who you think I am, but you've got the wrong guy."

Then, after a smack to his face, which was necessary to make my point, he was all, "I'll kill you, you psycho. I'll kill you."

Sure enough, as soon as I kneel in front of him, the pliers inches from his left nipple, his temporary silence ends.

"You stupid whore," he hisses. "You'll never get away with this."

He didn't call me a whore when I picked him up at the bar a few hours ago. On the contrary, he seemed more than eager for a night of extramarital fun. Too bad for him he's getting the exact opposite.

"With talk like that," I say through heavily painted lips, "how can the ladies resist you?"

Thick eyeliner and false lashes add to my camouflage, as does a long auburn wig which hides my chestnut, chin-length bob. The slinky dress I wore when I seduced him out of the bar and into my SUV has been replaced with cargo pants and a fleece hoodie.

I spread the jaws of the pliers and place them on his chest. Hopefully, with his head taped back against the chair, he can't see my trembling.

"I'll kill you," he seethes again.

I squeeze the pliers, not too hard—I don't have it in me to be that person—but enough to make him know I'm not messing around.

His obscenities ricochet around the empty barn. On my private piece of Massachusetts land, there is no one around for miles to hear him. Only the nesting birds on the roof that flutter away in alarm. He tries to squirm away from me, but not an inch of his body is mobile beneath the heavy tape. All he manages to do is nearly topple the chair over.

I catch him in time, my biceps straining against the load. Realigning the pliers, I squeeze his pec once more, not because I enjoy it, but because he did the same thing to his wife.

I know because I saw her in clinic. She's been a patient of mine for three years.

She has never confessed to his beatings. There is always an excuse of a fall, an open cupboard, a slip on their too-slick stairs. But I'm not blind. I know what the bruises and markings of domestic abuse look like. And the damage he did to her breast? The jagged cuts and gashes, all because he thought she was having an affair with her pastor, a man she had sought out purely for counseling (at least from what I'd surmised)? Well, that can't go unanswered.

He's back to his initial pleading. "I mean it. I'm not the guy you're looking for. You have to believe me."

I stare at the crimson tissue the skin around his nipple has become. "Now you know how your wife felt when you took your man-sized tweezers to her breast."

Or whatever it was he used. Once again, his wife wouldn't cop to the abuse. Gave me some flimsy story about getting cut by a wayward underwire from her bra.

Yeah, right.

I open and close the pliers in my hand. "My tool is a bit more primitive than yours was, but you get the gist."

The mention of his wife silences him. Nothing but the heavy breaths of a fearful man in pain follow. Even the hair follicles on his groomed chest prickle with anxiety. Or maybe it's anger. Judging by his searing stare, if he were free of his binds he would try to shred me to pieces. With his hands, with the pliers, with whatever he could find.

"How do you know my wife?" he asks. "You can't be her friend. She doesn't have any." He narrows his eyes and studies me, as if trying to figure out who I am. Even without my disguise he wouldn't recognize me. He is too important to accompany his wife to a doctor's visit.

"She doesn't have friends," I say, "because you control her every move."

I lean over and rummage through my duffel bag on the dirt floor. Aside from two lantern flashlights, which illuminate the barn nicely, the bag is the only object inside the old outbuilding beyond the wife beater's chair and the green tarp I rolled and dragged his sedated body in on.

The abuser's degrading name-calling starts up again, everything from the B word to the C word, but as soon as I pull the knife from my bag, those nasty words pinch off in his throat and tighten into a squeak. His eyes grow wide. He tries to shift the chair backward but manages only a few scrapes over the straw-littered ground.

Approaching him, I run the shiny blade over my palm. I'm still sticky with nervous adrenaline, but I imagine he's too scared to notice. I press the sharp tip of the knife against his neck. His yips become whimpers become begging.

"Please, please, I'll do anything you say."

"Anything?" Leaning close to his face, I drag the blade across his cheek, lightly enough to avoid drawing blood.

"Yes, anything!" His eyes dart back and forth in a downward direction, as if trying to follow the knife's path.

"One, you're going to admit you beat your wife."

"Yes, yes, I admit it," he sobs. "I'm sorry. She just makes me so irritated. She always—"

"Two, you're going to apologize to her." I step back and angle my head. "Honestly? If it were me? I'd report you and get you locked up in a place where *you're* the punching bag." I wink. "Or maybe something worse. How would you like that?"

Before he can respond, I rush back to him. His restrained body jerks as a whole. I poke the knife's tip under his chin. A drop of blood drips down the blade, but I don't worry about injuring him too deeply. I know where the major arteries are, and they aren't there.

"For some reason, your wife insists she still loves you. Says she'll deny everything if I report you." I harden my voice and pull the knife back. "But it has to stop. Got it?"

His expression is that of a toddler who promises to be good. If he could move his head, he would probably nod enthusiastically like one, too, anything to show his sincerity. Unfortunately, like a wise parent, I suspect that promise will be broken. With men like him it often is.

My made-up face shifts closer to his. "Because if it doesn't, if you don't stop controlling her, belittling her, speaking with your fists and your tweezers, I'll—"

A rustling outside the door cuts me off. A creaking follows.

I burst up and spin around toward the barn's entrance. My sudden alarm probably reveals my own nerves, reducing me in his eyes, but I can't help it. If someone were to find me here with a man taped to a chair, blood dripping from his chin, it would be all over for me. While I could deal with that —I'm pretty much done with this world, anyway—I would hate for my extracurricular activities to leave a stain on my colleagues or my patients. They don't deserve that, and that is not the way I want to go out.

The door creaks again. The bottom of it shifts. Although a crossbar dropped over the frame locks it, the wood—especially near the base—is rotting, just like all the other old boards in the place.

I hold my breath and grip the knife. My captive seizes the moment and starts hollering for help. I worry I'll have to silence him for good with my blade, but that can't be who I am.

How could someone find me here? Through an opaque but legit LLC, I own acres of this hilly land, accessed merely by a dirt road that has been canopied by trees over the years.

An old horse ranch, I believe. Maybe an apple orchard too. I don't remember. Agriculture wasn't what I had in mind when I bought it.

The base of the decaying door pushes inward. A heaving groan follows.

Just as I'm furiously plotting how to silence a witness on top of my prey (I'll need what's left of the sedative to drag the wife beater back to my Highlander), a cat pushes its head through a gap near the bottom, lifting the wood from the dirt floor, and scampers into the barn.

My relief is so swift it's physical, and I stumble forward. The cat, who appears to be part Maine Coon, albeit a petite one, with matted gray-black fur and a demure mew, slinks toward me, slowly at first and then quickly, weaving a path between my legs.

I squat down and stroke her under the chin. Burrs tangle her long tail, and abrasions cover patches of flesh where the hair has torn away. She smells of soil and stress.

"Aww, what's a pretty girl like you doing all the way out here?" I check her undercarriage to make sure I've chosen the right pronoun. "You hungry? Is that why you're so friendly?"

"Jesus Christ," Mr. Richy Rich Wife Beater says. His cries for help ceased the moment his only hope of rescue proved to be feline. "That thing could have rabies. You're crazy, you know that?"

I don't dispute either.

"And to think I almost pissed my pants over you." He snorts. "You're as weak as my wife. Just dressed up in tough-girl clothes, carrying big-boy weapons. When this is over, I'm going to grab you by the throat and teach you a—"

I spring up and hurtle toward him. The knife blade is back under his chin. "No," I spit out. "What you're *going* to do is leave your wife alone. Got that?"

Before he can answer, I stab the blade into his thigh, right through his creased Armani pants and into the muscular quads beneath them. Not deeply. Less than half an inch for sure, but he howls as if I've amputated his entire limb, maybe as much from surprise as pain. Not aware I was about to do that, I surprised even myself. Maybe I *am* becoming that person.

I yank the blade out and hustle behind his chair. I tilt it back. Blood blossoms to the size of a silver dollar on his slate-gray pants. No gushing because, again, no big artery.

His sobbing pleas return, his emotions as unstable as the angled position I've placed him in. His weight in the chair is heavy against my torso. The cat is back at my feet, meowing as if in approval, as if she, too, recognizes an asshole when she smells one.

With my mouth next to the wife beater's ear, my breath reeking of tension, I press the knife against his throbbing neck and say, "I'll be watching you. Following you. Stalking you. Even when you have no idea I'm there, I'll be there, and if you ever, *ever* so much as touch your wife again in any way that hurts her, I'll kill you."

I let my words sink in, my blade close against his flesh. His nose runs, and his chin quivers.

"And don't even think of mentioning this little…exchange to anyone."

Finally, I release him. It's obvious from his wild eyes and stricken mouth he believes me, but convincing him took longer than I expected. Better late than never, I suppose. I may not have made him piss his pants, but I definitely slapped the cocky out of his smirk.

After wiping the knife clean with a disinfecting wipe from my duffel bag, I dump it back in and grab a loaded syringe from the side pocket. I jab the needle into his arm. While I wait for him to conk out, I scoop up the cat. The fact she lets me pick her up proves how starved for food and attention she must be.

Knowing I shouldn't but unable to leave her out here by

herself, I rub her smelly, scabbed neck and say, "No worries, girl. I'll take you home."

What am I going to do with a cat? Especially since I might not be gracing the world's filthy presence much longer?

I shrug and gather my things.

That's a question for another day.

2

———

The morning traffic belches its way down Boston's Congress Street, and pedestrians stream around me on the sidewalk. Some are Bostonians heading to work. Others are tourists getting an early start on a day of sightseeing. The forecast of June sunshine and a high of seventy-eight degrees promises to make it a good one.

Crossing my fingers for a manageable patient schedule, I enter the nine-story granite building that houses my clinic. Since joining the staff of Congress Medical Clinic as a general internist four years ago, my patient load has snowballed. I'm grateful, but some days can be overwhelming. Congestive heart failure, chronic hypertension, diabetes—many jammed into fifteen-minute time slots in order to accommodate the volume of patients who wish to be seen. At least the work hours are better than my three years of residency training at Boston General, along with an additional year as chief resident.

What the Congress Medical Clinic lacks in creative naming, it makes up for in its proximity to my waterfront loft. Depending on how well I time the lights at the crosswalks, it's a twenty-minute jaunt at most, and the stroll over Evelyn

Moakley Bridge with its view of Boston Harbor and the downtown skyscrapers puts a little thrill in my espadrilles, one of the few things that still does.

Just inside the building's entrance, I stop for my usual hazelnut blend from the lobby's beverage kiosk. Monday is the judgmental barista's day off. Good. Seeing her four days a week is enough.

With coffee in hand, along with a leather tote bag slung over one shoulder and my workout bag over the other, I take the elevator to the fourth floor. A glance in its foxed mirrors reveals that my cropped pants and jeweled-necked blouse are already wrinkled.

Blowing at the heat rising from the lid's sip hole, I enter our glass-fronted waiting room, its ecru confines currently free of patients, and its magazines and patient fliers still orderly in their metal stands against the walls. From behind the reception counter, Alice Yun, our full-time RN, studies the computer screen with our young receptionist.

Spotting me, Alice rounds the desk, disappears into the hallway that leads to the exam rooms, and opens the inner door before I reach it. "Your schedule is overbooked. Had to squeeze a couple in. Sorry."

With my free hand, I reach into my tote bag and hand Alice a Mike's Pastry box. Inside are three cannoli, her favorite. "For staying late with me on Friday," I say. "I bought them yesterday, but they should still be fresh."

Her eyes light up beneath her stylish frames. "I'd eat them even if they were a year old."

"You'd be on the toilet for a week if you did."

She laughs and tries to break the seal on the white box. Setting my coffee on the front desk, I slip off my black paracord bracelet and unclasp the one-inch blade it hides.

Alice's hands fall still on the pastry box. "Whoa, I wouldn't have pegged you as the type to have such an...interesting accessory."

"It's not super pretty," I say, slicing through the tape and freeing the cannoli inside, "but it comes in handy for times like these."

After a few more pleasantries, I retreat to my workstation. At least two of my physician colleagues have arrived. I hear them rather than see them because each of us doctors is tucked away in a cubicle, five in total and scattered throughout the maze of exam rooms.

From what my ears tell me, Dr. Frank Goldberg, the man who started the clinic over thirty years ago but will soon be retiring, is down the hallway past the treatment room and to the left. He's chatting with Bo Linton, an energetic internist who's been doing locum-tenens work for us while Dr. Rishi Ganesh, another one of my colleagues, fights a battle with multiple sclerosis and only intermittently sees patients as a result.

Although I appreciate Bo Linton helping out during Rishi's absences, I've come to realize I don't much like him. On paper he's good. His training is impeccable, and he's spent the last three years working sporadic locum-tenens jobs so he can afford to do humanitarian work the rest of the time. Yet something seems off. Maybe it's because he came to see me as a patient a while back, and my professional world intersected with the personal. Or maybe it's because I don't like the way he looks at me, as if I'm an insect under his magnifying glass.

Likely it's my imagination. Lately everything seems off.

I power up my laptop and click open the Electronic Medical Records. Alice wasn't kidding about my schedule. Twenty-four patients, three more than I'm comfortable seeing in one day, and even that's pushing it.

My heart quickens when I spot the abused wife's name among my morning patients. It's been nearly two weeks since I drugged her husband and lugged him to my barn, his blood since cleared from the dirt floor and traces of his presence wiped from my Highlander (which, if not for my adrenaline and determination, I might not have been able to heft him back into). Not that it matters. He has no idea who I am. They never do. But it's still best to be careful.

I've spied on him a couple of times since. Watched him come and go from his office building a few miles away, fancy briefcase in manicured hand but gait less cocky and eyes casting furtive looks over his shoulder. I can't keep constant vigil on him, of course, no more than I can on any of my tune-ups. It's only important they *think* I am.

His wife is never far from my mind as I work through the morning patients: a rasping man with COPD, a wincing woman with shingles, an octogenarian transported from the free clinic where I volunteer my assistance one Saturday a month. Today the eighty-year-old's angina is so severe he should have gone directly to the emergency department, but according to the center's proxy, he insisted on only seeing "Dr. Hope."

Hope. My own name makes me sad. After everything I've lost, I no longer have much of it.

A three-minute window while Alice rooms a patient allows me a quick email check on my phone. I find two medical newsletters, an Amazon shipping confirmation, and the agenda for an upcoming HOA meeting. My inbox has plenty of spam emails too.

One of them catches my eye. I know what ur doing, it says.

No subject line. No link. Just that single sentence.

I ponder the message. One of those webcam threats maybe? The ones that claim to have caught us masturbating and promise to release the video to our contacts if we don't pay up?

I grunt. *Threaten away.* Not only is my laptop's camera covered with a small Post-It note, masturbation is a thing of the past. Like everything else in my life, it's lost its joy.

Alice exits the exam room and stirs me from my thoughts. She announces my next patient is ready.

The wife beater's wife.

I place my phone on the counter and grab my laptop. My shoulders tense over what I might find.

———

When I enter the room, the abused woman smiles broadly. It's the first time I've seen it reach her eyes. Sitting in a contented posture on the exam table, she smooths her too-large gown over her slender thighs and looks as though she hasn't a care in the world.

As I proceed through the appointment, which is a follow-up of her splenic hematoma, an internal wound we both know didn't come from a fall off her bike as she claimed but rather from the vicious punch of a cruel husband, I check more skin under her gown than is necessary. My neck muscles relax when I see no new bruises. No new scratches either or man-sized tweezer carvings. Though I have no reason to examine her breasts today, and her bra remains on, I'll have to assume by her giddy demeanor that Mr. Richy Rich Wife Beater has heeded my warning. At least for now.

Regardless, just as I do every time she comes in, I offer resources for domestic abuse. She assures me none are needed, and—here's another surprise—for once she doesn't deny the abuse.

"He's changed completely," she says, releasing a thick plait of hair trapped in the neck of her gown. "He apologized for his past…anger. Begged me to forgive him and promised it'll never happen again."

"And you believe him?"

"I do." She lowers her voice. "He was attacked two weeks ago. A mugger stabbed him in the leg. Cut his chest and neck too."

A mugger. *Right.* At least he kept his mouth shut about me.

Not that he's the type of guy who'd ever admit to being bested by a woman.

My patient shakes her head and adds, "He said it gave him a new outlook on life. He wants to be a new man, a better man, and I think he means it this time. He's even started going to church with me."

I suspect this might be a mountain of crap, but given her buoyant mood, as if still in shock over her good fortune, she clearly believes him.

"Well, you know I'm only a call away," I say. And I am. She's one of the patients who has carte blanche to my personal number.

Although I share none of her optimism that the beatings won't return, my spirit lifts nonetheless. This is why I do what I do. Why I make people pay for their wicked acts. If I'm lucky, she'll develop enough confidence during this honeymoon period of good behavior to leave him the moment his violent nature slithers back out of its snake hole.

During my lunch break, which is more of a five-minute pause to inhale a granola bar and have a quick pee, Dr. Terrence Williams stops by my workstation. He wears his usual skull-themed tie and holds a Tupperware container in his hands. At forty-two, he's closest to my age and was hired at the practice a couple of years before me. Like me, he did his residency training at Boston General. Unlike me, he's writing a spy novel and is convinced Idris Elba will star in it one day.

"Whoa, if you stuff that bar into your mouth any faster I'm going to be giving you the Heimlich." Terrence lifts the Tupperware lid. "Here. You get first pick since it's your patient who dropped them off."

I swallow a wad of crumbly granola and stare at the frosted cupcakes. "Ada again?"

Terrence nods.

Ada Jackson. The sweetest woman in the world and my favorite patient. A seventy-one-year-old retired teacher whose husband died last year from sepsis, sending her into a spiral of grief that's been the source of a number of clinic appointments with me.

I choose a white cupcake with pink frosting and a raspberry on top and put it on my counter for later. "I've told her she shouldn't bring gifts, that it's not appropriate, but she keeps doing it anyway."

"It's a cupcake, not a pharma-funded trip to Tahiti. Damn. Don't you wish the two of us had started practicing before they made those bribes unethical?"

We both laugh because we know he's teasing. Terrence is one of the most scrupulous doctors I've met. He's also the colleague I'm closest to here, and his wife, along with his eighteen-year-old daughter, who has sickle cell trait, are my patients. Each of us doctors at Congress Medical has a disease-area focus of interest, the enhanced knowledge in a particular subject aiding the team as a whole. Mine is in hematology.

"What's today's affirmation?" Terrence asks.

"Oh come on, really? I have patients to see."

"Check your phone app, Sullivan. I'm going to crack your cynicism if it kills me."

"And a daily affirmation is going to do that?"

"No, but it might make your glass half-full every once in a while."

I shake my head and grab my phone. "It says: *I don't need to be perfect.*"

Terrence spreads his arms. "See? It doesn't get more life changing than that."

I wave him off, and as we get back to work and the afternoon wears on, a lethargy takes root in me. So many people with so many problems, physical and emotional, some no fault of their own, others contributing to their ailments—not following treatment, not exercising, not putting proper nutrition into their mouths. I want to help all of them, cure them, fill their thoughts with puppies and rainbows, balloons and sunshine, but I can't. I am only one person, and the fact I can do so little sinks me deeper into my funk.

My last patient of the day, an empty-nest homemaker with an Etsy craft shop, is a lingerer. I finished her exam and relayed my thoughts on her gallbladder disease ten minutes ago, but she's still chatting away. That's okay. I use the opportunity to catch up on my electronic notes, nodding and murmuring at the appropriate times. Some people just need to talk, and like my favorite patient, Ada, this woman is lonely. She tells me her husband recently transferred to an office outside of Boston, and they now live "in the middle of nowhere."

"Should I give you the name of someone closer?" I ask. "Congress Medical is a long way for you to drive."

"Oh no, Doctor. You're well worth the trip."

Her words warm me, and I savor the feeling before it dissolves.

When she goes back to chatting, I return to the EMR, but moments later my typing slows. What's that she's telling me? About a neighbor?

"There are only a few houses where we live," she says, "and everyone else is gone during the day so no one else complains, but I hear that poor thing whimper. My neighbor doesn't get home from work—or boozing, or whatever he's doing—until at least seven. The dog doesn't bark much, just whimpers. All day long my neighbor leaves that poor German shepherd chained to a pole outside. Sometimes at night, too. I'm not even sure the animal has enough water."

I face my patient now, heat creeping up my spine, a different heat from the warmth her earlier praise gave me. I think of my new cat—Diva, I've named her—and what I might do if somebody hurt her. "Your neighbor?" I ask, clenching my hands.

"Yes, he's an awful man. Rude, calls me a witch, told me to

eff off when I threatened to call the police if he didn't take better care of his dog."

"That's terrible." Scenarios run through my mind. Turning back toward the EMR, I click open my patient's demographic page and find her address.

"I called the police anyway," she says. "Not that it did much good. What could they do? It's not like the dog barks loudly, just that sad whimper. They talked to my neighbor, and a day or two passed with the dog in the house. But then one day the jerk came home late, and the dog must have soiled in the house because…" My patient's lips quiver. "He kicked the dog out the door. I was outside and witnessed it, and now I can't get that yelp out of my head. He saw me standing there and told me if I call the police again, he'll hang the dog in my yard."

I swivel my chair toward her so abruptly it lifts off one of its legs. "Do you think he'd really do that?" I calculate her address's distance from my barn. Picture the old flagpole on the property. Wonder where I could get a sturdy chain.

She nods, and her tone grows even more fearful. "I have no doubt he would. At this point, I think the only reason he keeps the dog is to spite me."

I wonder how much her neighbor weighs. How much sedative it would take to transport him. How much height he has on my five-foot-seven frame. Drugging and lugging always comes down to logistics.

My heat grows to a flame as I realize I've found my next tune-up. These last couple of years, it's as close to passion as I get.

3

Inside the back room of a smelly makeshift gym in downtown Boston, my athletic tank top sticks to my torso, and sweat drips off my forehead. I assume the defender role. I prefer being the attacker, but as a woman my defense skills need to be equally strong, if not stronger.

My "attacker," a man with the body habitus of a Rockem Sockem robot and the personality of one too, comes at me with a high roundhouse kick. After six rounds of miscalculating my defensive counterattack, I finally nail the timing: a simple front kick to his groin before his foot smacks my jaw like it has the previous six times. If not for my face-saving headgear, I'd have an eggplant for a nose and a jigsaw puzzle for a jaw.

We don't mess around in Krav Maga class.

Judging by my opponent's grunt and failure to complete his roundhouse, I've landed my foot in his goods. He, too, is likely appreciating his protective armor, particularly around his groin.

We practice this attack-defend move a few more times, and although it seems to me that in a real-world setting no mugger or rapist is going to wallop me with a roundhouse kick, it's good to perfect my timing. We then move on to me trying—flailing?—to escape from an advanced choke hold. My faux attacker wields limbs of lead while I seem to wield nothing but trembling straw.

After class, our instructor, a survivalist with a cowlick, congratulates me on my progress and says I'll be a green belt in no time. I'm not so sure about that. I've been stuck at orange—the third level—for a while. But given I started the class only seventeen months ago, after an early tune-up gone wrong resulted in me nearly losing a tooth, I accept my instructor's warm fuzzy. We don't actually get awarded physical belts—it's only a certificate—but tomato, tomahto.

Ten minutes later, weary from my long day of patients followed by the ass-kicking martial arts class, I wince my way home, workout bag and leather tote slung over opposite shoulders. A trio of coffee-sipping tourists in matching T-shirts gives me the stink eye, or maybe they're simply repelled by *my* stink, but I smile at them and limp onward. Even at seven thirty in the evening, the summer humidity clings to my flesh.

When I enter the air-conditioned lobby of my high-rise condo in the Seaport District, I sigh in cool relief. After a nod to our doorman, Tony, I step into the elevator. Ten floors up, a glass of wine calls my name. *Soon*, I tell it, *soon*.

Having a loft, even a mere nine-hundred-square-foot one, on the tenth floor with a waterfront view is a luxury I don't deserve. I know this. Even my more-established colleagues can't pull off such a mortgage, not with Congress Medical's overhead and the often poor reimbursement we receive. But if giving up my loft meant getting back the people I lost, I'd gladly live in a box on the street.

The elevator dings open.

I'm only a short corridor away from that glass of wine.

I make it halfway when—

Uh oh.

My neighbor, Nathan Holt, peers out from his doorway

across from mine. Has he been standing there, waiting for the elevator bell to ding so he could catch me before I dart into my own unit? It wouldn't be the first time. He seems to know my schedule better than me.

For the sake of modesty, I pull a lightweight hoodie out of my workout bag and slip it on over my sweaty tank top. Finding a smile, I say hello. "The powers that be must have taken your advice. I see the broken tile in the lobby got replaced today."

He pats his thinning hair. "It was high risk. Someone could've tripped and broken a leg."

"We're lucky to have an actuary in the building."

He angles his head, as if trying to decide whether I'm poking fun at his occupation. When I reach my own door, he steps all the way into the hallway. "I can't turn it off. I'll be assessing risk until the day I die. Speaking of…" He rolls up his sleeve and thrusts his arm at me. "Does this look okay to you?"

In the two and a half years I've lived here, I've seen more of Nathan's skin than any neighbor should ever be asked to, but I set my two bags on the floor and frown in the contemplative concern he expects from me. Taking his elbow and raising his upper arm, I peer at the red papule that's sprouted on the flesh over his deltoid.

"Oh, that's nothing to worry about," I say. "Just a cherry angioma, a little vascular growth."

"You sure?" He pinches it. "I don't need to see a dermatologist then? Get it removed in case it's cancer?"

"I'm positive. It's tiny and not bleeding or irritated, so no treatment is needed."

"How did I get it?"

I smile. "These things pop up as we age."

"Okay, good. That's good. I turned forty-five two days ago."

"Happy birthday!"

"Each year ups my chances of a heart attack. We both know that risk. Do you think I should get an echocardiogram, just to be sure? Maybe a stress test?"

As if he were one of my patients—and I suppose here in our hallway he is—I offer my most reassuring voice. "Look at you: you're thin, you eat well, I've seen you in the building's gym. Plus, you've mentioned before that you have no family history of early heart disease. Trust me, Nathan, your risk is low."

He sighs in relief. This is what he needed to hear. "Thanks, Doctor. I'm sorry to be such a pain." His eyes turn sad behind his wire-rimmed glasses. "I try not to obsess so much, but it's a real challenge for me. I'm the guy who wore a mask in crowded places *before* the pandemic."

I give his shoulder a squeeze. "You're not a pain. You're just attentive to your body."

"Exactly."

We part ways, and I finally unlock my door and enter my unit.

I smell Diva before I see her. Or rather, I smell her cat barf, my patchouli air freshener not potent enough to cover the scent. Guess that means it's fresh. I go in search of the icky gift, striding past my sterile white kitchen into the tiny living room. The mess is easy to spot, just next to the floor-to-ceiling windows, beyond which a collection of boats sway in Boston Harbor.

At least this time Diva retched on the hardwood floor and not the area rug. Two nights ago my foot sank into a pile of rank ooze that had soaked into the carpet's white fibers.

"Here, kitty kitty," I call.

To my surprise, she sashays out of the lone bedroom to greet me, perhaps having finished another form of business in the en suite bathroom's litter box. She weaves around my feet, mewing softly. I scoop her up and nuzzle my face into her now-clean fur.

She's beautiful. Long haired, a mixture of black, gray, and white. Piercing eyes. Soft, full tail.

"Poor baby. Tummy still upset?" I cluck my tongue in sympathy. "It's okay. You're home now. *Mi casa es su casa.*"

Like a dog, she licks my cheek with a rough tongue.

"I knew we'd be a good fit," I tell her, the two of us heading off to my tiny laundry room in pursuit of paper towels and a disinfectant cleaner.

Shortly after I brought her home from my barn two weeks ago, I took her to the vet. Dr. Zale assured me Diva was fit and healthy but hadn't been spayed. She also had no microchip. Given the matted and excoriated state I found her in and how far away she was from any homes, previous ownership seemed doubtful. Or maybe I just preferred thinking that. After what took place in my barn, I couldn't exactly post *Cat Found* signs in the area.

Instead, I got her vaccinated and took away her ability to reproduce (*poor girl*). Aside from the urping, which a call to Dr. Zale confirmed might be a lingering effect of the anesthesia from the spaying or simply adjusting to a new home, Diva seems happy to be here. She ought to be, considering all the gourmet food and cat paraphernalia I've bought for her.

As I wipe the feline vomit off my glossy hardwood, an internal voice questions my choice. *What were you thinking? A cat? Especially with that bottle of pills in your bedroom?*

Tossing the soiled paper towels into the trash, I picture the mixture of opioids tucked away in my black lacquer nightstand, right next to my mother's silk scarf, my father's reading glasses, and the last book my fiancé ever read. Those sleep-inducing pills are my crutch. Or, perhaps more accurately, my exit door. A gateway into nothingness for when nothingness is all I want.

That day is coming. I feel its nearness. Sense its indifference. Indeed, my apathy's cloak is now a full body bag. All that remains is to zip it closed.

A long shower mutes some of my moroseness, and once the detritus of the day is washed off, I slip into loose-fitting lounge pants and a T-shirt. Back in the kitchen, I pour a glass of white wine, fill a bowl with pretzels, and then settle onto my cream-colored sofa. Diva joins me, but only after I make her promise not to barf on it. Dinner for both of us can wait.

When I grab the remote off the glass coffee table and click on the TV to a news station, I soon wish I hadn't. A video clip from a school board meeting flashes on the screen. Parents fight, shout obscenities. One man even throws a punch.

During sips of wine and crunches of pretzels, I stroke Diva's fur. "Think what they're role modeling for their poor kids," I tell her.

The next segment covers a politician outed for a long history of sexual harassment. I mutter another grunt of exasperation to my cat.

We continue like this for a while, me grumbling about the state of the world, the cat putting up with it in exchange for a full body rub. After a while, I can't take it anymore. I stab the power button on the remote with my index finger and silence the TV.

I should know better than to watch the news. Whatever positive energy the shower gave me deflates like an enema bag.

Exhaling hot air, I check another affirmation on my phone. Terrence would be proud.

I will only dwell on things that bring me joy.

The irony just makes me grumpier.

I grind my teeth and stare out the window at the darkening sky, pretzel crumbs dotting my shirt, Diva purring on my lap. My stainless-steel fridge hums in the background, and an occasional siren bleats from ten stories below. When the relaxed buzz of alcohol finally numbs my despair, I shift the cat from my thighs to the sofa cushion and retrieve my laptop from the small Atticus desk near the window. Curling back up on the couch, I open the computer and force myself not to sign into the patient portal.

"When you're home, you need to be home," Frank, our clinic head, often tells me. "Your patients can spare you for a few hours, and if they can't, that's what the on-call doctor is for."

I click open my email account instead, not having checked it since my fleeting respite in between clinic patients this morning. A string of new messages pops up. I sort through them, and once finished I return to my browser and connect to Google Maps. Before I type in the address, I hesitate, my fingertips hovering over the keyboard.

Should I? When I'm finally relaxed and numb?

I probably shouldn't.

I do it anyway. I type in my patient's address, the one whose neighbor abuses his German shepherd. Earlier, in the exam room while she was telling me the sad story, I studied her demographics page and burned her address into my brain.

Google Maps confirms she lives a distance from Boston in a less-populated area, just as she said. Street View shows only a few homes, partially shielded from each other by trees. I zoom in on the split-level closest to hers. Is this the one harboring a barbarian? The home's shoddy upkeep and junky yard, at least the part visible on Google Maps, suggest it is. Unsurprisingly, the front and side views reveal no pole or stake to tether a dog. It would most likely be in the back, which is a view Google Maps doesn't offer.

I toggle over to the yellow ranch home on the other side of my patient's house. The image is so clear it's as if I'm standing on the street myself, and as always I marvel at the lack of privacy the digital age has unleashed—but also at the gifts it offers someone like me.

The yellow house looks too far away from my patient's to be the one. It's doubtful she'd hear a whimpering dog from that distance. Plus, she mentioned she witnessed her brutish neighbor boot the German shepherd out the door, and, although I'm stereotyping, this one seems too tidy of a home. The tended flower boxes and pruned landscaping don't fit the profile of a dog abuser.

I swing back to the split-level with the junky yard. "Pretty sure we've got a Bingo match," I murmur to Diva.

With my body heat rising and my molecules tingling, I close out Google Maps. My screen returns to my inbox, and my brain starts weaving the web of a plan, the taste of revenge on my tongue.

"Oh, Diva," I say, stroking the cat, "the things I could do to this awful man. I could—"

A new email pops up in my inbox. The subject line reads: **Ignoring me?** I click it open and find only a single line: **First do no harm.** As I read the words, my muscles tense. I reach for my wine glass but find it empty.

Is the email spam? It has to be. And yet the reference to the ethical principle of medicine seems personal, as if the person knows my profession.

My gaze shoots to the sender's email address. Something about it seems familiar.

I stare out the window, trying to recall what it is. Then I remember. The email I received earlier in clinic, the one I assumed was a scammer blackmailing me over a nonexistent masturbation video caught on my webcam.

My fingers tap my keyboard. Next to me, Diva stops purring, as if sensing my growing apprehension. She jumps off the couch and swishes off to the kitchen.

"You'll be disappointed," I call out, barely cognizant of my words, too focused on opening my spam folder and searching for the email message I condemned there earlier. "I haven't fed you yet."

There it is. The email from this morning that I assumed

was spam. No subject line, just a body that says: I know what ur doing.

Tonight's message is from the same email address: *iseeyou1003@bxmail.com*. When I glanced at it earlier today, its significance didn't register. But it does now.

I see you.

1003.

The walls of my loft shrink in on me. My condo's number is 1003. The same number in the email address.

Coincidence. It has to be.

Because the alternative is too awful to ponder.

4

Shortly after 5:00 a.m. the next morning, I jog along the Boston Harborwalk. Sunrise is still a few minutes away, and the pier is mostly deserted. Just a singular jogger here and there.

Another half hour's wait would have been smart—plenty of people out and about by five thirty or six—but my fragmented sleep left me restless and on edge, and a whirring treadmill in the building's gym won't cut it. I don't have to be at the clinic until eight. That gives me plenty of time to run through the Seaport District to Charlestown and back, most of it along the waterfront.

The wooden planks thump beneath my Nikes, and the wind, still crisp at this hour, bites through my zipped hoodie. On my right, Massachusetts Bay breaks angrily against the docks, and the gathering seagulls squawk in protest.

As I watch them swoop down, their webbed feet landing on the boardwalk, something scrapes behind me. I look over my shoulder, but no one's there. Up ahead, a jogger stretches his quads, and I'm relieved to spot another person.

Despite my best efforts to find my zen and enjoy the

morning air, yesterday's strange emails repeat in a constant loop in my mind.

I know what ur doing.

First do no harm.

And that email address: *iseeyou1003@bxmail.com*.

It all seems so personal.

An email account could be traced, couldn't it? But if the sender used a public computer, like at a library, and a burner phone to verify the email account, any attempt at identification might be pointless. Plus, if he—or she—truly knows what I've been doing in my barn, they would be confident I won't scurry off to the authorities to report them. Not when it would bring unwanted attention my way.

A figure darts in my peripheral vision. A glance to the glass building on my left reveals only a cluster of thin trees and a nearby bike share. With growing unease, I increase my pace. At least the man who was stretching his quads moments earlier has started jogging. If I maintain his pace, he'll serve as a safety net. A second ago, he looked back at me, but his face was nothing but shadows in the predawn light.

Who sent those emails?

Who could know of my…after-hours interest? My land is remote, the barn far from prying eyes or ears, the old house that initially occupied the property long since burned down. Between my salary and what my mother and father left me, she an investment banker and he a science professor, I was able to pay cash for the place.

And what, exactly, is the emailer's motive? Blackmail seems the most likely, an ugly game that could go on forever, but the alternative—exposure—is unthinkable. My professional reputation is the only thing I have left. Besides my new cat, that is.

Mr. Richy Rich Wife Beater surfaces in my mind. I replay squeezing his chest with a pliers and stabbing him in the thigh. Vicious moves even for me. Is he my email stalker?

No. The look in his eye when I brought the knife down was pure terror. Seeing me again is the last thing he wants.

What about the cheating husband I exposed eight months ago, the one who got rough with his conquests? I treated one of those women in clinic for a torn perineum. I'd arranged for his wife to show up at the hotel he'd booked for us. I texted her the location from his phone while he was in the bathroom and then stalled him off with three whiskey sours. After enough time passed, I cracked open the room's door. He was too drunk to notice and too busy drooling all over me, pinching me through my clingy dress and slapping my ass, asking me if I could feel how hard he was, how much he wanted me. When his wife stormed in and saw her husband lusting over another woman, grenades exploded from her eyeballs.

I hightailed it out of there and left him to her wrath. Judging by the howling and cursing that carried down the hallway, she was no shrinking violet like my patient is. She screamed she was going to kick his nuts to the curb and take all her money with her. She was tired of supporting his "waste of space as a man."

So yeah, there's little doubt he would love to blast some revenge my way.

But I was well-disguised. I even spoke with a French accent, my year in the Peace Corps after high school improving my linguistic ability, so it seems impossible he discovered my identity and has now decided to stalk me.

In the breaking daylight, the jogger up ahead looks over his shoulder once more. He wears a knit cap, and his running jacket is zipped high to his chin. His ongoing presence reassures me. There is safety in numbers.

With sweat trickling down my spine, my mind wanders back to my first tune-up, a woman in Target eighteen months ago. Inexperienced and green in the way of vigilantism, I acted impulsively, something I no longer do. My sessions now take place in the barn. But at the time, the woman's actions infuriated me, and nothing silences my grief better than revenge. It's that rush of satisfaction I get from knowing that at least *someone* is paying for their crime.

The woman in Target was forcing her daughter, who was maybe eight or nine years old, to shoplift, having her slip things into the large tote bag slung over the woman's shoulder. It was clear the child didn't want to. The fear and confusion on her face were easy to read, and I doubted it was the first time she'd been ordered to steal.

Angered by what I was witnessing, I grabbed a hat and sunglasses from the accessories department and made my way toward them. While pretending to run into the woman, I plucked her wallet from her gaping purse propped up on the cart and slipped it into my coat pocket.

"What're you blind or something?" the woman snapped at me when I bumped into her.

After apologizing for my clumsiness, I notified security about the thefts. While a plainclothes guard confronted the mother, I retreated to the bathroom with her wallet and took a picture of her driver's license and credit cards, my fingers shaking like an octogenarian's. I couldn't believe what I was doing. I was terrified I'd get caught. When I finished, I turned the wallet in at the customer-service counter. Told them someone had dropped it near the toilet. Then I bolted out of there.

A week later, wearing a disguise of a blond wig, heavy makeup, and a padded suit from a costume shop under my clothes to boost my size-six frame to a size fourteen, I drove to the address printed on her driver's license and waited for her to get home. A knife filled my hand, and my knees bounced in anxiety against the steering wheel. Yet I felt an unfamiliar thrill of excitement too.

When she pulled into the driveway, I confirmed she was alone and then wormed my way into her Volkswagen Jetta with a flimsy excuse. Once in the passenger seat, I held the knife to her neck and demanded she stop forcing her daughter to steal.

I wasn't going to use the weapon, of course I wasn't. Not only was I a novice back then, the punishment wouldn't have fit the crime. But the sharp blade served as a good deterrent, and I reveled in the adrenaline rush it gave me. Nothing but pure electricity coursed through my blood.

I lied to the woman and told her I had access to her bank accounts. I swore I'd drain every one of them if she ever mistreated her daughter again. The mother's freaked-out expression suggested she very much believed me, and I'd be surprised if she reverted back to her old ways after I left. I'd also be surprised if she's the source of the mysterious emails.

But what about the guy—

Another scrape and movement to my left. Like before I see nothing. Just a building under construction. Up ahead lies the bridge to Charlestown, and I'm now on the sidewalk instead of the boardwalk. Even though foot traffic in the area has picked up, the street I'm jogging along remains deserted.

The runner is no longer in front of me.

Where did he go?

Thinking I should head back to the safety of my loft—I've jogged over two miles now—I turn around and quicken my stride.

Before I make it ten feet, someone pulls me off the side-walk and yanks me over a two-foot construction barrier in front of a brick building.

I land hard on all fours on the concrete. Pain shoots through my kneecaps, and the cement rips my Lycra leggings. When I cry out, a hand covers my mouth. It tastes like metal and grime, and the person behind me reeks of body odor.

I bite down on the sour-tasting flesh. My attacker yelps but doesn't release me, just forces my body all the way flat on the rough pavement. Beyond the construction barricades, cars pass by, but from our low position the drivers won't be able to see us.

Restrained on my stomach, I jerk my head back to see if my assailant is the runner who was in front of me, but all I catch is blondish hair before he smashes my face into the ground. Tiny pebbles of concrete rip into my cheek.

Blond hair. No knit cap. Not my runner.

Lying on top of me, the attacker grabs at my leggings. Given my forced prone position, I feel this rather than see it. Whether he's pulling my jogging pants down to assault me or to search for money, I don't know. He could be desperate for either. Maybe he's desperate for both.

But there's one thing I know that he doesn't.

I know myself.

I know what I'm capable of.

I stop resisting. My body falls limp. Using his surprise at my sudden laxity, his breath hot on the back of my neck, I crack my head back and aim for whatever part of him hovers behind my skull. Given the growing traffic, I hear nothing but car engines, but when his hold on me loosens, I assume I've struck something tender. A nose. A throat. Maybe an ear.

Under his weakened grasp, I free my arm, reach behind me, and squeeze his balls through the crotch of what feels like cotton chinos. This time I do hear a cry, and when he rolls off me, maybe realizing I'm far too much trouble, I leap up and kick his face while he's down.

His lip splits from the blow of my sneaker, and blood pools out. His nose, too, is bleeding, probably the recipient of my earlier head butt. He curls into the fetal position. Although this appears to be a sign of surrender, I'm tempted to give him a punch to the throat just in case. In Krav Maga, they teach you to fight dirty. It's a woman's best defense, and it's a skill a woman with my pastime needs. But my assailant looks so wasted and pathetic, his face bleeding, his clothes tattered and stained, that I stop short. As quickly as my fight-or-flight adrenaline surged when he jumped me, my empathy sends it packing.

Maybe he really did just want money. Hoping for a twenty, a ten, anything to get him what he needs. Booze? Drugs? Simply food and shelter?

I believe I have a good sense for people—Terrence, my colleague, calls me the character whisperer—and although I might be dead wrong about my attacker's intentions, I'm convinced he's not my mysterious emailer. Nor is he the jogger in front of me who seemed to vanish into the waterfront air. No knit hat. No jogging clothes.

Slowing my labored breaths, I dig into the hidden pocket of my legging's waistband and pull out a twenty-dollar bill. Its purpose was to buy a breakfast sandwich after my run, but this disheveled man appears to need it more than me.

I drop it on the ground next to him, wishing I had more to offer. Then I hop over the construction barrier that hid us and limp off. I think about reporting the attack—know that I should—but until I learn what my online stalker wants, any police attention my way seems unwise.

As I hobble away, my heart still pounds faster than it should. My throat still threatens to close off. My nerves still jitter.

But that's okay.

It's nice to at least feel something.

5

HIM

He grinds his teeth and crumples up the overdue rent bill, its threat of eviction one more kick to his already KO'd soul.

People like her never own up, he thinks. *They destroy lives and go on living their own without a shred of remorse.*

He tosses the wadded bill across the basement apartment, aiming for one of the crusted and stinking takeout containers on the kitchen counter. It bounces off the sink instead, inside of which dishes pile high like Jenga blocks.

She's the one who should be paying my goddamn bills.

He thinks about his life. How it has spiraled down the toilet of his mildewed bathroom for the past six years. Hers, meanwhile, soars higher. Waterfront loft, respected medical practice, patients who think she's Jesus reincarnated.

He visited her clinic once. Scheduled an appointment for his alternating bouts of diarrhea and constipation, which were sometimes so bad he worried he'd never shit normally again. He could barely take a walk after eating a meal without buckling over in a cramping spasm.

She diagnosed irritable bowel syndrome, mixed type— IBS-M per his printed checkout summary. Gave him a full bag of medication samples and spent an extra fifteen minutes counseling on nutritional changes so he wouldn't have to fork over money he didn't have for a dietitian.

"This should save you some cost, at least," she said, smiling, both her chair and her attention swiveled toward him instead of her laptop.

Good bedside manner or not, he hated her. And okay, the treatment helped a lot. So what? Just because he plans to ruin her doesn't mean he can't benefit from her skills, skills she developed from the patients she practiced on along the way.

And the patients she killed. Or at least, the *patient* she killed.

He's tried to let it go. For six years, he's tried. Even saw a therapist when he could still afford it. Yet his inner turmoil grew. Still grows. First helplessness, then anger, then hatred. Wash, rinse, repeat. Over and over and over again.

He drops to his couch and buries himself face down on a cushion that smells like soy sauce and ass. A low-grade groan rumbles in his throat. If only he could find peace.

Soon. Maybe soon.

He finally started following her eight months ago. Although acting out on his obsession with her might be his final descent into madness, he can't help it.

Then he caught a break. A break so startling he thought he was hallucinating.

She beat and stabbed a man out in the middle of nowhere in an old barn. He witnessed every incredible moment.

It was a Tuesday night. He'd been following her, just as he'd followed her several times before. After her SUV pulled out of her loft's parking deck one evening after clinic, he maneuvered his old Chevy behind her and tailed her to a bar on the outskirts of Boston.

When she stepped out of her vehicle in front of the upscale nightclub, he got quite a shock. It wasn't her form-fitting dress or high heels that surprised him, although they were an atypical choice from her usual style. It was the long auburn wig and the face full of makeup that startled him. They made her unrecognizable. Her usual vibe was an understated but professional Anne Hathaway. But that night? She was a sultry Christina Hendricks.

Intrigued, and for once not focused on his own internal pain, he waited in his car across the street from the club. An hour later she reappeared, but this time with a man in a tailored suit. One of his arms was around her shoulders. The other groped her like a guy who thinks everything is his for the taking.

When the two of them climbed into her Highlander and drove away, he followed behind in his Chevy, driving for the better part of an hour. Under a vibrant sunset, urban landscape morphed into suburban homes and then into rural and wooded terrain. Finally, her SUV pulled onto a dirt road and disappeared into a copse of trees.

Knowing he'd be spotted if his car followed her in there, he pulled over to the side of the highway and headed on foot in the direction she drove. After about three quarters of a mile, he spotted a barn, her SUV parked near it.

As he approached the outbuilding, he heard a man screaming and cursing. He froze, both in fear and confusion. Then, tentatively, he advanced and peered through a crack in the wallboards. Quietly, barely daring to breathe, he watched, transfixed. What he saw shocked him.

You're not who people think you are at all, are you, Dr. Sullivan?

He fumbled for his phone and recorded what he could between the one-inch slat. For a few minutes, a mangy cat sniffed around his feet, but he didn't dare shoo it away in case he'd be discovered. Finally, the animal gave up and pawed its way into the barn.

He recorded a little longer, and when it appeared the doctor with the sweet bedside manner and bag full of free medication was finishing up with her torture, he slunk away and prayed the snapping branches beneath his feet wouldn't be noticed.

Once safely back in his car, he drove off. For the first time in six years, he smiled. He'd just been given a gift.

Now it was his turn for payback.

6

From the backseat of my Highlander, Diva's sonorous breaths rise above the nearly imperceptible hum of the hybrid, which idles near the dog abuser's home on a quiet but ugly street on the outskirts of an industrial suburb. Given Thursdays are my light day, the afternoon devoted to administrative duties, I bowed out of clinic early to stake out my next asshole tune-up.

Diva is in her cat carrier. I'm in a blunt-cut wig and massive sunglasses. Around us, the sun burns bright and hot, more like a July day than a June one. I've yet to see a soul exit or enter a home.

One might assume cats and cars don't mix, but Diva shatters that myth. The steady drone of tires over pavement as we left Boston seemed to soothe her. Or maybe she was simply relieved not to be left alone in my condo. For a stray, not to mention a cat, she's surprisingly social. Dog-like, even. Her urping has stopped, and her contentment with her new living arrangement is obvious.

I was smart to invite her into my life. We're simpatico, the two of us. Two low-key feminine packages with agreeable personalities who prove looks can be deceiving.

I sip my spiced chai tea and scan the neighborhood behind my dark shades. Dying trees line the street and shield the widely spaced homes. Only my patient's house and the dog abuser's share any proximity. Hers, a one-story ranch, shows attentive care, with flower boxes in the windows and a trimmed lawn. His, a split-level modular, is rundown, and just like my sneak peek on Google Maps suggested, junk litters its yard. A gas can sits next to a rusted lawn mower. An aluminum shed leans to one side. A stack of old tires spills onto the driveway. Presumably, the dog is in back, hidden by the house.

I squeeze my door release but don't yet open it. A hesitation holds me back. Not because I'm afraid the dog abuser will be home—my patient mentioned he doesn't return until seven—but because I worry about unseen eyes watching me.

A week has passed since the strange emails popped into my inbox, so maybe the sender has grown bored. Moved on to new territory. It's possible I misread the whole thing. Made it personal when it wasn't. It could have been some anonymous emailer trying to get a rise out of a random recipient.

Still, the tightness in my throat, the churn in my belly, the dampness in my palms—they're all there no matter how much I try to deep breathe them away. Maybe that's what my electronic stalker wants. Me, looking over my shoulder like some slasher-movie victim, wondering when the whir of the chainsaw will come.

I glance up at my rearview mirror. Nothing behind me but the rutted and neglected road. No cars, no dog walkers, no delivery people.

Loosening my grip on the Highlander's door handle, I remind myself I can only act on what I can control. Isn't that what those dumb affirmations tell me?

Avenging a mistreated dog is something I can control.

Cooing a promise to Diva that I'll be right back, I slip my cross-body purse over my head and exit the vehicle. I smooth my cotton pants and look around the still-deserted neighborhood. A name tag pinned to the left breast pocket of my understated blouse identifies me as a real estate agent. It's generic, but so is my excuse if I'm encountered: I'm simply checking out property requested by a client but must have the wrong address.

Avoiding the walkway leading to the abuser's front door, I traipse at a wide angle through the dandelion-stippled grass on the other side of the driveway, hopefully dodging any front door camera should there be one. I round the strewn tires, pass the tilted shed, and head toward the backyard. Before I even see the dog, I hear him. A whimpering, mournful cry. When I reach the back of the house and lay eyes on the German shepherd chained to a metal stake under the hot sun, my nostrils flare, and heat floods my face.

Bypassing an old car engine and scattered tools, I rush through the backyard toward the dog. No fence, electric or otherwise, contains him. Only a heavy chain clasped to his collar, wound so tightly around the stake that the shepherd has barely a foot of movement. His water bowl, unreachable at three feet away, contains a half-inch of fluid. Dog turds litter the dead grass.

"What the hell?" I cry out, unable to contain my horror.

Why in the world would someone have a dog only to leave him outside alone all day? Maybe even all night. What kind of a monster lives here?

"Oh, you poor, poor thing," I sputter through a tight throat. Still, I slow my pace as I approach him. He is a German shepherd, after all.

He rises to all fours, as best he can with his reduced range of motion, and bares his teeth at me. From this higher stance, it looks like *he* is actually a *she*.

In a display of defense, she barks at me, but her guard-dog act is weak, either because of my nonthreatening approach or from her own exhaustion in the heat.

I inch a few feet forward. Her barking quiets into a low growl.

"Good girl," I coo, my tone tentative. "Don't worry, I won't hurt you." A few inches closer now. "What a pretty girl you are."

Actually, she's not pretty at all. Hairless patches dot her coat, and a scab festers on her hind leg. One of her eyes oozes green muck.

When I'm less than two feet away, she drops back down and whimpers. I close the remaining distance between us and squat, offering soothing words as I pet her. Then I guide her up and walk her around the stake to unwind her.

Free from her tight tether, she trots to the water bowl, and in an instant the meager offering is gone. Spotting a hose, I hurry to the back of the house and turn the water on. As I drag the green tubing to the dog's bowl, I search again for a camera. Thankfully, there isn't one.

I fill the bowl and return the hose to the back of the house. All the while, my brain rapid fires a conversation with itself:

You can't leave the dog here.

But I'm only doing surveillance and confirmation. I can't take her with me. Not yet, anyway.

But you can't leave her here.

Where will I put her? I have a nine-hundred-square-foot loft in the city.

But you can't leave her here with this monster.

Just as I turn the water off and think, *Screw it, I'm taking her,* a car door slams from what sounds like the driveway.

I freeze.

From across the backyard, I look at the dog.

She looks at me, her posture crouched and her body shaking despite the heat.

I can't take her now. I have no idea who this man is, how big he is, how ruthless he might be to a trespasser. Just because I conquered the transient who attacked me two days ago doesn't mean I can take this guy. Neither the pepper spray in my purse nor the tiny blade in my ripcord bracelet will do much good against a violent giant. How far might he go if he catches me stealing his dog? For all I know, he has bodies buried in this weedy ground.

I mouth the word *sorry* to the German shepherd and promise I'll come back for her. Then I round the house on the opposite side of the driveway and speed walk my way to my SUV, grateful I parked it closer to my patient's house than this one. Hopefully, the guy is taking a leak in his bathroom or grabbing a beer, oblivious of the fake real estate agent who just scurried across his yard.

Once inside my still-idling vehicle, the air conditioning on high for Diva who startles awake in her carrier at my abrupt entrance, I press the accelerator too hard with my summer loafer and squeal away. Not until the dog abuser's house is gone from my rearview mirror do I exhale.

That was close. Too close. I'm not even wearing my full disguise.

I *will* rescue that dog, I will. But I'm also going to make that man pay. He needs to be persuaded—sharply—that he will never own a pet again.

Ever.

The farther I drive, the hotter my anger grows. I stab the radio's *On* button but immediately stab it back off. I can't take any depressing news or hopeless songs. Instead, I drive and seethe. Aside from my occasional anxiety, like just now at the man's house, I seem capable of only two emotional states: anger or apathy, apathy or anger. Oh, and let's not forget despair. I'm so sick of bastards. So sick of idiots. So sick of good people dying and assholes thriving.

As we clear the industrial suburb and make our way back to Boston, I say to Diva, "Humanity sucks. It absolutely s-s-sucks." My fury unmasks my old stutter, something that hasn't happened in at least a decade. "Goliaths pay no taxes while millions of people can't feed their kids. Skeptics refuse medical advice up to their dying breaths. Politicians flip-flop on a dime, doing and s-s-saying anything to get reelected." My verbal diarrhea floods out, and the road blurs before me. "Travelers punch flight attendants. Bigots attack people because of the color of their skin or their sexual orientation. Men beat their wives. Women force their kids to steal. Ogres torture helpless animals. And if that's not enough, the earth is burning. It's flooding. It's melting."

I'm in full-on rant mode now, barely registering the cars that pass me on the highway. In the rearview mirror, Diva sits wide-eyed in her carrier. I continue to rave.

"My mom beats colon cancer only to die because some prick crushes her and Dad in a hit and run. Come. The Fuck. On." My hands slam the steering wheel with each word. The tires swerve into the next lane. I jerk my SUV back between the broken white lines and try to force a sliver of calm into me, but calm is impossible. All I can picture are my dead parents.

Three and a half years ago, only six months after I started at Congress Medical Clinic, my mom and dad's car flipped multiple times and landed in a wooded ravine where it remained unseen overnight, both bodies trapped inside. From the autopsies, the pathologist deduced my father had lived a few hours longer than my mother, who was killed instantly and nearly decapitated. In other words, the man who loved nothing more than doing Sunday morning crossword puzzles while his wife tapped away on her Excel spreadsheets next to him had to stare at his mangled spouse, the love of his life, for three agonizing hours.

The monster who hit them drove away, never to be found. Never to be brought to justice.

Tears sprout to my eyes. I blink them away, but it's no use because after I push down the images of my parents, Manuel surfaces instead.

"Manny," I whisper. His name chokes off in my throat. "He got me through that year, Diva. Without him, I don't know what I would have done. He kept me sane, you know? Dreaming of your decapitated mom every night doesn't exactly make for sound sleep."

I shift to the left lane to pass a crawling MINI Cooper and glance at Diva in the rearview mirror. She licks her front paw and watches me through the metal grates of her carrier.

"Not knowing who killed my parents—*still* not knowing— eats at me every day. Was it some boozer? Some amped-up jerk flying a hundred miles an hour? Some Instagrammer who couldn't put down her goddamn phone? Manuel was my rock, my lighthouse. But then"—I slam my palms against the steering wheel again, making Diva jump—"hello, shit world, goodbye fiancé! The kindest man in the world gets leukemia and dies eight months later from an overwhelming infection."

A sob thickens my throat.

"And then, and then…" I struggle to form the words. "And then the universe says, 'Hey, we ain't done with you yet, missy. Let's take that little eight-week fetus from you too, the one Manny was miraculously able to give you despite being on chemo."

At the memory of my miscarriage two years ago, shortly after Manuel's death, I can no longer speak. I realize I can no longer see, either, because tears have blinded me. I drive out of sheer muscle memory, but then a long blast of a car horn startles me into focus. I swing back into the right lane, grateful my exit is ahead.

Get your shit together, Hope.

I do some deep breathing, even though it's never helped me before. Neither has medication. Or therapy. Or an affirmation app.

Anger or despair. Revenge or apathy. These past few years, that's all I know.

Terrence, my colleague with the laughing-skull ties and

publishing aspirations, says all this cynicism is going to lead me to darkness. If he only knew the half of it.

But I get through my days well enough. In me, people see what they want to see: a dedicated, smiling doctor who lives by the Golden Rule. Even if that smile, like my driving, comes from muscle memory and not true joy.

I release my death grip on the steering wheel and apologize to Diva for losing my cool. Then I take the exit that leads me to downtown Boston.

Enough with the whining. It's undeserved and doesn't suit me. I'm independent, have plenty of money, and am more privileged than I have a right to be.

Over a year and a half ago, after taking down a thief who tried to steal my elderly patient's purse, I realized there was a much more productive way to deal with my anger. My first tune-up on the woman in Target clinched it in my mind. The universe didn't need my wallowing. It needed my action. So I made a pact with myself: Take control and change what I can, or get off the pot and step through the exit door.

"But don't worry," I say to Diva, as if she can read my thoughts. "I can't leave this world just yet. We've got work to do. A dog owner needs an attitude adjustment, and a German shepherd needs a new home."

I nod, as if reassuring myself as much as the cat.

"That, we can control."

7

———

Tuesday's clinic moves slower than a sloth in a horse race. Restless and distracted, wanting nothing more than to get revenge on the dog abuser, I work through a schedule full of chronic patients, few of whom are making any progress in their disease course.

I had hoped to perform his drug and lug Saturday evening, two days after confirming he was indeed deserving of it, but my arrival at his place that night was poorly timed. Or maybe perfectly timed depending on how you look at it. As I slowed my Highlander a block away from his cluttered yard, a couple exited a Ford Focus that was parked in his driveway.

A son and daughter-in-law? A daughter and son-in-law? A niece and a nephew? I had no clue, but as I cruised past Saturday evening, my window lowered to catch their words, I overheard the younger man thanking the dog-owner—who turned out to be a short, wiry, middle-aged monster and not the giant-sized monster I'd imagined—for letting them crash at his place for the next few days. That meant their departure would be today or tomorrow, depending on the male visitor's definition of "a few." To give myself a little cushion, I'll wait until tomorrow night to carry out my plan. In the meantime, I itch and burn to free that German shepherd, despite my daily affirmation app promising me that: *Self-control will reward you.*

Yeah, tell that to the poor dog.

At least one of my patients is doing well today. Janelle, a thirty-one-year-old information technologist who works at Boston General, saw a revolving door of doctors for over a year before coming to me a few months ago. Her chief complaint was chronic abdominal pain and nausea, along with emotional instability and body aches. She was practically in tears, but tears of frustration rather than distress.

"I suppose you're going to write me off too," she said to me during her first appointment last March. "Say it's all in my head, or it's hormones, or it's stress, but believe me, I was fine before all this started. They see a woman, a woman of color at that, and they immediately assume it's psychosomatic."

Her turmoil was obvious, and she wouldn't be the first woman with chronic symptoms to be dismissed, so I performed a complete history and physical examination and asked to review her past medical records. Even though my own enthusiasm has been muted of late, I still enjoy a good diagnostic puzzle.

Janelle handed over a file of printed visit summaries and lab work. "I won't hold my breath. I'm only here because a woman at my gym swears by you."

"I promise I'll do all I can to find out what's wrong."

And I did. After spending two hours reviewing Janelle's records, both from primary care physicians and gynecologists, along with her blood tests, I called her at home on a Wednesday evening for more information. I'd found some of her red blood cell indices to be mildly abnormal.

She seemed both surprised and pleased by my call. After several minutes of trying to deduce with her any heavy-metal exposure, I learned she had purchased some earthenware in Mexico on a cruise a couple of years back. Knowing that terra cotta clay can sometimes contain lead and discovering that she used the bowls and plates on a regular basis, I asked her to come back in for more blood work. A short time later we had the diagnosis: lead poisoning. Rare in an adult nowadays, but not impossible, and also not unheard of to present as chronic abdominal pain.

Today is Janelle's second follow-up after chelation therapy—and disposal of the earthenware—and she claims she feels like a new woman. "You ever need anything, Dr. Sullivan, you give me a call. Not sure what a techie can offer you, but I'll do my best."

Her grin buoys me, and although pleased to have helped her, I find the diagnostic solve doesn't give me the boost it once did.

"My focus area is hematology," I say, shrugging. "So I was just lucky to spot something in your blood cells the other providers didn't."

"Take the win, Doc." Janelle raises her impressively toned arms. "Take the win."

I try to, I really do, but all I can think of is freeing that German shepherd and kicking its owner's ass.

By the end of the day, I feel as deflated as an overused gym ball. My colleagues have all departed, each having a significant other or kids to go home to. Me? I have a cat, which I guess is more than I had three weeks ago.

As I sit on the stool at my workstation, laptop in front of me, Manuel flits into my head.

"You're being melodramatic, Hoppy," his beautiful soul would tell me. "I'm the pathologist. Let me be the weird one." And then I would grin, knowing he was right. Even weak and nauseated from chemotherapy, he loved to make me laugh.

"Staying late too, I see."

The unexpected voice makes me jump. My knee strikes the underside of the counter, my joint still sore from my tussle with the transient, and I yip in pain.

I put a hand over my heart as my colleague, Bo Linton,

approaches. Tall, sandy-haired, strong jawline. He's not only a real doctor, he could play one on TV.

"You scared me," I say, my pulse racing. "I thought everyone had left."

"Sorry. Didn't mean to sneak up on you."

"Thanks for filling in for Rishi again," I say, for lack of anything better.

"No problem. I'm happy to do locums for you guys as long as you need me."

Which hopefully won't be much longer, I think.

Once again I wonder why Bo's gaze makes me squirm, and once again I tell myself it's because I saw him as a patient before he took this locum tenens job. Fingers crossed, he won't schedule with me again. Once was enough if we're to maintain a professional relationship.

He hovers near my workstation, puffing out his chest beneath his checkered button-down, a shirt that looks more Target than Nordstrom. He smooths his full head of hair.

Oh sweet Jesus, is he going to ask me out?

Suddenly I'm happy he was once my patient, even if it was only for one visit. I'll claim ethics precludes me from meeting him for a drink.

At last, he says, "Okay then, I'll see you tomorrow."

I force a smile and twist the paracord bracelet on my wrist, careful not to unclasp its small blade. Not until Bo is gone from the hallway and the back door clicks shut do I exhale my pent-up breath.

I stare at the open chart in my EMR, the clinic silent and darkened around me. Then I double check my last patient note, sign off on it, and deliver my medical findings into the ether.

After gathering my belongings, I leave through the back door like Bo did and lock it behind me. Although this hallway exit is supposed to remain locked at all times, occasionally one of us forgets, which incurs the wrath of our normally good-natured office manager.

While I wait for the elevator to return me to ground level, I check my email on my phone. A deluge of messages greets me, but only one of them makes me freeze.

Sent ten minutes ago, the email is from that same unnerving address: *iseeyou1003@bxmail.com*. The subject line reads: I'm still here.

The elevator doors ping open, but I don't move. They close again, and the lift leaves without me.

Swallowing, I press open the email.

You haven't responded yet. Did you think I'd forget about you?

What is going on here? I wonder, but then a pinch of anger joins my worry, and I stab out a response: What do you want? Money?

To my surprise, the sender answers immediately, as if he or she has been hovering over the keyboard, waiting for me to reply. We need to chat.

About what?

In person.

"Right," I mutter out loud. I'd be a fool to meet up with an online stalker. Still, I can't help but wonder what he wants, assuming it *is* a man. An in-person meeting suggests there's more going on than a "pay me ransom or I'll take over your computer" sort of thing.

Regardless, I type: Never going to happen.

The reply comes swiftly: Then I'll release what I have on you.

What in the world is this person talking about? What, exactly, do they think they have on me?

I shake my head and push the elevator's down button to call the lift back.

This person is fishing. That's all. Maybe he or she does know who I am. Maybe they've even been one of my patients. How hard is it to find someone's personal email? Probably not hard at all. Same with my address. But if the sender had something incriminating, they would be more specific, and if they think I'm going to fall for these tactics, they'll be sorely disappointed.

Just as the elevator arrives, I stab out a definitive: Fuck off.

Then I step inside the lift, click a few tabs on my phone, and block *iseeyou1003@bxmail.com* from ever contacting me again.

8

The following morning begins early with a 7:00 a.m. meeting at Boston General. Although my four colleagues and I no longer round on inpatients—the facility has hospitalists for that—we still need to stay up to date with hospital developments, so we take turns to attend. This month's meeting falls on me, after which I'll carry back any relevant news. It was supposed to be Rishi's turn, but given his come-and-go MS symptoms, I offered to attend in his place.

I arrive a few minutes early and head to the continental breakfast buffet. After filling my coffee cup, I pile a small plate with fruit and yogurt and take a seat behind one of the long conference tables in the auditorium. All the while, my thoughts hash out tonight's revenge act.

The glimpse I caught of the dog abuser on Saturday confirmed he's not much bigger than me. A routine dose of an intramuscular sedative should be enough. I have a small supply at home, pilfered here and there from our treatment room, where we keep the drugs on hand for any procedures that need a bit of calming. The vials' left-over volumes are less monitored than the drug-dispensing cabinets in the hospital.

I rarely use injections in my drug and lugs, though. One,

because I don't like stealing from our supply, and two, because roofies usually do the trick. But entering the dog abuser's home and seducing him probably won't be an option, unlike the wife beater who was easy. Once I'd learned the Armani-suited guy's after-work routine, I hit on him in his preferred bar, his ego never allowing the possibility that I could be anything but attracted to him. As I pressed up against him, acting all lovesick, I dropped a couple of pills into his drink. Plop plop, fizz fizz. I'm not proud to have a contact who can get me rohypnol, but without it, there'd be no trips to my barn, and thus, no justice.

Tonight, however, a syringe will be needed. Along with a quick zap of my Taser.

My revenge thoughts are broken as Kim Lombardi, one of the hospitalists, sits down next to me in the auditorium. I chew a spoonful of yogurt and raspberries and try to force the dog abuser from my mind.

"Any Fourth of July plans?" Kim asks in her flat cadence.

The holiday is still over two weeks away. I haven't thought that far ahead. I shake my head and am about to respond when Dan Knudson, another hospitalist, plops down on the other side of me and cuts me off.

"How's it hanging, ladies?" Before either of us can respond, he speaks over me and says, "Hey, Kim, I saw your sister won some big award in transplant surgery up there at the Mayo Clinic."

"Her brother was named CEO of Jenzell Pharmaceuticals too," I pipe in.

Dan looks impressed. "Wow, you working on your Nobel Prize yet?"

Kim shrugs noncommittally, her toffee-blond hair pulled back in a messy bun, her blouse a boxy linen. She doesn't like talking about her accomplished family, but Dan does it anyway. I know this because the three of us were residents together, Kim two years behind me and Dan one. The two of them dated briefly, and the whole thing got messy. I tried to stay out of it, but that was difficult considering we were an enmeshed family during our training, whether we liked it or not. Dan is a competent doctor but surprisingly childish and cluelessly entitled. He thinks his side jokes don't rub the wrong way, but they often do. Like now. He's a horndog, too, finding double entendres in everything. Back in residency, he would joke about threesomes—as if any of us female residents would ever take him up on it.

He shifts to me. "So, Hope, what's going on in *your* life?"

The way he emphasizes the word *your* makes me uncomfortable, as if he knows something I don't. Paranoia on my part? Probably. But that email exchange yesterday put me on edge. I hope I did the right thing in blocking the sender.

"Fine. Stay mysterious." Dan winks as the president of the Medical Staff takes her position behind the podium four rows below us. "Oh, by the way," he adds quickly, "a patient I discharged is transferring to your clinic. It's within walking distance from his home, so I gave him your name. I think he's coming in this week to see you, but watch out. He's a difficult one."

I don't get a chance to ask in what way the patient is difficult—demeanor? medical problems? communication issues? —because the med-staff president starts the meeting.

Guess it'll be a surprise.

Ninety minutes later, I'm back on Congress Street, hurrying into our clinic's building. My brow is damp with perspiration from the brisk mile walk, and my lightweight sweater sticks to my skin. Once inside, I tug at the fabric and stride up to the lobby's coffee kiosk. Interacting with the big-haired, judgmental barista is the last thing I care to do, but I want—need —more caffeine.

True to form, she's already trashing someone.

"And you should see how fat she's gotten," Miss Judgie says to her fellow barista, who straightens when I approach. Her expression suggests she doesn't enjoy her coworker's gossip any more than I do.

After getting my coffee, I pass by the law office on the ground floor and head up to the clinic on the fourth, my mind back on the dog abuser. Usually I'm better at compartmentalizing, better at focusing on the task at hand, but the ogre's behavior has me on edge. Every moment I delay on getting to him is an extra moment of misery for the dog. I can only hope the presence of houseguests led to a temporary improvement in the German shepherd's treatment.

Tonight. Just make it through to tonight.

To avoid encountering the day's first patients, who will be in our waiting room by now, I sidestep the glass front of our clinic and enter through the back hallway. The only people I see on my trek through our maze of exam rooms are our nurse Alice, who's weighing a patient, and my colleague, Dr. Irene Montgomery. She's chatting on the phone at her cubby, describing her *cah*'s engine troubles, her Boston accent thicker than the rubber tires on that *cah*. We wave to each other in greeting.

According to my EMR schedule, my first appointment of the day is a new patient: a forty-three-year-old man with a skin boil. I click open the tab that holds his outside medical records, which have already been scanned in for me to peruse. As soon as I see his recent hospitalization for pneumonia, I realize this is the patient Dan Knudson mentioned to me at the hospital meeting. Judging by the man's lengthy problem list, it is now understandable what Dan meant by the patient being difficult. High blood pressure, autoimmune disease, recurrent infections. Multiple drug allergies too. At least today's skin boil should be easy to manage.

When I enter the room and introduce myself, the first

thing I notice aside from him wearing a mask, which, considering his medical history, is a wise choice, is that his height and build are similar to the dog abuser's. I calculate the sedative dose I'll need for tonight.

Focus, Hope. Focus.

After reviewing the patient's past medical history with him, he says, "My pneumonia is all better. The only thing I'm here for today is this." He lifts the side of his Homer Simpson T-shirt and points to a walnut-size boil on his abdomen, its red base topped by a tense, yellowish hue.

Despite my best efforts to concentrate on his problem, I picture the German shepherd in the junk-filled backyard. Does she have any boils that need to be lanced?

"…could've gone to urgent care for it," the patient is saying, "but I figured it would be good to get established with you anyway. You can drain a boil, right?"

"Yes."

"Good." A clump of his gelled hair flops over his eyes and lands on his mask. He pushes it back. "But I can't have any penicillins or cephalosporins. Too allergic."

With my laptop in hand, I usher him back to the treatment room, where I numb and prep the tissue area. All the while he tells me about his numerous hospitalizations ("kidney infection back in March") and his allergic reactions ("such bad throat swelling they almost had to intubate me"), but my thoughts keep drifting to the German shepherd, who I've taken to calling Shelly in my mind.

Is she thirsty right now?

"…my thyroid was all out of whack…"

How hot is it supposed to get today?

"…and my God, the hives, so many hives…"

Is her chain wound up again?

"…doxy and clinda too…"

Not much longer, Shelly, not much longer.

"You okay, Doctor?"

I snap back to the patient on the table and realize I'm still compressing his boil, even though no pus remains. Alice, who entered the treatment room a few minutes ago to collect the culture swab I swiped over the wound, stares at me from behind her jeweled eyeglasses.

"Um, yes. Yes, I'm fine." My face warms in embarrassment at my mind-wandering. "Just want to make sure I got it all. Let me prescribe you an antibiotic, and we'll get you on your way."

I step to my laptop on the counter near the sink and return to his electronic chart. Alice leaves with the culture tube and its pus-drenched swab. While I review the patient's home instructions with him—wound care, dressing change, what to watch for—I type in a prescription for clindamycin (*no penicillins or cephalosporins—check*) that will go to the patient's pharmacy, which Alice has already entered into the EMR.

Then, with my mind back on poor Shelly the shepherd, I hit *Send*.

9

Not far from my barn, I grab the chain attached to the collar around the dog abuser's neck and yank it. The wiry man flops over sideways onto the grass, and a wheeze sprays from his mouth. Maybe the collar is too tight. I don't take pleasure in that, but at least I gave him more than twelve inches of wiggle room from the flagpole, unlike what he gives his poor dog.

In my long-sleeved, padded unitard, which plumps up my linen suit like Spandex in reverse, I squat down next to him. A knife rests in my hand in case he gets grabby, but given I've duct-taped his wrists behind his back, that seems unlikely. I bound his ankles too. My disguise, including my prosthetic nose and chin, are too warm for the mid-June evening. Rivulets of sweat drip down my crevices.

On the horizon, the sun sets in glimmering rays of orange. Without another soul for miles, there's no one to hear us. If he tried crying for help during the night or while I was at work, it was pointless.

I fan my arm toward the hilly and wooded terrain. "How are you enjoying yourself? Are my accommodations up to your standards?" I give another sharp tug on his chain. "At least it's pretty. That's more than your dog gets. Nothing but old tires and corroded engines for her."

The abuser is too weak to offer much, but he does manage to rasp that he'll kill me and then calls me a crazy— insert C word—just like the wife beater did last month. His neck cords jut out beneath the leather collar, and his face, which is burned and chapped from being in the sun all day, bloats like an overripe tomato. Although lean and short, his muscle definition is impressive for a man in his fifties, and I imagine him pumping out a couple hundred push-ups a day. If he were my patient, I'd commend his commitment to fitness.

I check my watch. Unlike with the wife beater, my hands aren't shaking. Is that because I am beyond furious with this man for abusing his dog or is it because I am getting unhealthily comfortable with all this?

"Twenty-three hours and thirty-four minutes," I say. "I guess that's long enough to make my point, don't you think?"

He doesn't respond, just lies on his side in his T-shirt and grass-stained jeans, breaths heavy, wrists taped together behind him. Although he might not want to give me the satisfaction of a response, it's obvious his anger is only a cover. A wariness sharpens his eyes, and his gaze flits back and forth between the six-inch blade in my hand and my altered face, as if he is fearful of what I might do.

"Then again, maybe I should just leave you here. It's not like Shelly"—I hold up my knife-free hand—"Sorry, that's my name for your German shepherd. It's not like Shelly gets to pack up her crate and go home."

The uncertainty in his eyes grows.

The moment I finished clinic yesterday, I hurried back to my loft and drove to the dog abuser's house. Dressed in the same costume I'm wearing now, with the fake realtor badge pinned to my blazer and a syringe full of sedative in my pocket, I rang the guy's doorbell. After giving him some nonsense talk about a property evaluation, I showed myself in and shot him with my Taser.

Once he was twitching on the floor, I jabbed the sedative into his arm, put him on the green tarp I keep in my SUV for these occasions, and dragged him out his side garage door and into the back seat of my car. Took a fair amount of heaving and huffing, but he's not much heavier than me, and my upper body strength is first-rate. It's the bigger ones who give me grief. I have to dope them up lightly first and then coerce them into my car by a number of means—seduction, a personal threat to out their behavior, a knife—whatever is best suited for the occasion. It's not until they are in the vehicle that I can fully sedate them.

Was I nervous someone might be watching me last night? Yes. Especially since the email sender appears to know my condo number. But I was careful and vigilant, and that includes putting a fake license plate on my car like I always do during my tune-ups. I'm confident I was alone. Even if those emails *do* mean someone is on to me, I had no choice but to act on the dog's behalf. I had to risk it. Otherwise Shelly would still be tied up outside instead of being cared for at a shelter. To be safe, though, I will put future tune-ups on hold. At least for now.

When we reached my barn, I fitted the dog abuser with a collar ($29.99 from Petco) and a chain ($44.99 from Ace Hardware) and hooked him up to the flagpole. I slipped a padlock between two chain links near the pole and did the same around his collar's attachment. It seemed unlikely he'd free his hands while I was gone, but if he did, I wanted to make sure he couldn't remove the chain and break away.

And then I left.

For twenty-three hours and thirty-four minutes.

No food. No water. No shelter. Just him, the overnight insects and wildlife, and the daytime sun. Same as his dog gets.

He must have freaked out when he woke up from the sedative last night and found himself chained to a flagpole, wrists and ankles bound.

"Thank goodness it didn't rain," I say to him. I place a hand over my padded bosom in mock relief and sit back on my padded butt. "Then again, if it had, you would have been able to enjoy the full sensory experience your dog gets." My tone hardens. "Day in and day out."

I reach over to touch his burnt cheek, but he flicks his head away.

"Guess I should've left you some sunscreen. Maybe some lip balm too. Shelly doesn't get any comforts, though, so why should you?"

I stare at his moist crotch and the ground around him.

"You wet yourself, and I'm sorry for that, but at least you're not sitting in your own shit like Shelly."

I scoot back and reach into the backpack I brought with me. I pull out my water bottle, a big thirty-two-ounce container. Uncapping it, my eyes never leaving his, I take a long, cool drink. Then I yank out a chocolate nut bar and start eating.

"You're insane," the dog abuser sputters. He manages to push himself back up into a seated position and leans against the flagpole.

My forced calm vanishes. "Insane? Me? You want to know what's insane? Having a dog when all you do is ignore and mistreat it."

I duckwalk back toward him, his gaze glued to my knife. I hadn't planned on cutting him, but I'm tempted. His dog has wounds and scabs all over. Why shouldn't the abuser too? But I hold myself back. With every tune-up, I fear the line between the brutes and me grows thinner. I have to be careful not to cross it.

"Shelly is fine, by the way," I spit out. "Thanks for asking."

He squints his eyes but offers nothing.

"I dropped her off at a rescue shelter and told them I found her wandering in a field. I would have kept her myself, but it's not practical."

I would have, too, if not for my HOA forbidding large dogs and the terror a German shepherd might instill in Diva. I don't want my cat leaping out the window into Massachusetts Bay.

"They promised they would patch Shelly up and find her a good home," I say. "She's a beautiful dog and too beaten down by life to be much of a threat. They checked her for a microchip, but I was pretty confident a bully like you wouldn't have put one in. Who knows when Shelly was last seen by a vet?"

The man's squint intensifies, and a deep groove forms between his wiry eyebrows, half of which have gone gray. "Who. The hell. Are you?"

I don't begrudge him the question. It's the one I hear most often. I also don't give him an answer. Instead, I crouch close to him and run the tip of my blade down his cheek. His narrowed eyes grow wide, and I feel his body tense. He has no idea what I will do, and honestly, I don't either. I'm too caught up in the rush of revenge.

"If you ever," I whisper into his ear, "ever, ever, ever, even *think* about getting another pet, I will gut you. I will drag you back out here and gut you."

My knife drops to his trim belly. This time, he can't hold back his sharp inhalation of fear.

"Because I'll be watching you. Do you understand?" When he doesn't respond, I shout into his ear, "Do you understand?"

He bobs his head *yes* so frantically it thumps against the flagpole. On contact, the metal reverberates like a gong.

Satisfied, I rise, return to my backpack, and retrieve another bottle of water. This one contains two roofies, but a man without water for nearly twenty-four hours will suck it down without a thought. The rohypnol, especially at that dose, might knock him out longer than the sedative did, but I didn't dare add only one tablet and risk him not drinking the whole thing.

I needn't have worried. Once I cut his wrists free with my knife, he snatches the bottle from my hand and slurps down its contents.

Squatting once again, I wait for him to get drowsy. He needs to be out before we leave. I can't drag him to my car otherwise, and I don't want him seeing our location on the drive back.

It's okay. I have plenty of time. Diva has been fed, her litter box cleaned, and she has pretty much claimed my loft as her own.

I close my eyes and revel in the dopamine surging through my brain and body. In these moments, seeing one more bully get their due, everything else vanishes. Challenging patients, global poverty, children shot in schools, bigots, inept politicians, cryptic emails from unknown senders, murdered parents, buried fiancés, miscarriages—all of it disappears.

For a heartbeat, a long and wonderful heartbeat, I feel something more than nothing and everything less than anger.

I feel joy.

I feel useful.

I feel life.

10

———

For lunch the next day, I get a full forty-five minutes, enough time for Terrence and me to stroll a few blocks to Quincy Market for a bite to eat, a rare treat for a Friday. Usually there are too many last-minute patient add-ons for us to go anywhere. Had Terrence known that a mere sixteen hours ago, I dragged a doped-up dog abuser into the cargo space of my Highlander and delivered him back to his trashy home sans German shepherd, he might have admitted me to the psych ward instead.

We sit on a bench near Faneuil Hall, the building's historic red brick and arched windows a steppingstone to American independence. Tourists enter and exit, their phones poised for pictures. The sky is overcast and the air humid, but none of that lessens Boston's appeal.

A clump of onions falls from my gyro onto the sidewalk. Terrence chuckles and bends over to scoop up the mess with a napkin. His tie, a collection of dancing skeletons, grazes the ground.

He tosses the soiled napkin into a trashcan two feet away. "Your afternoon patients will be grateful you lost a few onions."

"Still better than Frank's breath at the end of the day."

We both laugh at my joke. As much as we love our soon-to-be-retiring senior partner, he'd be wise to indulge in some late-afternoon mints.

"How's the book coming?" I ask.

"Writing a novel is harder than I thought it would be."

"Most things are. You and Stel ready for Kayla to hit the college trail in a month?"

"No. Especially Stel. Those two are tight."

"That's what happens when the rest of the family pumps out testosterone. Your women gotta stick together."

Terrence smiles, but it's a sad smile. "Just wish she would've chosen a school here, not upstate New York. Hope the health center there is good."

"She'll be—"

The staccato chirp of my mobile cuts me off. I wipe Greek sauce off my fingers and pull the phone from the pocket of my cotton skirt.

The screen flashes an unknown number. I'm tempted to let it go to voicemail, but I bought a fancy cat tree for Diva from an online pet boutique yesterday. It's possible there's a problem with the order.

I mouth a *sorry* to Terrence and answer the call.

"Hello, is this Dr. Hope Sullivan?" a deep, no-nonsense voice asks—a voice that most definitely doesn't sound like a boutique-pet-store order gone wrong.

"Yes…" I say slowly.

"This is Martin Hernandez. I'm an investigator for the Medical Board. Is this a good time?"

The Medical Board? Shit oh shit oh shit.

"Sure," I say, standing and then immediately sitting back down on the bench. Terrence looks over at me, his expression questioning.

"Dr. Sullivan, we've had an anonymous complaint lodged against you, but before you—"

"Oh my God, when? Why?"

"Not long ago. The complainant claims you were…under the influence during a patient encounter, but—"

"I've never used any substances at work. Ever!"

My outburst garners a few stares. Next to me, Terrence asks if everything's okay, but his voice is distant and warped.

"Before you get too alarmed," Mr. Hernandez says, "let me explain that I have some...concerns about the validity of this complaint, which is why I'm taking a more informal approach, but you'll still receive a letter of notification this afternoon. I have to look into it."

"How will you do that?"

"I'll interview you, your colleagues, that kind of thing."

My stomach tightens, and the gyro threatens to come back up. Terrence puts a calming hand on my forearm, but I'm anything but calm.

"The fact the anonymous caller didn't submit a formal complaint through proper channels," Martin Hernandez says, "means we have no way to verify the caller's concerns with more details, nor do we have any medical records to check."

"It's bogus. I can tell you that right now."

"It very well might be. It wouldn't be the first time a disgruntled patient has made a false claim. Or maybe a claim they believe has merit but really doesn't, so as I said…"

Martin continues to speak perfectly understandable sentences about getting a drug test from me, meeting with my coworkers, determining if this is indeed a frivolous claim, but I barely catch any of his words as a whole. Instead, the turmoil in my belly swirls faster, and my mind makes a sickening connection.

The emails.

I consider interrupting Martin, telling him someone is out to get me, that this person must be the source of the anonymous complaint, but I can't reveal that yet. Not until I know what the sender knows. What he or she has on me. If the

Board got wind of my tune-ups, a suspended license would be the least of my worries.

So instead, I murmur agreement at Martin's suggested time to meet, give him the name and number of our office manager who can schedule interviews with my colleagues, and tell him I'll submit a sample for a drug test whenever he wants.

When we end our call, my fingers fumble over my phone screen for my email app.

"Hope, what's going on?" Terrence asks.

A few tourists are looking our way, probably wondering if the woman on the bench is about to stroke out.

I ignore both my colleague and the tourists.

I open the email app, convinced my electronic stalker is behind the complaint. He or she is trying to derail the only thing that still tethers me to this world: my professional reputation.

Yep, there it is. Fifth in a surge of new, unread messages is another email from my stalker, this time from a new address since I blocked the old one. It was sent two hours ago.

The new email address is *dontignoremedoctor@bxmail.com*.

The subject line reads: I'm still watching.

And in all caps, the body of the email shouts: THIS IS WHAT HAPPENS WHEN YOU IGNORE ME.

With shaky fingers, fueled by shock and fury, I type out a response: Fine. I'm listening. What do you want?

Then I press *Send* and wait.

11

HIM

From his desk, he reads the doctor's email asking him what he wants. What should fill him with relief, or at the very least satisfaction, having finally gotten her attention with the complaint to the Medical Board, fills him only with anger.

Anger over her initial dismissal of him. Anger over her tone that he should be grateful she's giving him her time (because he *does* detect a tone in her email). Anger over what she took from him.

He squeezes the mouse so tightly its plastic casing cracks. His whole body writhes, as if he has a million worms burrowing under his skin.

What do I want? What do I want? I'll tell you what I want. I want you to see my pain, to hear my pain, to feel *my pain. That's what I want.*

He types none of this, though. Merely rocks back and forth at his desk and picks at his arms. He'll give her no specifics, no details. He wants her to stew for a bit. He has seen her looking over her shoulder as she leaves clinic. Spied on her while she jogs. Eyed her from across the street as she enters her fancy condo high-rise.

Good. She should feel the threat, especially considering

that incriminating video he has of her on his phone. After what she did to him, any suffering on her end will be mere ounces of pain compared to his tons.

Still, he'll cut down on his spying. She might catch on, and he can't risk her getting him before he gets her.

He shifts his hands back to the keyboard, fingertips at the ready. Finally, he types his response:

She was smart, she was successful, she was beautiful in every way, and your negligence took her from me. No, worse than negligence, your rushed indifference. Your failed diagnosis.

And now you will pay.

12

———

Wednesday morning I stand at my granite island, chewing toast I barely taste and reading today's useless affirmation on my phone app: *My needs matter.*

The last five days have been hell. The anonymous Board complaint and my stalker's cryptic but threatening email, to which he hasn't yet followed up, have turned me into a fidgety, wide-eyed version of myself.

Guess I *can* feel more than apathy and anger. I can feel angst. I can feel fear. I can feel my reputation is worth hanging on for—and not just mine. My colleagues', too, because anything that stains my standing will also pollute theirs.

Maybe in a twisted way, I owe my stalker a thank you. Dormant emotions have woken up in me. Now, if only I could feel peace.

Another thing that makes me want to dive back under the covers this morning is that Kim Lombardi, the hospitalist, called me on Monday. One of my patients was admitted to Boston General with a severe drug reaction. It was the complex new patient I saw last week, the one Dan Knudson sent me. The man was allergic to the clindamycin I prescribed for his boil. Apparently his wife picked up the prescription and doled out the first pill to him, alongside his pastrami sandwich, not recognizing the drug's brand name printed on the bottle. It differed from the generic name.

But clindamycin wasn't included in the allergy list Alice had compiled when she roomed the patient, nor from his recent hospitalization with pneumonia. I know that because the first thing I checked after hanging up with Kim was that list. That means I must have missed the allergy in his outside records. Or worse, maybe he mentioned it to me, but in my distraction over getting revenge on the dog abuser, I didn't hear him. Either way it's on me, not Alice or the hospital nurse.

Now, as I cling to Diva near my door, my bag over my shoulder, my cropped pants and summer sweater-set giving off a confidence I don't feel, I wonder if today will be the day the Board brings me down. Or maybe it'll be my incompetence with the allergic patient that seals my professional coffin shut. Or it could be my own hubris for thinking I can take down assholes without ever being discovered.

And yet how can I stop? My tune-ups are like oxygen to me, and the guilt I'd feel for not helping a battered wife or an abused dog or a girl forced to shoplift by her mother would summon my exit-door pills more swiftly than I could swallow them.

"See there?" I say to Diva. "I can feel *guilt* too."

The cat squirms, and I lower her to the hardwood floor, to which her claws have not been kind. Unlike me, she's grown bolder each day, pronouncing herself queen of my loft.

That last email suggested someone close to the stalker died at my hands, but I don't know how that can be. The only patient deaths I've experienced in my four years at Congress Medical were patients who either died of old age or because of a prolonged illness. Those deaths occurred in the hospital or in hospice, and I wasn't involved in their care beyond outpatient visits. Their deaths saddened me, but only a few were unexpected.

And now you will pay, the stalker's email said.

When? When will I pay? And how? I've sent three emails asking him to clarify what he means, defending myself as to the impossibility of what he's accusing me of, but I've heard nothing back. His sudden silence has left me in a constant state of fight or flight.

I've decided to assume it *is* a man sending the threats. The message didn't seem that of a woman, although I could be mistaken. In reality, the person could be any gender identity, but picturing the stalker in my mind helps me process the threat.

After a few more minutes of rumination, I force my legs to move and exit my condo. I'm two feet into the carpeted corridor when Nathan, my actuary neighbor—who must have made some good investments to afford this place—steps out of his loft. Possibly, he was staring out his peephole until I left, wanting to time our departures.

My lips find a smile. "Good morning, Nathan."

"Let's hope so." He transfers his briefcase to his left hand so he can tap his leg with the right. "My calf cramped up three times last night. Awful pain. Do you think I'm deficient in something?"

While we drift toward the elevator, I discuss the healthiness of his diet and the extreme unlikeliness of a nutritional deficit.

"I was reading about autopsies the other day," he says, smoothing a few wayward hairs off his forehead.

Uh oh.

"The article said you can still have a heart attack if your coronary arteries are normal."

"Well, so to speak, maybe. Other factors can lead to a

myocardial infarction." I'm unprepared for this discussion at seven thirty in the morning, especially when I'm already on edge. Manuel was the pathologist, not me. Hopefully, my response will end the conversation.

It doesn't. Just as the elevator pings open, Nathan says, "I also read that if you inject someone in the eye to kill them it could be missed. You know, in forensic medicine."

My shock must be visible on my face because as he holds the elevator door open for me, he apologizes. "Forgive me. I get lost in facts sometimes."

We step inside the lift, its cottony scent compliments of an air-freshener tucked up in the corner.

Nathan's expression is contrite. "Just trying to distract you with conversation. You seem stressed. That's not good for any of your organs."

I'm moved by his concern, not to mention his perceptiveness. "I'm fine, thank you, but as for eyes on autopsy, I wouldn't know about that."

Fortunately, the elevator stops on the sixth floor and two more residents get on, ending the morbid banter. When we exit the building, a sunny June day greets us. A light breeze lifts my hair and carries the briny smell of the bay fused with the exhaust of passing traffic. I'm relieved Nathan needs to go left while I go right.

Before he heads off down the populated sidewalk, he pulls a bran muffin covered in plastic wrap from his sport coat pocket. The baked good is crushed on one side but mostly intact.

"Here." He glances down shyly. "I made a fresh batch last night. You look like you need it more than me this morning."

He darts off before I can thank him. Touched again by his thoughtfulness, I remind myself that underneath his health-focused rants lies a kind man. Some good people still exist in the world. They're not all monsters.

I tuck the muffin into my bag and hurry off to clinic. Twenty minutes later, when I'm in line at the coffee kiosk with the other professionals who work in the building, I listen to the barista with the big hair gossip to her coworker. Any fleeting affection for humanity I had vanishes.

"It's just near the corner on Piedmont Street," she says as she froths up a latte. "It's one of those booth-rental places. My stylist says it's better than being employed by some greedy salon owner." The barista hands the latte to the customer, and as soon as she's taken the order for the woman in line in front of me, her chatter returns. "She stays late for me every Tuesday. Does a wash and full blow-out and locks up when we leave. It's because I tip her so well." The barista, whose nametag reads Kirsten, lowers her voice conspiratorially. "Given her penchant for designer bags and shoes, I know where those tips are going. Between you and me, she should really stay in her price lane."

"Well, not everyone has a sugar daddy like you," her coworker says. She takes my order, and we share a smile.

My smile doesn't last. With coffee in hand, I cross the lobby to the elevators, my low-heeled pumps clicking on the marble flooring. I hope I make it through the day.

With only one hour of clinic remaining, my second to last patient cancels, and I find a window to call Martin Hernandez, the investigator from the Medical Board who's looking into the anonymous complaint. Although I know who's behind the bogus accusation, Martin doesn't, and my inability to explain it to him makes my jaw ache with frustration.

As I wait for him to pick up, I slide my chair all the way inside my workspace to hide in my cubby. The counter presses into my stomach, but I don't care. If I could shrink down to the size of a pen, I would.

Martin interviewed my physician colleagues: Terrence, Frank, Irene, and even Rishi from home. Each one assured me the complaint is ridiculous, but it didn't lessen my embarrassment. Bo, our locum tenens doctor, was also interviewed, but he hasn't mentioned anything about it, probably because he feels he doesn't know me well enough to weigh in. Our RN Alice, the LPNs, our office manager, and our receptionists were similarly questioned about my conduct, and they stand behind me as well. Still, whenever I walk by them, I sense lowered voices and a shift in conversation, as if they've been discussing me behind my back. My face burns a constant shade of red. It appears embarrassment is another emotion I can feel.

When Martin Hernandez answers, I ask if there have been any developments. He assures me everything looks good.

"I'm staring at your negative drug screen right now," he says. "Thank you for submitting it so promptly. Helps support your case."

Does my case need supporting?

"Each of your colleagues swears they've never seen you use any substances beyond the occasional glass of wine at dinner parties—and never at work." He stresses that last part, and I begin to believe he's on my side.

His next words are even more reassuring. "Since the caller never identified himself, and given the testimonies of your colleagues, including your residency program director—"

"You went that far back?" I cut in. No doubt Dr. Connor "Cocky" Casey, my former program director, enjoyed that conversation. Something to lord over me.

"I'm very thorough and efficient." Martin's voice sounds like he's smiling. "So between my interviews and your spotless professional record, I feel comfortable writing this complaint up as lacking merit. In other words, frivolous. I'll prepare my ROI—that's Report of Investigation—by tomorrow morning and pass it on to the investigator supervisor. She'll then send it to the Board secretary, and if everyone's in agreement, it'll be filed away."

"So it won't go on my record?"

"It will remain confidential and won't be docketed, no."

I exhale so heavily Martin laughs on the other end.

"Relax, Dr. Sullivan," he says. "This happens more than you realize. Mixed in with all the legitimate complaints are everything from minor grievances like outdated magazines in the doctor's waiting room to full-out lies. Someone seeking to settle a score."

If only Martin Hernandez knew how spot-on he was.

I thank him for moving so quickly on this, which I can't imagine is the norm. Still, my relief is not one hundred percent. Whether the complaint is docketed or not, I'll still be on the Board's radar. How can I not be?

As soon as I hang up with the investigator, a text from Kim Lombardi comes in: **Your allergic patient is doing okay. He's over the worst of it, but FYI, he's pissed. At both you AND his wife.**

Although I'm grateful the hospitalist keeps me routinely informed via text messages—she considers us better friends than we are—her message only makes me feel worse. How could I have messed up so badly?

"Hey, Hope, there's—"

At the sudden interruption, I swivel my chair too rapidly and almost fall over. Bo quickly rights me.

"Whoa, you okay?" he asks, his body pressed against mine in support. His sandy hair is tousled after a long day, and his basil eyes match the hue of his shirt.

I jump up to distance myself from him. "Jesus, you have to quit sneaking up on me."

I didn't mean to sound so hostile, but my heart is somewhere in my throat, and I'm struggling to swallow it down. When I see the wounded look in his eyes, I curse my overreaction.

Terrence rounds the corner, likely wondering what all the commotion is about.

"I'm sorry," I say to Bo, but before I can add anything else, he holds up a hand. A basket dangles from his fingers. Through cellophane, I see a box of tea and some cookies.

"I just came to give you this," he says, his posture stiff. "I was at the front counter when it was delivered. Told Sarah I'd bring it to you on my way back."

He plops it on my counter and hurries back to his own workspace down the next hallway.

Terrence approaches me. "Bad day?"

"Try bad week." I sink back down on my chair and pluck the card off the gift basket. Alice appears with my next patient, and I indicate with a nod that I'll be ready.

"Maybe take it easier on Bo," Terrence says. "I know he's a bit…Ken-dollish…but he's an okay guy."

"He reads war history and wears trail shoes with faded suit pants."

Who's the judgmental one now? I imagine the barista saying to me.

Terrence frowns. "Don't judge a book by its cover. Well, the man cover, not the actual war-book cover." He lowers his voice and leans back against my counter, his elbow brushing the gift basket. "Between you and me, he used to have a problem with alcohol. Then something happened to scare him straight—maybe a patient died, not sure—but he's been volunteering at a youth shelter ever since." Terrence raises an eyebrow. "Told me that in confidence, by the way."

I mime zipping my lips to let him know Bo's secret is safe with me.

"And that's not all. His sister died a while back. They were twins."

Great. Now I feel even shittier.

"Who's the basket from?" Terrence points to the small

card in my hand which I still haven't opened. "I'm betting Ada again."

Thoughts of my favorite patient soften my mood. Even though she knows she's not supposed to bring me gifts, today's present probably stems from my squeezing her in this morning for a medication check. She has a history of congestive heart failure, and it's so well controlled on digoxin that she refuses to let me switch her to a newer drug. I just wish it would heal the sweet woman's heartache too. If the world was full of Ada Jacksons, I wouldn't need to do what I do on the side.

I open the card and read it out loud. "Thank you for all your care. From your most grateful patient."

"Ada it is then." Terrence laughs and gives my shoulder a squeeze. "That complaint is bogus, and the Board will see that. Relax. You know we've all got your back."

My throat tightens at Terrence's support, but all I manage is a weird cluck.

Ninety minutes later, when all the patients have been seen and most of the staff have left except for Bo and Irene, I head to the break room and boil water for the tea Ada dropped off. Once it's steeping at my workstation, I get down to what I've been itching to do all day: rack my brain for any patient whose death I could be responsible for.

The first to surface is a man with Alzheimer's who died two months ago from pneumonia. The oral antibiotic I'd initially prescribed didn't stave off hospitalization. Dan Knudson told me the organism was resistant to everything, and the man's death was inevitable. There is also my patient who died unexpectedly on the ward last year. A sudden cardiac arrest. For weeks, I fretted I had missed something in his outpatient diagnosis.

But the stalker's email said *she*. I take a sip of tea and pull up the email on my phone to reread it for the hundredth time. She was smart, she was successful, she was beautiful in every way.

It was a woman he lost, someone close to him.

And your negligence took her from me, he accused.

Who? Who did I take?

A mother? A daughter? A wife? I have no idea how old my email stalker is.

I lean back in my chair and close my eyes. Thinking and sipping, sipping and thinking, the mug warm in my hands, a refuge against the cool air blasting from the air-conditioning vent above my head. My somber brainstorming pauses only briefly, when Irene calls goodbye, leaving Bo and me alone in the clinic.

A sixty-year-old patient of mine passed away last year after a long bout with breast cancer, but I rarely saw her during the end stages, her care shifting to her oncologist.

A fifty-four-year-old woman I'd been treating for familial hypercholesterolemia suffered a fatal heart attack three years ago, but that wasn't a result of poor medical care. It was a result of poor genes.

Irene had a young woman die from heart failure after severe anorexia nervosa, and Terrence lost a patient to lupus, but although I'd seen each woman in clinic when Irene and Terrence were unavailable, I can't think of anything I might have done that contributed to their demise.

Regardless, I make a written list of all these women and a few more that come to mind. Once I reach a standstill, I wake up my laptop screen. The EMR pops back into view. I click the search tab and hesitate.

Accessing medical records is tricky. Gone are the days when doctors—and nurses, and receptionists, and everyone else on staff—had full rein to patient charts. HIPAA, the Health Insurance Portability and Accountability Act, came and limited that freedom, and rightfully so. But along with HIPAA (and electronic records) came restrictions that cripple me now. Big Brother is watching. Big Brother knows who accesses a chart.

Having treated all the women on my list at least once or

twice, I could justify reentering a couple of their records. But all of them? The women are deceased. What justification do I have for reopening their charts? I could claim research, but I've submitted no formal application, and I'm not sure that would fly.

Like Diva with her paw, I scratch behind my ear. Bo flashes in my peripheral vision and gives me a quick nod good-bye. He scurries away before I can apologize for my earlier behavior. Probably wants to steer clear of me, and I don't blame him.

I return to the patient list on my counter. The fifty-four-year-old woman with familial hypercholesterolemia seems the most likely candidate for perceived mismanagement, so I risk opening her chart. Given it has been inactivated due to her death, I might be drawing more attention my way. *Great.* All I need is to be reported to the Board for chart-snooping.

After fifteen minutes of perusing her records, I find nothing.

I yawn. Twice. Desiring more caffeine, I drain the last of my tea and head to the break room to steep another cup. When it's ready, I grab a cookie from Ada's gift basket and return to my workstation with both mug and treat, hoping they will revive me. I close the woman's chart, not daring to access any others. If my email stalker is trying to drive me crazy with helplessness, he's succeeding.

In my growing fatigue, another thought comes to me. What if the stalker is referring to a patient from an earlier time? Back when I was a resident? A med student, even. Lots of patients I cared for as a trainee died, not because of my mistakes, but because I rotated through wards housing Boston General's sickest patients—the ICU, the cancer floor, the burn unit. I'd never be able to remember all their names. Or what if it's a patient from my work at the free clinic?

Too tired to think, I struggle to focus. I yawn and then yawn again. I still have today's charts to complete, charts of very much alive patients. My energy should be devoted to them.

I drink more tea, and when I can barely keep my eyes open, I drink some more. I open Spotify on my phone, select a peppy tune, and rise from my chair and start dancing. It's a good way to release endorphins. Got me through plenty of long nights on call. One song is all I need, and I'm alone in the clinic, so who cares? The janitor won't arrive for a while.

But even my dance moves grow sluggish.

What is wrong with me?

I roll my hips, trying to get in the groove, but my vision doubles.

Scared now, I grab the counter. Am I having a stroke?

I look to the right.

I cry out in alarm.

Bo Linton is standing there in our maze of hallways, not twelve feet away, staring at me, a look of…what—longing? pity? sadness?—on his face. I didn't hear him return. How long has he been lurking there? Watching me?

"Whaaaa…?" I start to ask, but my lips and tongue are thick and uncooperative. My body sways, but not from the music.

And then it hits me. *Oh God.* Terrence said Bo lost a sister. A twin sister? Could I have…? Was it me who…?

"I forgot my phone," Bo says. "I—Hope, are you all right?"

As soon as he rushes toward me, I scream. Or at least I try to.

Because someone else is behind Bo.

I fall to the ground. My vision is blurred, my brain foggy, and my eyelids cement slabs, but yes, there are definitely two people in front of me, one with a green shirt and tall, the other hidden in jeans, a hoodie, and a medical mask.

Bo makes it halfway toward me when the person behind

him sneaks up and cracks him over the head. I don't see with what. I only hear a sickening *thump*.

Bo's body drops to the tiled floor.

The stranger approaches me.

My heavy eyelids close.

13

HIM

S he sits there restrained to a chair, ankles strapped to the wooden legs, hands bound behind her back, head lolled forward in her induced sleep.

Just like that man she tortured in the barn, Michael thinks. *Well, not* just *like.*

She's not in a barn. She's in the living room of Michael's mildewed basement apartment, the only place he can afford, and even that's in doubt with his twice-missed rent payment. Another difference is that he used plastic ties instead of duct tape. Somehow that seemed more dignified, not that she deserves dignity.

His knees bounce a rapid rhythm against his own chair positioned four feet away, and his teeth grind back and forth. His impatience for her to wake up is a twelve on a scale of one to ten.

He already went through her phone, having brought along the leather tote bag he found in her workspace. Fortunately, there were no security cameras near the exam rooms, not that he'd likely be identified in his hoodie and mask. He used her face to open the phone screen and then found her personal number, the only detail he didn't yet have. He added it to his contacts under the name *Killer*.

He holds a knife in his hand, just like she did to the man in the barn.

Could he really use it? He's not sure. Certainly not as callously as she did, as if stabbing a person's thigh were nothing more than stabbing a bloody steak. Granted, from what Michael overheard of their exchange, the guy beat his wife. He probably got what he deserved. On some level, Michael feels a sliver of respect for the doctor.

But then he thinks about his wife. His wife didn't beat anyone up. She didn't deserve to die.

And for that, Michael must make the doctor take responsibility. At the very least, she must acknowledge what she did and feel some remorse. His wife deserves to be more than an insignificant, forgotten footnote in the doctor's privileged life.

If he can't make her do those things, then he'll make her pay. Make her atone for her clueless disregard of his wife's life because if he doesn't, his own grief will swallow him whole. There'll be nothing left of him but the dust that coats his shabby furniture and the mites that burrow into his thread-bare carpet.

He closes his eyes and waits.

14

I blink open my eyes and struggle to keep them that way. It's dark. Blurry. Mostly shadows. Where am I?

My mouth feels like a dried-out sponge, and my arms ache all the way down to my fingers, which tingle painfully when I try to move them. Something smells funky, like a pile of wet gym towels. My eyelids fight to close, and a dizzying fatigue threatens to sink me back into my groggy slumber.

I blink a few more times, and a figure materializes in front of me.

I jerk back, but my body has little give. I'm sitting, that much I can tell. My hands are bound behind me, and when I try to move my legs, I feel nothing but resistance. Something tight binds my ankles

"Where am I?" I croak to the figure in the shadowy room. From the shape of his body and the way he sits on his chair, legs wide, it's clear he's a man, but I can't see his features in the dark. "Who are you?"

He doesn't answer.

Squinting, I try to make out my surroundings. Shapes of furniture behind the man. A couch, maybe a desk in the corner. To my left, a glowing light of…what?…a microwave?

On my right, the faint illumination of a streetlamp slips through a high window.

Then I remember what happened.

My gaze darts back to the shadowy man whose legs bounce up and down on the chair. "You…you were in the clinic."

Oh God. Bo.

"Where is Dr. Linton?" My lips feel flabby and sluggish. "What did you do to him? Is he okay?"

The man in front of me still says nothing. Just keeps fidgeting in his chair.

"You better not have hurt him." My voice grows louder, stronger, my tongue loosening up.

It's a dumb thing to say, because I saw Bo go down. Cracked over the head with something. A single blow isn't always enough to knock a person out. Did Bo suffer worse? More blows? Punches? My throat pinches with guilt. Whatever happened to him is because of me. Because of the stalker I first chose to ignore and then stupidly thought I could manage. How did the guy get into the clinic? Was the back door unlocked? Maybe he snuck in after Bo came back for his phone.

"What do you want?" I ask.

My captor's body falls abruptly still, and he finally speaks. "How does it feel to get a taste of your own medicine?"

"What? I don't…"

It hits me. I'm tied to a chair. I've been drugged. He must have seen my performance in the barn, and he's replicating it. His emails suggested he had something on me.

"Bravo." Outrage fights its way through my hazy fear. "You roofied me. Or something." I replay the last hour in clinic and try to piece together how he did it.

After a few imagined scenarios, it comes to me. The tea. No plastic wrapping covered the box. Easy to crush something up and slip it into those tea bags, the tea I thought was from

Ada. *Thank you for all your care*, the note said. *From your most grateful patient.* I realize now—*a little late, Hope*—that no name was signed. I just assumed it was Ada given her history.

My mistake might be understandable, but if my legs were free, I'd kick myself for being so gullible. Then I'd kick the man in front of me. A good, dirty Krav Maga kick.

As if reading my mind, he bounds up from his chair. I shirk back but regret my weakness.

He doesn't come for me. Instead, he stomps off in the direction of the glowing light and slaps at something on the wall. Track lighting fills the room.

My eyes close against the brightness. When I open them again, I realize I'm in a basement apartment. Small living room with a sagging couch that holds my tote bag, a desk in the corner topped with computer hardware, a kitchenette to my left, its laminate countertops cluttered with empty beer bottles and takeout boxes. Near the hopper window to my right, a moist stain of mold darkens the wall.

The man steps back into my line of sight, and I finally get a good look at his face.

"Manny!" I cry out.

As quickly as I think I see my dead fiancé, my logic returns.

This isn't Manuel. The stubble, the olive skin, the intensity of those dark eyes—those parts looks like my Manny. The rest —the narrow jawline, the stained T-shirt with the logo of some tech company, the too-loose jeans on a too-thin body— those don't look like Manny at all. Nor do the scratches and scabs on this guy's arms, which he digs at now like a patient with skin-picker's dermatitis. I realize, too, that this isn't the man who attacked me on my run, which was only two weeks ago but feels like twenty.

Something else dawns on me. "I've seen you in clinic. For your stomach issues." My surprise makes me sound like an imbecile.

"I've been watching you for a while, Dr. Sullivan." He stops picking his arms and starts pacing the tattered carpet. "Quite the double life you live."

I don't bother to deny it. What's the point? "Whatever you've seen me do, whatever I *have* done on my own time, I assure you they've all deserved it. Dog abusers. Child abusers. Wife abusers."

At the word *wife*, the guy pauses his agitated pacing. A weird noise, not quite a sob, not quite a choke, emits from his throat.

His wife. His wife has died.

And he thinks I killed her.

My stomach tightens. If that's the case, I might not be getting out of here alive.

15

———

My abductor resumes his pacing and skin picking, back and forth in front of me. Pace pace pace. Pick pick pick. My arms ache behind my back, and my fingers still tingle, but at least they're not numb. I assume a plastic tie binds my wrists, because a glance down reveals the same thing around each of my ankles.

"You don't know why you're here, do you?" His tone drips with disdain. "You go about your life, alive, healthy, rich, no idea of the pain you've caused."

"I'm sorry, but I don't under—"

"You don't understand? Oh, poor baby." He halts and thumps his chest like a crazed Tarzan. "She was everything to me, everything, and you took her away. Then you went on with your life as if nothing happened."

"Your wife? If you tell me a little about her, I might remember." My heart races. I'm not used to being on this side of revenge. "Was she a patient of mine?"

He mimes a face at me. "Did you need a medical degree to put that together? Of course she was a patient of yours. She was pregnant, you know. With twins."

His voice cracks, and I realize what I heard earlier wasn't disdain. Not entirely, anyway. It was grief.

"We wanted to get settled in our careers first. She was a lawyer. You're not the only one with a fancy job, you know." He doesn't give me time to respond. "But she had a family history of early ovarian failure, and when she turned thirty-three, she started to panic that if we didn't try soon, she'd never be able to have kids."

His speech is urgent, as if he needs me to hear his pain.

"At first, it didn't work. She couldn't get pregnant. I told her she was enough for me, but she was determined."

While he keeps talking, I pump my forefeet, trying to restore circulation. I wriggle my hands behind my back. Not as snug as I'd first thought. Maybe the tingling in my fingers is more from the awkward positioning than from too tight of a bind.

"I suggested IVF, but she wasn't ready to go that route. Not yet…"

With my wrists crisscrossed, I realize my paracord bracelet is within reach. My bracelet with the small, hidden blade. Maybe I can cut myself free.

"…but then it was like a miracle. We found out she was pregnant. That was the happiest day of my life. That and the day we got married. She was the love of my life. I know that sounds stupid. Trite, even. But she made life worth getting out of bed for. When you're always swimming in darkness you need someone like that, you know?"

I do, I think but don't say. *More than you realize.*

I flit my fingers over the bracelet, trying to find the release clasp. Before I can, the man rushes toward me.

"And then you killed her. Six years ago, you killed her and my babies."

I shrink back at his outburst. His face is so close I can see the capillaries in his eyes and the shadows of poor sleep underneath them.

"Six years?" I fumble with the roped fabric of my bracelet. "How…I was a third-year resident back then."

I try to remember her. A younger woman's death should stand out. My fingers temporarily pause their hunt as my mind combs through the ICU patients who died during my residency. I need more details.

"What happened to your wife? Please, maybe I can reassure you—"

"Reassure me? Ha." He points to his computer equipment. "I tried to let it go, I did. Tried to bury myself in work. I had a great job in tech. Now though? Now I can barely pay rent on this shitty apartment from the few freelance jobs I land, people who're too stupid to know the computer fix they need is only a Google search away."

He drops down in front of me. His erratic, up-down behavior makes me nervous. This is a man who has nothing to lose.

I keep twisting my wrist, my fingers searching for the bracelet's clasp. There isn't much leeway in the bind, but there's some. I twist more, more, my fingers running over the fabric cords. The plastic tie cuts into my flesh. More, more…

There's the release tab.

"I can't eat," the man says, waving his knife around. The blade is at least six inches longer than the one I'm trying to free. "I can't sleep. I can't think." Tears sprout in his eyes. "I miss her so much. Every day. Do you know what it's like to lose someone you love so deeply? To lose all hope in life?"

As much as I want to escape, a flood of sympathy washes over me. Empathy, too, because I do indeed know what it's like to lose hope. We wear the same shoes, my abductor and I, only his ended up marching to me, while mine were marching to assholes.

"So I started watching you," he says. "Following you. Knowing I had to make you pay."

"I'm so sorry." I click the blade open, careful not to drag it over my skin. "I've lost people too. My parents. My fiancé. My...my..." I can't bring myself to say *baby* and risk the emotion it holds. Escape is what matters now. But if he only knew how similar we are. "I understand that black hole, a hole that devours every one of your molecules until you stop caring about living at all."

He falls still and stares at me, as if he didn't expect that response. For a moment I believe he might let me go. Then his lip curls, and his need for vengeance returns.

I quietly pull the inch-long blade out from my paracord bracelet and press it against the tie binding my wrists. My movements are awkward but careful. If I drop the bracelet, it's all over.

"What happened to your wife?" I ask. "Help me remember, and I'll try to explain things better."

He seems to debate this for a minute. He rises from his crouched position and returns to the wooden chair that matches my own, about four feet away. "She got a blood clot, but you were too busy. Too many other patients you paid more attention to. Maybe she wasn't rich enough, important enough, special enough."

That comment riles me. *I treat every patient the same,* I'm about to retort, but my tongue cuts the words off. Do I? I believe I do. I pray I do. But could I suffer from unconscious bias? Don't studies suggest we all do?

Or were we simply overwhelmed on the ward that night? I think back to six years ago.

"Was she in the ICU?" I ask, still cutting the plastic tie with my blade. Twice it slips, and twice my fingers do a panicked clench to keep the bracelet from falling to the carpet.

He scoffs and jabs his knife in the air. "She never made it that far. She *should* have been, but she was on the general medicine ward, left alone in her room. Ignored. Everyone rushing to tend to everyone but her. And during that time, during those awful minutes before she was moved, that clot shot to her lungs and killed her." He makes a guttural sound. "Killed my twin babies."

I swallow. My mouth fills with sand. I keep cutting the plastic tie. A vague memory forms in my mind. A pregnant woman, mid- to late-thirties. Died awaiting transfer to the ICU. I remember something with Risk Management. An investigation. A presentation at Resident Report, but she wasn't my patient. Yes, I remember now. She wasn't mine.

"She wasn't my patient," I blurt out, cutting faster now. My wrists are looser, close to being set free.

"I saw you!" He jumps up from the chair again, the knife swiping close to his leg. "I saw your name all over her chart. Dr. Hope Sullivan. *Hope.* Such a cruel irony because there was no hope for my wife. Risk Management claimed it was a 'tragic but unforeseeable event,' and every lawyer I consulted agreed. Liars, all of them."

"No, no." I try to remember the details. All the while I cut the tie with my tiny blade. Cut, saw, cut, saw. Despite being a basement rental, the apartment is warm, and perspiration dots my brow. "I might have been the senior resident on call that night, but a junior resident would have been her primary doctor. That's who would have overseen her care."

Who were the junior residents on with me? I wonder. *Who?* There would've been several. Boston General's internal medicine program has dozens of residents. Maybe it wasn't even an internal medicine resident. Maybe it was an ER resident, or a family practice resident rotating through our wards, or a visiting doctor not associated with Boston General.

"What was your wife's name?" I ask.

Snaaaap.

The plastic tie breaks. My wrists fall free. I keep the blade between my fingers and pray he doesn't notice my arms' newfound laxity.

"You think the fact you were just the senior resident on call that night excuses you?" he says. "Are you *kidding* me?"

He's right. It's a cop-out.

I'll try to make it right with him, I will. I'll find his wife's records, get to the bottom of it, get him compensation if I can. Just acknowledging the negligence—if indeed it occurred—might go some way in healing him.

He stands a couple of feet in front of me. I can't do anything with my ankles bound. I need him closer.

"*Balık baştan kokar,*" he says.

I don't understand his words, but my mind focuses only on escape now. He takes a step forward and squats down again. A few inches more, and I'll be able to reach out and touch him.

"That's Turkish for 'a fish rots from the head down.'" He taps his knife against my knee. "One of my grandmother's favorite sayings."

My abductor has no accent, but his Turkish sounds legit, so maybe his grandma taught him the language.

"Do you know what that means?" He inches closer.

I squeeze the small blade of my bracelet between my thumb and first two fingers, ready to use it. I answer his question. "It means I was the supervising resident, so the buck stops with me."

"For all I know, you've killed other patients too. Maybe on purpose. I've seen what you can do. I have it on video."

If he moves one inch closer, I'm confident I can cut him.

"I swear I haven't," I say, ready to swipe. "What you… what you saw in that barn…he was a bad man. A terrible man. Don't you see? I'm not that different from you. I'm trying to get justice too."

"Then maybe that means I need to kill you."

He closes the last tiny distance on his haunches and raises the knife. Flips it this way and that, the track lighting reflecting off its shiny blade. He doesn't stab it toward me, and I'm not sure he truly intends to hurt me. My gut tells me he doesn't have it in him, that deep down he's too kind, too good of a person. His eyes hold more pain and sorrow than murder.

But I can't take that chance.

With the swiftness of a cat, I swipe my freed arm around and rake my blade across his neck.

16

———

I don't slice deeply. My only intention is to disarm him long enough to escape my ankle binds and flee his basement lair.

Disarm him I have, for in his shock over my surprise attack, one of his hands darts to his neck, and the other drops the knife. Blood slips between his fingers from my cut, and he stumbles back.

I dump my body forward and scoop up the knife. Quickly, I cut the plastic ties that tether my ankles, surprised by the sharpness of the blade.

By the time I look up again, he's lunging at me, left hand still pressed against his neck. He swipes a right jab at my cheek, but whether he's an unskilled fighter or merely an unenthused one, he manages barely a clip which I deflect.

I burst up. The table chair falls back on the carpet. Before I can run to the door, the neck of my sweater pulls against my throat. He's wadded the fabric up in his hand, and my body jerks back like a vaudeville act yanked off the stage.

Instinctively, my dirty fighting skills take over. I flex my leg and land a forceful backward blow onto his kneecap. When his hold on my sweater loosens, I spin around and deliver a fisted punch to his nose. The cartilage crunches beneath my knuckles.

He howls and backs away, blood dripping from his nostrils. My adrenaline surges, and when he holds out his hand, it's only too late that I consider he might be crying *uncle*. Instead, my amygdala detects a threat before my forebrain catches up, and I swing around and smack a roundhouse kick into his throat.

Krav Maga.

Fight dirty.

It's a woman's best defense.

My abductor drops to the outdated carpet, both hands now at his neck in the universal sign of choking. He flops onto his back, his body writhing, his narrow jaw working back and forth. Wheezy gasps erupt from his mouth, and when his dark eyes widen in fear, I see Manny right before aggressive leukemia stole his life.

Oh shit, what have I done?

The man struggles to breathe. How badly have I injured him? Have I crushed his windpipe? Simply bruised his cartilage? Damaged his larynx?

I squat next to him, press my ear to his mouth, and stare at his chest. It's difficult to tell how well he's moving air. His lips aren't blue, so that's reassuring.

He needs help, though. Help I can't deliver here alone in his basement. But neither can I risk being found here.

His writhing stills, but his gasping persists. A tear streaks down his cheek, and at the sight of it, my own eyes threaten to well up. I don't know his story. Who he is. I don't even know his name. Have I killed him? Killed him for doing what I myself have done? Seeking justice for someone wronged?

"I'm going to get you help," I say. "I promise."

Not wanting to use my own phone—assuming it's still in my bag on the sofa—I roll the man onto his side to maintain his airway and find his cell in the back pocket of his loose-fitting jeans. I hold it in front of his face, and the screen unlocks. While I wait to be connected to 911, I realize I have no idea where I am.

I pat his other pockets for a wallet. A driver's license would tell me who he is and where he lives. No wallet.

Phone to my ear, I dart to the kitchen counter and spot a piece of mail beneath an empty pizza box. It's addressed to "Current Resident." When the operator picks up and asks what my emergency is, I sputter out the address on the junk mail and tell her a man can't breathe and needs help. Then, while she's still speaking, I cram the envelope in my bag and grab a dishtowel bunched up by the sink. I wipe my prints from the phone and slip it back into the pocket of the stranger I've incapacitated.

Grabbing my bag off the sofa, I'm relieved to find my own phone still inside it. Whether he's looked through it or not, I don't know. I race to the door but then halt. Returning to the living room, where the wide-eyed man is thankfully still breathing, I swipe the cut plastic ties off the floor, along with my bracelet and his knife. The knife I wipe clean of prints and place in the sink. The bracelet and ties go into my bag. Finally, I return both chairs to the table in the small kitchen and wipe those down too. I don't want him to get questioned about why he has restraints in his home or signs of a struggle. Keeping him from getting arrested for abducting me is the least I can do.

I exit the basement door, which is a private entrance, and bolt up the concrete steps into the night. To my enormous relief, sirens materialize in the distance.

The next five days drag in slow motion.

I see patients in clinic Thursday and Friday.

I visit Bo in the hospital Friday night, grateful he remembers nothing about the attack but ashamed his head injury is because of me.

I spend Saturday pampering Diva and letting her continue to take over my loft.

I attend my Sunday Krav Maga class and go see the patient whose allergic reaction to clindamycin landed him in the hospital due to my mistake. He is being discharged but wants nothing to do with me, his clipped responses to my questions proof of that. As I leave the internal medicine ward with my head lowered and my cheeks burning, Dan Knudson, the hospitalist on duty, tries to reassure me a medication error like that can happen to any doctor.

On Monday morning, I lend a supportive ear to my neighbor, Nathan, first peering at his new scalp lesion and then listening to his heart for a nonexistent arrhythmia.

And now, at 7:00 p.m. on Monday night, the summer sun still bright and the temperature warm, I am driving to a suburb west of Boston, where I have been assured by the animal shelter that Shelly has found a wonderful home. I want to see it for myself.

None of these visits or activities serve as a distraction. Thoughts about the grieving man I left wounded in his dreary basement apartment last Wednesday torment me, and I'm dying to know how he's doing. Like a ghosted lover, I continuously check my email, praying to see a new message from him, but nothing comes.

The irony almost makes me laugh out loud. A couple of weeks ago I told him to fuck off. Now I long for him to reach out.

Did he die? Is he in a hospital? Is he back home, plotting his next act of revenge against me? If that's the case, I can't really blame him.

As my SUV idles at a red light, still in Boston proper and a good distance from Shelly's new digs, I realize I might never know my stalker's fate. Without having his name, I can't call hospitals and ask for him, and a Google search of his address didn't reveal his identity.

Thinking I might find out who he is from my patient schedule, I went back through months and months of appointments, looking for any male patients under forty with irritable bowel syndrome, which is what I had seen him for. Someone named Joe Smith fit the description, and it was only then I realized how fake the name sounded. The address "Joe Smith" provided was made up too. He paid cash for the office visit, claiming to have no insurance, so no credit card or other identifiers were on file. If I knew the name of his wife, that would help, but he never supplied that either.

Driving past red-brick rowhouses on Tremont Street, I flash back to the savage kick I gave the man's throat. I wince and rub my own. The fact I might have fatally wounded him renders me hollow.

At least Bo's subdural brain bleed was small, although his head remains wrapped in a bandage and his concussion could be months away from fully healing. He has no memory of the attack, and because of privacy concerns, the clinic's only security cameras are in the waiting room and in the corridor outside the front door. Everyone, including the police, believe Bo was alone when the intruder entered from the unlocked door in the back. I wasn't about to counter otherwise.

Although my stalker was wrong to clobber Bo over the head, I am convinced his true intent isn't violence. That might be naive on my part, but it's what my gut tells me. If given the chance to talk things out like grown adults and not vengeful cretins, I think the two of us would find we're more kindred spirits than enemies.

Then again, maybe I'm full of shit. Maybe I only feel this need to protect him because I feel guilty over what I did to him. Maybe also because he reminds me of Manny, at least the gentle side of him I imagine exists but didn't get the chance to see.

Whatever it is that motivates me, I need to find him.

Finally, I break free of the sluggish city traffic. Tightly packed homes and businesses give way to strip malls and then to winding roads and wooded residences. Fifteen minutes later, my GPS tells me the German shepherd's new digs are only two streets away.

Sure enough, when I round a second bend of oak trees and hydrangea bushes, I find the colonial house with a well-maintained lawn that matches the address the animal shelter gave me.

To my relief, two kids toss a Frisbee to Shelly in the front yard. She catches it in her mouth and trots back to the children, but not before doing a little celebratory spin.

The boy pets her and laughs. "Good job, girl, good job." The girl hugs her around the neck and says, "I love you, Maggie."

Maggie. It's a good name. Maybe even better than Shelly.

Gone is the dog's heavy collar and chain. Gone is the misery in her eyes.

I feel a hint of a smile on my face.

At least I did something right.

The following day, I exit the exam room of my last patient of the morning and return to my work counter. While I type the patient's note into the EMR, my abductor's fate is never far from my mind.

It has been six days since I kicked his throat. Six days without communication. Six days during which I might be a killer and not know it. But hey, according to my daily affirmation: *I don't have to be perfect to love myself.*

I pluck a peppermint from the pocket of my white doctor's coat, which I wear today because I can't get warm. As the mint burns my tongue I think of my father. He kept a jar of the candies in his science lab. Although they were never my favorite, I can't seem to quit them now.

For the fifth time, I check my last patient's allergy list. When I finally assure myself it is a safe drug for her, I send a prescription for cyclobenzaprine to her pharmacy of choice. The muscle relaxant should help her muscle spasms. If only I could take it to ease my own restlessness.

With my thoughts racing all over the place, the last thing I need is more caffeine, but I ditch my white coat and dart down to the lobby's coffee kiosk all the same. Mostly I'm avoiding my colleagues, even Terrence. I'm still embarrassed by the false claim my stalker made to the Medical Board twelve days ago and the resultant investigation. Plus, our entire staff has been on edge since Bo's attack, and if they draw me into another discussion about the intruder and who it could have been, I worry I'll reveal something I shouldn't. Best to stay quiet and play dumb.

As I cross the lobby's marble floor, I pass one of Terrence's patients, a woman who recently started chemotherapy for breast cancer. Her hair has started to thin, not yet enough for a wig or scarf but enough to be noticeable. I nod to her in passing.

Nearing the kiosk, which currently has no line, I grimace when I hear what the judgmental barista named Kirsten is saying to her coworker about Terrence's patient.

"…she should style it differently. It looks *awful* hanging straight like that. She could be a pretty woman if she used better product on it." Kirsten, who is still staring off at the woman with cancer, flutters her lips. "If that was me, I'd wear a wig."

At my approach, the nice barista elbows her coworker. Kirsten dons her fake smile. "What can I get for you?" she asks me.

My jaw clenches so tightly I can barely verbalize my order. Miss Judgie is every elementary kid who mocked my childhood stutter and every middle- and high-school girl who called me "zit face" because of my acne. Doesn't matter that both conditions resolved and that by graduation none of my classmates remembered my awkward phases. *I* remembered. *I* still carried the burn.

What if Terrence's patient overheard the barista? As if the woman's life isn't difficult enough—cancer in her forties, three kids at home. Who is this big-haired, loud-mouthed server to make such a cruel, opinionated comment? She probably doesn't know the woman is sick, but that's no excuse. How would she like it if someone talked about her that way? How would she—to quote my abductor—like a taste of her own medicine?

My blood boils hotter than the coffee she pours me, and in this momentary rage, all my restless thoughts cease except for one: a remembered conversation from last week about the barista's weekly wash and blow-out with her stylist who rents a booth. "It's just near the corner on Piedmont Street," the barista boasted. "She stays late for me every Tuesday."

Today is Tuesday. Tonight, the barista named Kirsten will be in a booth in a salon loft near the corner of Piedmont Street.

A calm I haven't felt in days returns. So, too, does that invigorating electricity that makes everything else seem okay. This is what I need. This is what might restore my balance. It's only a small wrong I'll right, but it might still make a dent. A tiny, little dent in our endless inhumanity.

I smile and take my coffee.

18

───────

Piedmont Street is narrow and insulated by buildings, many of them bricked and multistoried. The one I'm waiting in now is smaller and more decrepit than the others but, more importantly, it's empty. Apart from the booth-rental salon on the main floor, the upper level houses an accountant's office and a shoe-repair shop, both of which are closed for the day.

Inside the stuffy confines of Style Your Way Salon, on one of six adjustable chairs in one of six booths, each fronted by a mirror and a counter, I stare out the window and keep watch for Kirsten. Out on the street, parked vehicles form a long queue, but the sidewalks are quiet. I spot only a young couple holding hands as they pass by. My loaded duffel bag sits near my feet. In the windowless back room, two shampooing sinks protrude from the navy-blue wall. From one of their porcelain bases hang prepared strips of duct tape.

When I arrived fifteen minutes ago, I told the barista's stylist she could go. I said I was Kirsten's friend and that Kirsten had an emergency and asked me to stop by to deliver the message. I told her I worked nearby so it was no bother.

The stylist didn't put up much resistance. Didn't even ask

what the emergency was. She simply packed up her products and supplies and made haste, probably as happy to be free of the late appointment with the gossipy mean girl as I am to soon be setting her straight.

After the stylist locked both the salon door and the main door behind us, I pretended to walk away. Once she was gone, I rounded the building and reentered through the same side window I'm staring out now. I had unlatched it while the stylist was gathering her supplies.

I noted only one security camera, back in the tiled entryway. After I climbed back in through the window, I had to walk past that camera to wedge magazines in both the building's door and the salon's door so that Kirsten could enter, but my disguise is good, and no one could identify me if they check the recording later. If there had been an alarm system, I would have had to make a plan B.

Dressed in my padded bodysuit, which I have covered with a long-sleeved blouse and a gauzy, floor-length skirt, I'm unrecognizable. A quick glance in the mirror on the opposite side of the window confirms this. Green contacts camouflage my caramel-brown irises. Over-the-top makeup contours my face into angles and shades it doesn't normally have. My long auburn wig hides my chin-length bob. It's the same wig I've had since residency, having bought it for a skit for our faculty roast.

Still, to be on the safe side, a balaclava mask with holes only for my eyes sits like an expectant child on my lap. I can't have Kirsten recognizing me. Although an intelligent person might be able to put two hairs and two hairs together and realize I heard her mocking the cancer patient this morning, I don't believe Kirsten is in that category. She is too self-absorbed. Even after all this time, I doubt she knows I'm a physician on the fourth floor of the building. I never wear my white coat outside the clinic—too pretentious—and honestly, I'm not sure she would be able to pick me out of a line-up as someone she serves on a regular basis.

I glance at my phone. Seven forty. I don't know the exact time of her appointment. That detail wasn't shared.

I don't have to wait long. Twenty minutes later, Kirsten clicks her three-inch heels down the sidewalk outside the window. Her slender thighs barely touch beneath her tight skirt. Her long hair looks a bit oily and flat and could indeed benefit from a "Style Your Way."

She'll get one, all right. Just not the one she had in mind.

The main building door heaves open, and I imagine the barista wondering why there is a magazine in its frame. I wipe my palms on my flowing skirt, hurry into the lavender-scented bathroom, and pull on a pair of gloves from my blouse pocket.

The inner salon door squeaks open. Heels tap on the entranceway tile.

My hair follicles tingle, and my cells spark with electricity.

The heel clicking slows.

"Hello?" Kirsten says. Then, more tentatively, "Mindy? Are you in here?"

Hidden inside the bathroom, I alter my voice and call out, "Come in. I'll be right out." Hopefully, between my altered pitch and the barrier of the bathroom door, she accepts that it's Mindy. "Just make your way to a sink."

The footsteps speed up again and click their way into the windowless back room.

"I'm in such a need of a fix-up," Kirsten says. "Not even July yet and the humidity is killing my hair. I was in beauty pageants in high school. I have a reputation to maintain, you know." She laughs, as if her joke is funny. "You should've seen some of my customers today. Talk about needy. Most of those pimply Gen Z-ers are still suckling on their mommas' teats."

Bold words considering Kirsten is still suckling on her sugar daddy's bank account.

I slip on the balaclava mask and reach into the deep

pocket of my skirt and clutch my stun gun. Unlike my Taser, the stun gun has to be used at close range, but I used my last Taser cartridge on the dog abuser and have yet to receive the new one I ordered. The shock and pain the stun gun inflicts should at least be enough to still Kirsten while I apply the duct tape. An intramuscular injection of a sedative would take a few minutes to kick in, and I can't wait that long to restrain her. Plus, I hate to waste my precious supply.

I lick my lips and open the door. A small voice nags at me—*Are you sure you should be doing this? With so much attention already your way?*—but I cast the warning aside. No time for that now. With my stun gun raised and ready, I rush to the sink where the barista is still standing.

She cries out in alarm. No doubt an armed, plump woman wearing gauzy clothes and a balaclava mask would have that effect on anyone.

Before she can stop me, I press the stun gun into her neck and shock her with fifty thousand volts of electricity. Her muscles stiffen, and her face contorts into a rictus of fear and disbelief. The ammonia scent of urine follows, and I have to bite back my natural compassion or I'll risk not finishing the job.

I don't have long before her stunned paralysis resolves—I only gave her a quick zap—so I lower her onto the sink's reclining chair, rip my pre-cut strands of duct tape from the porcelain underbelly of the adjacent sink, and secure her wrists to the armrests. Another piece of tape goes across her mouth before her cries can return. Finally, I secure her ankles to the chair, just as I did with the wife beater in my barn last month, and just as my stalker did to me six days ago.

Winding the tape above the straps of Kirsten's designer heels, I hear that annoying inner voice again:

You're escalating.

Stabbing the wife beater.

Torturing the dog abuser.

Shocking a woman who uses words, not fists.

This needs to stop.

Again, I ignore the voice of reason that asks whether this barista's crimes fit the punishment. If I back out now, she won't learn her lesson.

My face sweats inside the knit balaclava, probably streaking my makeup like the Joker's. Some movement returns to the barista, but she is too well taped to do much beyond shift her trunk.

She moans against her mouth-covering, but her voice is muffled. Her gaze shoots to her expensive purse on the floor and then back to me. I interpret this as a bribe to pay me off and leave her be.

I retreat to my duffel bag several feet away and withdraw scissors and hair clippers.

"Beyond that stun gun, nothing I do will hurt," I say to reassure her. "At least not physically. It's a psychological lesson you need."

Kirsten's eyes widen at the site of my hair-cutting tools, and her muffled protests grow more forceful.

I set the clippers on the sink and tap the scissors up and down on my gloved palm.

"You're a beautiful woman on the outside," I tell her, the knit mask puffing out with my breath. "Tall, nice figure, thick hair, pretty complexion."

She straightens her torso in the chair, and the duct tape over her mouth stretches taut. Good grief, I think she's trying to fight back a smile. That response alone tells me I'm doing the right thing.

"But on the inside?" I say. "On the inside, you're ugly. So very ugly."

The tape over her mouth loses its tautness.

"You belittle people, gossip about them, judge them."

She jerks her body, tugging at her restraints, but the tape doesn't budge.

I step to the side of her, so close that my skirt touches her silky blouse. I grab a chunk of her dark hair. "You need to worry less about what your boyfriend can do for you and more about what you can do for yourself."

Holding her head still, I spread the blades of the scissors over a thick mass of hair and cut close to her scalp. A foot and a half of hair falls to the white floor.

Her moans become a choked wail.

I cut another chunk off. The mirror in the booth across from us gives her a front-row seat to the show.

"So here's what I want." I lop off another big chunk of hair. "I want you to quit looking down your nose at everyone." *Snip.* "I want you to treat others with respect." *Snip.* "I want you to stop judging every goddamn thing people do. People who are just trying to survive life." *Snip, snip, snip.*

The floor is a mossy patch of black at my feet. With every yank and snip, the barista's sobbing intensifies. When her hair is nothing but a blunt shag, I drop the scissors into the sink and pick up the clippers instead.

At the sight of them, she shakes her head vigorously, something she didn't dare do with pointy scissors near her scalp.

"What I want," I continue, holding her skull firm against my padded chest and adjusting the clipper's blades to the closest setting, "is for you to take a long, deep look at yourself and work on being a better person." At the push of a button, the shears whir to life. "A kinder person. One who helps others instead of only herself."

The clippers buzz their way around the barista's scalp, which, uncovered by all that hair, is as prettily shaped as the rest of her.

"Volunteer at the food bank. Feed a homeless person. Visit the animal shelter."

She watches herself in the mirror and moans beneath the tape around her mouth. The fact she seems more bothered by my alteration of her appearance than by my attack itself tells me she is a lost cause.

If that's the case, why am I doing this?

When her scalp is at last covered by nothing but a soft dusting of dark stubble, I turn off the clippers and toss them into my open bag on the floor, which is far enough away to avoid her hair garden. Scissors back in my hand, I cut the duct tape around her right wrist, but only about halfway through.

"That should get you started." I toss the scissors into the bag. "Once I'm gone, bend over and rip the rest with your teeth." I click my own teeth a few times under the balaclava mask to demonstrate. "With one hand free, you can work on the other one and then your ankles. But"—I pull her head back and force her to examine herself in the mirror across from us—"maybe now you won't be so quick to judge others."

I kick her purse across the floor into one of the rental booths so she can't call anyone too quickly, at least not until I've made my escape. Then I rip the tape from her mouth.

She cries out in pain, but before she can make any other sound, I clap my gloved hand over her mouth. "If you scream, my scissors will do more than cut your hair, got it?"

She nods and, to her credit, says nothing. Maybe there is nothing left to say.

When I retrieve my duffel bag and stand upright to leave, I catch myself in the mirror. I wonder who this disguised madwoman in a balaclava is. If Manuel were alive, he wouldn't recognize her, nor would he want to.

In that Style Your Way mirror, my troubled eyes tell me what my heart already knows: *This tune-up doesn't feel so good.*

I stare back at the reams of dark hair on the floor and then at my prey. Like a trapped wolf gnawing at its own flesh, she gnashes at the tape on her wrist with her teeth, trying to free the first hand.

Where is my sense of victory? Of justice? Of improving humanity?

Where is my escape from apathy?

I feel nothing. Absolutely nothing. Well, nothing but a growing sense of shame.

Did my stalker taint the one activity that helps keep me alive? Or, like everything else in life, has the intoxicating effect simply worn off?

I picture the exit-door pills inside my nightstand drawer.

Maybe that means it's time.

19

HIM

Michael blinks open his eyes. White ceiling, white bedding, white walls, an old television set jutting from the one in front of him. He swallows, but it hurts so much, he doesn't dare do it again.

His left elbow feels full. When he moves it, something tugs at his flesh. Slowly, to avoid worsening his dizzy fog, he turns his head and finds an IV catheter in his arm, hooked to a fluid bag suspended from a pole. He rotates his head to the other side, just now noticing the *blip blip blip* of a monitor, and when he inhales, a sterile scent bypasses the oxygen prongs in his nose.

I'm in the hospital.

Why?

How?

He swallows again, unable to avoid it, and his throat aches so badly he wonders how it's functioning at all.

And then he remembers.

A woman. In his basement apartment. One minute he was in charge, the next she was free. Cutting, punching, kicking.

He reaches up to the bridge of his nose. No bandage

there, but the touch alone makes him wince. His hand travels to the side of his neck. A soft dressing covers the area where Dr. Hope Sullivan cut him. That's not what hurts, though. It's the front of his throat that feels like a thousand stabbing needles.

The force of her kick floods back to him. The instant pain. The absence of breath, the wind knocked out of him. The taste of blood.

How am I still alive?

Who found me?

How did I end up here in the—

A woman in a white coat and surgical mask enters the single room and cuts off his thoughts. A doctor, it seems. Michael's gaze sweeps her pea-green blouse, her shapeless pants, her shoulder-length hair with sandy highlights and slightly crooked bangs. His immediate thought is *forgettable*, a forgettable woman.

He's not sure why that's the first thing to come to mind. Maybe it's because Jasmine always measured people by how memorable they were. "He moves like a cat burglar," she'd say. "You don't even have to see his face to recognize him." Or, "Her laughter is so soft and pretty, like a blanket I want to curl up in."

Jasmine. His wife. Beautiful Jasmine, gone forever. *She* was memorable. If she were more forgettable, maybe he wouldn't be walking the earth in such torment.

Michael realizes the doctor is speaking to him, her voice a Midwestern monotone.

"…very lucky to be alive." She flicks his IV bag near the tubing's insertion. "You woke up briefly an hour ago, but I'm not sure you remember."

No, he doesn't remember. He tries to respond, but nothing but a rasp comes out.

"Shh," the physician says. "Your throat was badly injured.

Your vocal cords were damaged. We almost had to do a tracheotomy, but the anesthesiologist was able to intubate you."

Her words might be jargon to some, but Michael understands them. They are words he heard when his wife fought for her life in the hospital six years ago.

"We extubated you last night. You've been out for a week." The doctor must intuit Michael's question as to what day it is —or rather night, judging by the darkness pressing through the gaps in the window blinds—because she adds, "It's the last Wednesday of June."

Michael blinks and tries to process it all.

"At first your unconsciousness was from the trauma." The doctor crosses her arms. "We worried you might have been deprived of oxygen for too long. Then it was from the heavy sedation we gave you while you were on the ventilator. Your heart rhythm has been acting up, too, but hopefully we've stabilized that for now."

A petite, thirty-something nurse comes in. She apologizes for interrupting and introduces herself as Polly. "Just need to change your IV bag."

Once she finishes, she asks Michael if he is comfortable. He shakes his head and scowls because no, he's not fricking comfortable. She adjusts his pillow and asks if that's better. Then she inspects his IV line.

Her actions are gentle, caring, and he feels bad for being surly. Her eyes crinkle around a smile, her cheeks petal pink above her mask, and she pats his arm soothingly. When she does, he spots a bruise on her wrist peeking out from the sleeve of her scrub jacket.

"Maybe you could order an extra dose of pain medication?" Polly asks the doctor, who's checking something on her phone. "Now that he's awake and more aware?"

The doctor nods, and when the nurse leaves, the doctor

surprises Michael by sitting on the edge of his bed. She's so close to him he has to raise the arm with the IV tubing and rest it on his chest. He finds her proximity uncomfortably intimate.

"That's your PICC line." She points to the IV in the crook of his elbow. "Allows us to deliver fluids for a longer time than a peripheral IV."

As she's talking, a strange sensation washes over Michael. A feeling of déjà vu, as if he has met this woman before. Hard to tell with her medical mask on, but her toneless voice is familiar. He opens his mouth and tries to ask her name. Maybe she gave it to him when she came in, but his mind had been wandering to his wife.

"Wha…na," he rasps out. He points to her name tag, which is enfolded in her white coat.

She smooths her coat and tugs the tag. "My name?" When Michael nods, she says, "I'm Dr. Kim Lombardi."

The name means nothing to Michael, and yet she's familiar to him, more so with each passing minute. He focuses on her eyes, wondering where—or if—he has seen her before.

"You're lucky the paramedics got there when they did," she says. "They found your wallet in your bedroom and were able to identify you. Otherwise you might have been a John Doe, because no one has come looking for you."

Michael finds that a cruel thing to say, but he knows it's true. He has no one. Like Jasmine, his mother has passed on, and he hasn't spoken to his father in years.

"You're not out of the woods yet though, Mr. Yerli," the physician adds. "Time will tell whether your speech comes back." She pats his hand, but her touch isn't soothing like the nurse's was. "I know it's no fun being here. I was in and out of hospitals as a child in Nebraska. Had a heart defect that required a lot of surgeries, so I understand. So many people take their good fortune for granted, don't they? They don't realize how great they have it."

Michael shrugs, his shoulders one area that doesn't hurt. He wishes she would get off his bed and leave.

Where do I know her from? Kim Lombardi.

Seems like a name he wouldn't forget.

His pointed stare must get through to her because she stops talking about his possible need for speech therapy. "Mr. Yerli, are you okay?"

How do I know you? his brain pesters.

"Mr. Yerli?" This time, his name rolls more slowly off her tongue as if she, too, has made a connection. "Yerli. That name sounds familiar."

"Weee mehhh bfr," he rasps out, only the first word of his attempted *we met before* enunciated.

They squint at each other, eyebrows pinched, the doctor still perched on his bed.

Then, like lightning bolts colliding, recognition seems to hit both of them at the same time. Her eyes widen, and his breaths grow even more labored.

It's her.

It's the doctor who took care of my wife.

Not Hope Sullivan, but the junior resident at the time. Face a little fuller. Hair now with highlights and wispy bangs. With his injuries, including a nose that must be bruised and swollen where Dr. Sullivan punched him, Dr. Lombardi might not have recognized him either. Now, though, she might remember hearing his last name from her encounters with Jasmine, even though Jasmine had kept her maiden name.

But wouldn't he remember seeing a *Lombardi* in his wife's medical records? Had he missed it? Or did the doctor have a different name back then?

They blink at each other. The *blip blip blip* of the heart monitor next to Michael's bed captures his pulse, which skyrockets from allegro to prestissimo, much like the piano pieces Jasmine once played.

Jasmine. This doctor took care of my Jasmine.

For the past six years, Michael has homed in on Hope Sullivan, the name that stood out in the chart, but a new name comes to him now. It's not *Lombardi*. It's something else, a name he can now match to her face and voice.

Does that mean…

Have I been focused on the wrong doctor this whole time?

20

———

Late Wednesday night, dressed in cotton pajamas and sipping herbal tea, I sit at my desk near the window and stare out at the harbor. The city lights cast shadows on the moored boats, their gentle rocking a hypnotic distraction from the patient notes I should be completing.

If I'm lucky, the visual motion will put me to sleep. A good snooze has been hard to come by this past week, and after last evening's tune-up at Style Your Way Salon, all I can see when I close my eyes are the barista's shock of hair on the floor and the look of horror in her eyes. Needless to say, she wasn't serving coffee in my building today. The other barista had to fend for herself behind the counter. This morning, my daily affirmation preached: *I will forgive myself for my mistakes,* and I wish like hell I could embrace it.

Diva weaves her way around my slippered feet, mewing softly. I scoop her up and stroke her soft neck. It's amazing how quickly we've become attached to each other.

Nathan seems to like her too, which surprises me, considering his hypochondria and germaphobia. When I came home last night, the cat darted out at the exact moment Nathan opened his door. He wanted me to check his knee, but instead Diva shot into his loft. He went in search of her and returned a few moments later with her in his arms, cooing to her kindly. Only after he handed her back to me did he ask about Toxoplasmosis. I assured him that his brief feline interaction would pose little risk of it.

With the cat purring in my lap and sleep not coming, I turn away from the window and back to the EMR on my laptop. I click open Ada Jackson's chart, the lovely patient who most certainly did *not* drop off the tea that led to my drugged-up demise. She called earlier in the afternoon for an appointment, complaining of vague back pain. She needed a refill of her digoxin too. Although I had no openings, I worked her in, just as I always do.

"It's between my shoulder blades, Doctor," the seventy-one-year-old woman said, right before offering me a lemon drop from a small tin she keeps in her purse. "My lower back too. Well, all over, really."

Finding nothing specific on exam, I reassured her it was likely muscular in origin. Nothing a little ibuprofen couldn't relieve. "Maybe you slept on it wrong," I said.

"Or maybe it's all in my head."

I helped her off the exam table and back onto the chair next to the counter. "Ada, you know how I feel about that phrase. Even if our symptoms are caused by our emotions"—I looked pointedly at her—"like grief, it's all legit. Our bodies produce hormones and chemicals, and no matter what the trigger is, the physical pain they cause is very much real."

She took my cold hand in her warm one and squeezed it and, after listening to my treatment plan, surprised me by saying, "You look a little down, dear."

"Oh. Just tired, I guess."

She tilted her head as if not buying my excuse. "Well, if you ever need to talk, you know who to call. Let me doctor *you* for a change."

Her maternal warmth melted me, and I almost crawled

into her arms there and then. Oh, what I wouldn't give to embrace my mother again. As I replay our encounter now, I hope Ada lives to be a hundred and one, because I don't want to live in a world where she's gone.

As I'm about to sign off on her chart, my cell phone rings. It's over on the coffee table, and I'm tempted to let it go—Diva won't be pleased to be disturbed from my warm lap—but it could be one of my patients. I've given my personal number to several, but it's surprising how few use it, as if not wanting to abuse the privilege.

"Sorry, Diva." I settle the cat back on the floor, rousing her from her sleep. "Duty calls."

The number is Boston General's. I wonder if one of my patients has been admitted. Maybe an ER doctor or hospitalist is about to give me bad news.

Please don't let Allergy Man have been readmitted.

"Hello? This is Dr. Sullivan."

At first I hear nothing but the blipping of a cardiac monitor.

"Hello?" I repeat.

Breathing fills the line, as if the caller has just lifted the phone to their mouth. Heavy, coarse breaths. My senses go on high alert.

A raspy voice tries to say something. "Achhhhe," is all I hear.

"I'm sorry?"

"Achhh..."

"Who is—" My own words catch in my throat. I know who it is. Know it like I know the heart pumps blood through the aorta and the spleen rids the body of old blood cells. "Are you the man who abducted me?" I whisper.

Another rasp. It sounds like a confirmation, but I can't be sure.

I grip the phone and stare at Diva. She's back at my feet near the coffee table, as if sensing my disquiet.

"Are you the man who abducted me?" I repeat. "Grunt once for yes, twice for no."

I feel stupid for saying it, but it works. One grunt follows.

"Oh thank God, you're alive." I sink to my cream-colored sofa. "I worried I killed you."

Two grunts, and the dark humor in it almost makes me laugh.

"So you're at Boston General?"

One grunt confirms he is.

I listen to his raspy breaths, no doubt compliments of my throat kick, and wonder why he's calling me. Is it a threat? Unlikely, considering he's in the hospital. How did he get my number? Maybe he hunted inside my phone while I was conked out in his basement.

I don't get the chance to ask because, with great difficulty it seems, another harsh vocalization croaks through the phone. "Accchhheerrr."

I imagine my abductor's face red and strained, his neck veins bulging in order to get the word out, and yet for the life of me, I have no idea what he's trying to tell me.

"I'm sorry. I don't understand. Ache? Are you in pain? Do you need more—"

"Hey, you shouldn't be trying to speak." It's a woman's voice, distant at first, and then growing in volume as if she's approaching the patient's bed. "Not yet."

I recognize the monotone as Kim Lombardi's. She must be the hospitalist on duty tonight.

"You can try again in a few days," Kim says. "When there's less swelling."

I'm about to call out that I'm on the line. Kim could help answer my questions about the guy. But I hold back. How would I explain my connection to him? I can hardly say he abducted me, or that he assaulted Bo, or that he claims to have proof of the revenge acts I've performed. At best I'll be an accessory to Bo's attack for not coming forward, and at worst I'll be arrested. Kim might act overly friendly to me at times, but I doubt she'd be my strongest defender.

"Are you all right, Mr. Yerli?" I hear Kim say through the phone.

Yerli. Finally, a surname for my abductor, but it doesn't ring any bells. I don't remember having a patient with that last name, either six years ago when his wife died or now. I wish Kim would say his first name.

The patient's breathing grows louder, his grunts more frenetic, and then abruptly they stop. Kim's voice fills the phone. "I'm sorry. Michael can't talk right now."

Michael.

Michael Yerli.

"He'll have to get back to you."

His name still means nothing to me. His tortured state from the night I was his victim, however, does. He wore a look of powerlessness and futility, one I understood because before I took charge and found an outlet for my own grief, I used to wear it myself.

As before, I feel a sudden, inexplicable sense of protectiveness for this man, a fiery urge to help him, to safeguard him.

I don't get the chance.

Kim disconnects the call.

21

After Michael Yerli's startling phone call, I cross back to my laptop on the desk by the window and abandon any thoughts of going to bed. Diva, on the other hand, has retreated to the other room and is probably already in feline dreamland.

The EMR is still open to Ada Jackson's chart. After signing off on her clinic note, I click the search bar and type in the name *Yerli*.

It's a long shot, but three patients pop up. Since our EMR interfaces with the hospital's system, they could be patients of our clinic, the hospital, or both. None of the names look familiar—certainly no Michael. Two of the three Yerli patients are men, so that rules out Michael's wife, and the female Yerli's date of birth, which comes up with the search, indicates she'd be ninety years old now.

This is as far as my snooping should go. Even if a female patient with the last name of *Yerli* had a date of birth that could fit Michael's wife's, I'm not technically permitted to open her chart. HIPAA allows for the sharing of health information between providers treating the same patient, but if I'm *not* treating that patient, I can't open their electronic medical record and snoop around, not if I want to keep my job.

A patient fitting Michael's wife might be a gray area for me. I was the senior resident on call overseeing the junior resident taking care of her, so she was my patient in part. But questions could still be asked if my snooping were discovered. I should have a reason for accessing her records, one that's a little less scandalous than "her husband was stalking me."

Regardless, the hypothetical is a moot point. None of the three patients listed on the screen in front of me could be Michael's wife.

I lean back in my chair and rub at a tense spot in my neck. How can I find her information, especially without knowing her name? Equally important, *why* do I want to find her information? Is it sheer curiosity on my part? Is it to prove my innocence? Is it to bring solace to a tormented man?

Maybe it's all of the above. I've spent the past three and a half years craving answers for my parents' deaths. Discovering who hit them and forced their car into a ravine won't bring them back, but at the very least, it might fill that endless, aching, questioning hole in my chest. Knowing their killer is out there, free as a feather in a breeze, not paying for his or her crime, heats my blood to the boiling point.

So yes, I know how Michael Yerli feels. If my finding answers for him keeps him from becoming me (the shameful image of the barista and her piles of hair pops into my brain yet again), then that alone is worth my trouble.

I pluck a pencil from the holder on my desk and roll it between my fingers. A thought of how to proceed comes to mind. Michael told me his wife's case went to Risk Management, the hospital department that works to mitigate any potential legal threats. If I could get access to a list of cases I was involved in as a resident that went to Risk Management, I could look for a pregnant woman who died of a pulmonary embolism.

The fact I barely remember the case suggests I was only tangentially involved. If I were her primary doctor, a pregnant woman dying on my watch would haunt me for life, but if I wasn't her primary doctor, who was? And how can I get access to a list of Risk Management cases from six years ago?

I chomp on the pencil and swivel my desk chair, hoping an answer will come to me. When one finally does, I groan.

Dr. Connor "Cocky" Casey.

The program director of the internal medicine program at Boston General.

Starting a year before my internship, he's held the position for nine years. Although more than competent at the job—forward-thinking, innovative, open-minded—his good looks and his talent as a college athlete, which won his soccer team more than one championship, imparted in him a gift-from-God complex. This complex shines for the ladies, and rumors abound about a few starstruck residents (and two medical students—*ew*) who were more than happy to play a round of Doctor with the program director. Although I don't think he ever initiated crossing that superior-subordinate line, he didn't exactly wave the moral flag of "we shouldn't do this" when someone else did.

Like many men of his ilk, however, he was more interested in the women who didn't fall at his feet. Women like me. He never acted on his impulses, especially once I started dating Manuel, but I read his body language loud and clear. A brush of my elbow here, a little double entendre there.

I never took the bait, and to his credit, my unspoken rejection of him never reflected on my evaluations or my selection for the chief-resident year, but I was always aware the implied offer to sleep with him remained on the examination-room table. Even now, it's still in every lingering smile at hospital meetings, every wink at a casual joke, every touch of a hand on my back in a chance elevator meeting.

Dr. Connor Cocky Casey, oh he with his Irish blue eyes

and wavy black hair, would have a list of all the resident-involved cases that landed in Risk Management.

As much as it fills my mouth with a lewd taste, it might be time to take the program director up on his between-the-lines offer. The last I heard from a doe-eyed resident who rotated through my clinic last winter, the man is still happily single.

If I use the excuse that I'm considering conducting a research project that looks at resident-involved vs. attending-involved Risk Management cases, he might just buy it and help me out.

The question is, at what price?

22

———

On Friday afternoon, I step out of the elevator but avoid the coffee kiosk. The judgmental barista is back, and given it's only been three days since I left her with nothing but a moss of hair, I give her props for returning so soon.

Although she wears a long wig that resembles the real thing so much it must have cost her boyfriend a bundle, her expression is less smug and not a word of judgy gossip crosses her lips, at least not while I'm in the lobby. All I hear as I keep my distance is, "Can I help you" and "That's a beautiful sweater."

Maybe I did some good there after all, but the whole thing still eats at me. I went overboard. Fell deeper into my personal sea of darkness. I could be at risk of discovery, too, because she must have reported it to the police. She doesn't have the same motivation to keep quiet about her attack like the wife beater and dog abuser do. Just because I haven't spotted anything in the news about a Bostonian getting her head buzzed by a madwoman doesn't mean the cops aren't looking for said madwoman this very second.

I was careful, though. Wore gloves and a first-rate disguise. So I'll be all right. This time, anyway.

Pushing Kirsten and her hair—or lack thereof—from my mind, I exit the building that houses Congress Medical and spill onto the crowded sidewalk. I closed my schedule early this afternoon in order to do two things I would rather not do: visit Bo in the post-discharge rehab facility and schmooze Dr. Conner Cocky Casey in the administrative building of Boston General. As expected on the first day of July, the heat clings to my skin like a wet wipe. Gathering clouds suggest rain is ahead, and I'm grateful for the umbrella in my leather bag.

As I beeline toward Boston General, less than a fifteen-minute walk from my clinic, crowds of tourists swallow me whole and prevent what little breeze there is from reaching me. By the time I arrive at the rehab unit, I'm sweaty and limp. Despite my slim-fit pants and silky summer blouse—and no, I'm not proud of using a tarted-up appearance to achieve my ends with Cocky Casey—I won't beguile anyone with a wet-dog look, so I slink into the bathroom on Bo's floor to freshen up.

Reveling in the air-conditioning, I pull out my makeup bag and apply more than my restrained usual. I plump up my bobbed hair, apply cherry-almond lotion to my hands and around my neck in lieu of perfume, and smooth my blouse. I'll wait to undo an extra button until I've finished with Bo. My colleague doesn't need my seducing. He only needs my apology, which I can't give because it would implicate me in his head injury.

Once I have upgraded from wet dog to acceptable human being, I head down a bland hallway lined by handrails. Nodding at a nurse behind the desk, who I recognize from my residency days, I pause outside Bo's room and gather my resolve before stepping in.

Inside, the sandy-haired man with the Ken-doll face sits in a chair angled toward the window, his hospital bed neatly made. His head is no longer bandaged, but sutures remain visible on his scalp behind his ear from the attacker's—my abductor's—second blow. It was the hit on the top of the head that caused his small brain bleed.

A book titled *Unbalanced: Wars and the Health Disparities They Create* rests closed on his lap, and Terrence's clichéd words of not judging a book by its cover come back to me. Or, in this case, judging the reader, as I had assumed Bo's interest in military tomes meant a fascination with war, when maybe it actually represents a desire to better understand its human effects.

He must hear the soft tap of my ballet flats because he turns toward me. A smile soon follows, and he shifts his chair away from the window to face the door. He's dressed in cotton sweatpants and a T-shirt that reads *Where There's a Bed, There's Hope*, with a logo I assume represents the youth shelter where he volunteers. It dawns on me he might mistake my visit for something it's not, which will only heighten his interest in me, but I can't do anything about that now.

"Nice to see you," he says warmly.

"How much time have you got left on your sentence?"

"Hopefully, they'll release me tomorrow. They want to do a follow-up scan and make sure the hematoma hasn't reaccumulated."

I nod, and we chat for a few minutes about clinic patients we've both seen, Fourth of July plans (of which I have none, beyond learning what I can about Michael's wife), and a quick foray into the latest political fracas at which I'm surprised he and I share the same view.

Still, our conversation is stilted, and he appears distracted, as if something weighs on his mind. I suppose getting attacked will do that, and I worry his seeing me might trigger a memory I don't want awakened. He can't know I was in the clinic when he got clobbered, or that I was drugged and hauled away by Michael. It would raise questions I don't want to answer.

Maybe this visit was a bad idea.

Thankfully, when I ask him if his memory surrounding the

attack has returned, he shakes his head. "No, I'm thinking that's gone forever."

A few more awkward seconds pass, and just as I start to say, "Well, I should probably get going," he speaks over me, his hands clenched on the book in his lap. "Hope, I was wondering if, well, after I'm out of here, we could—"

I raise a palm to cut him off. "I'm going to stop you there. We're colleagues. We need to keep it professional. Besides"—I puff air out of my cheeks—"I'm not dating material." I want to add the words *because I'm a ghost inside* but don't.

"Um, no, that's not it, but…"

My face heats in embarrassment.

"There's uh…" He stares at his book. "Oh man, how am I supposed to do this?" He pauses again. "There's, ah, there's something I need to—"

The rehab room's bedside phone rings, and its shrill tone makes both of us jump. At the same time, Dan Knudson enters the room, the hospitalist either a friend of Bo's or his doctor back in the hospital. I use both of the interruptions as an opportunity to make my exit. Although curious about what Bo was going to say, I'm too embarrassed by my assumption he wanted to date me to stick around and find out. Besides, I need to get over to Cocky Casey's office.

I greet my former resident colleague, salute a goodbye to Bo, and leave them both with the ringing phone.

Inside an office with an executive desk, a wall full of diplomas and certificates, and a Pac-Man arcade game tucked away in the corner, Dr. Connor Cocky Casey shares none of Bo's hesitation.

He leans back in his chair, glances down at the cleavage I've unleashed, and says, "It really is good to see you again, Hope. Really good. I felt like a schoolboy when my secretary said you asked to stop by." His dazzling irises match his sky-blue shirt, and his dark hair curls into an attractive tousle.

I lift an eyebrow. "What? Not even a pretense of professionalism?" At least he didn't mention his questioning by the Board during Martin Hernandez's investigation of me, so a big kudos to him for that.

His gaze falls on my silky blouse again. "You come see me, dressed like that, on a Friday at five—I'm pretty sure it's not to complain about the last resident we sent you."

"Juanita was great. Nothing to complain about there."

"I rest my case."

Cocky Casey winks, and as always I marvel at his ability to be selectively randy. It's as if he harbors a perverted sixth sense about when to lay on the charm and when to act the program director he is. If I were wearing a hat, I would tip it to him.

"Actually," I say, "I came to ask you a favor."

He grins and runs a phallic-shaped pen through his fingers. "I like the sound of that."

"I'm considering a research project—"

"Well, that's dull."

"A research project that looks at all the resident-involved patient deaths referred to Risk Management in the past ten years. I'm sure a lot of resident-involved cases get reviewed by Risk Management, but I'm only looking at patient deaths."

Program-director Connor Casey reappears, and a groove forms between his eyebrows. "Why are you interested in looking at that?"

I shrug. "Just want to compare resident-involved vs. staff-involved incidences of at-risk cases."

"That seems like a project full of finger-pointing. Not sure how our faculty physicians would feel about that."

"It's not to name names. It's to get an idea of whether resident-involved cases get…" I'm making this up as I go along, having overestimated Cocky Casey's five-o'clock hormones. "If they get…"

"Poorer care? Better care?" He stops massaging the pen. "You know as well as I do that attendings oversee every case. I'm not sure how you can separate the two. And as you said, a lot of cases get booted to Risk Management. Doesn't imply poor care or negligence by the health-care provider. It's simply a proactive stance taken by the hospital." He crosses his arms. "Have you gotten IRB approval yet?"

Shit. Casey has kept his job for a reason. The randy switch is turned off.

"Look," I say. "I just need a solid from you. I promise it's not to target any one person. You have my word on that." I lean forward and run the tip of my tongue over my strawberry lip gloss. "We could talk more about it over drinks."

Cocky Casey stares at me. Seems to ponder the idea. After a beat, his arms uncross, and the pen in his hand starts moving again. The corner of his mouth lifts, and, with relief, I notice his randy switch is back on. "At my place?" he says.

Double shit.

"Only if you bring the list with you," I answer.

"Hmm, thank God for computers, right?" He lifts an eyebrow. "I can have that compiled and printed in no time."

Five drinks, six hours, three condoms (one torn in haste before its placement), and two surprisingly good shags later, so good that they make me wonder why I've avoided his advances for so long, I hop into an Uber outside Cocky Casey's East Boston condo. The list I requested from him burns like a branding tool in a side pocket of my tote bag, right next to my stash of roofies. Before I realized I might actually enjoy a tumble in the sheets with the program director, I considered dumping them into his wine as soon as he handed the goods over.

I left the drugs where they were, though. Not only could knocking my former program director out come back to bite me, it would have stolen the first bit of escape I've had in months. It's been a long time since I've had sex.

Did I just whore myself out? Maybe. But there are far less pretty specimens to sell my soul to, and, according to today's affirmation: *I believe everything happens for a reason.*

At least screwing someone won't get me arrested.

23

When I return to my loft, Diva slinks toward me, first slowly, with an attitude that says, "How dare you come home at 1:00 a.m. and make me miss dinner?" and then more quickly, as if deciding she'll catch more Fancy Feast with sugar than with salt.

"Just chill, pretty thing." I open a can of moist cat food. "I left you plenty of dry stuff. It's not my fault it doesn't meet your culinary standards."

After I spoon the slimy blob onto a clean dish, the salmon odor clearly more intoxicating to her than it is to me, I point to my leather tote on the granite island. "Got what I needed. You'd be proud of me."

Knowing neither of us believes that's true, I pad my bare feet to the bedroom and peel off my clothes. Though I'm eager to see the list of patient names Cocky Casey gave me, I'm equally eager to shower. I step under the hot stream and soap away the dried sweat and lingering scent of my whoring.

Once back in my creamy white living room, I grab a remote from my desk and close the blinds, the harbor lights disappearing from view. I don't usually bother to lower the window coverings. Who's going to see me from ten stories up? But tonight, at this late hour, I want to be alone with my prize.

Retrieving Casey's list from my bag, I step over Diva, who's now licking herself on my area rug in a most unladylike fashion, and settle onto my sofa to scan the names.

Several patients are listed. I requested ten years' worth to cover my tracks—not that the promiscuous program director likely bought my research lie. I only asked for patient deaths, though, so that reduced what could have been pages of Risk Management cases to only one and a half. The only year I'm interested in is the year I was an R3—a third-year resident. That would be six years ago, which is when Michael claims I killed his wife, even though I was merely the senior resident on call.

A fish rots from the head down.

On the list, I find seven resident-involved cases of patient deaths that were referred to Risk Management that year. Three women, four men. One of those three women might be Michael Yerli's wife.

If only Cocky Casey would have included the residents involved in each of the women's care, but he didn't. He only supplied the patient names and the year of Risk Management involvement.

The three names are Elizabeth Biddercombe, Jasmine Bonnet, and Michelle Shaw. Learning more about them will require searching their EMR charts, which leads me right back to the HIPAA barrier. How much am I willing to risk a violation to uncover what happened to Michael's wife?

"What do you think, Diva?" I rest my head back against the couch. "Do I take the risk? Or maybe the better question is, will I be able to live with myself if I don't?"

Diva stops grooming and stares up at me. I take her pointed look as a go-ahead to proceed.

Returning to my desk, I wake my laptop from sleep. Once logged into the EMR, I search the first of the three names on my list and discover there's only one Elizabeth Biddercombe in the system. Her birth and death dates show up on the screen alongside her name. She was forty-two when she died six years ago. Could be Michael's wife, I suppose. He mentioned they'd struggled with infertility.

Next I type in Jasmine Bonnet. Another possible fit, maybe a better one because she'd be forty-three now were she still alive.

Finally, I type Michelle Shaw into the search bar, but too many charts with that name pop up on the screen. A few of the age dates could match Michael's wife's, but I'd have to go looking haphazardly among them.

Wanting to open as few charts as possible, I start with the first name, Elizabeth Biddercombe, and pull up her death summary. The woman died of massive trauma due to a car accident. Not Michael's wife then. Although I'm curious why she ended up in Risk Management, I don't snoop any further. Maybe I can pass this one off as an accidental chart access.

Shifting to the second name on Cocky Casey's list, I open Jasmine Bonnet's chart and find the autopsy report. I scroll down to the cause of death.

Pulmonary embolism.

Anticipation tingles down my spine. This must be her. Michael mentioned his wife shot a clot to her lungs.

Strange, though. According to the pathologist, Jasmine Bonnet didn't suffer a saddle-type pulmonary embolism. Not even a massive one, certainly not the type that leads to death. Just several smaller ones.

To confirm I have the right woman, I open the demographic information. Listed as the Emergency Contact is *Michael Yerli, Husband.*

Bingo. A sad Bingo, at that.

I pause to reflect on Michael's loss. To lose a spouse is tragic enough, but to believe your doctor caused it must be maddening. The thought I might have had something to do with it is downright crushing.

My fingertip taps my mouse. "What do you think, Diva?"

The cat leaves the area rug and jumps up on my lap at the desk. The scent of seafood lingers on her whiskers.

"Seeing as how I've already entered her chart, I might as well keep going, right?"

For the next few minutes, I review Jasmine's hospital summary report, which in this grim case is a death summary rather than a discharge summary.

According to the note, Jasmine arrived at the emergency department complaining of shortness of breath and was admitted to the general medicine ward for observation. At the time, neither her early pregnancy nor the pulmonary embolism had been diagnosed, although the latter was among the possible causes of her symptoms. Both conditions were later found on autopsy.

Although back in his basement apartment with me, Michael accused the hospital staff of ignoring Jasmine, the summary note doesn't suggest that. Rather, the preliminary labs and vital signs show she was in stable condition until a few dips in her oxygen saturation prompted a larger workup, which resulted in the diagnosis of a hypercoagulable state. Unfortunately, before her abnormal clotting could be stabilized by blood thinners, she shot another embolism up to her lungs and couldn't be resuscitated.

I sink back in the desk chair and absorb this information. Why don't I remember any of it? How could I forget doing cardiopulmonary resuscitation on a woman in her thirties that we later learned was pregnant? With twins. Six years isn't that long ago.

I stroke the cat. "No way would I forget something like that," I murmur. Yet, other than a vague Resident Report presentation that comes to mind, I have no recollection of being directly involved in Jasmine's care.

I scroll the rest of the way down the summary report to see who wrote it. When I spot the physician's name, my hand falls still on Diva's back.

Hope Sullivan, MD.

Me.

I shake my head. I would remember writing this note, I'm sure of it. And yet there my name is, as plain as the cat in my lap. The only other explanation I can think of is that someone accidentally wrote the note while logged into the EMR as me. When they went to submit it, my name would be recorded as the signing physician.

Did I forget to log out of a ward computer? Did another resident then sit down at that same terminal and start writing Jasmine's note under my profile?

That smells fishier than Diva's breath.

With growing unease, I close out the death summary and find the initial history and physical report. I scroll down to the admitting physician.

Not me. It was a resident named Kimberly Baker.

My confusion deepens. I open one of the progress reports. There are only two of them because, sadly, Jasmine died the next day. The only thing I can find relevant to me is a brief mention that the patient's admission was discussed with the senior resident on call, Hope Sullivan.

So I *had* been briefed on her condition, but it was before the woman's downward turn. If Jasmine was only mildly hypoxic at first and not yet in distress, then I would have told the junior resident to order lab tests and keep me posted with any new developments.

But I don't remember being kept posted on anything. Not Jasmine's pregnancy. Not her cardiopulmonary resuscitation. Not her ultimate demise. I only remember bits of the case from Resident Report a few days later.

The notes are dated early July, almost six years ago today. That's the time of resident turnover all over the country. First years become second years. Second years become third years. Third years move on to wherever their next professional chapter takes them.

I would have just been starting my third year of training. What was my first rotation that month? If it had been an outpatient assignment, I would have only been covering call the night Jasmine was admitted and wouldn't have been there the next day when she coded and died. And I certainly wouldn't have written her death summary.

I close my eyes and pull up my final year's schedule in my mind. Rotations blur in my thoughts. Then I remember. Rheumatology.

I was rotating through rheumatology the month of July. I remember because Dr. Chow planned to go on maternity leave in August, and I wanted the chance to work with her before she did.

So no, I would not have been on the ward the next day when Jasmine worsened and died. I would have been in rheum clinic with Dr. Chow and would only have heard about Jasmine's death later.

Does that excuse me? Not at all. Could I have missed something while the junior resident presented Jasmine's admission to me? Yes. Especially at the beginning of the new training year and especially if we were swamped.

Jesus, did I screw up?

Focused back on the EMR, I review Jasmine's hospital course and labs once more. They confirm she was stable during the night while I was on call. It was the next day she deteriorated. How, I don't know. The pharmacy record shows blood thinners were started shortly after her hypercoagulable state was detected. It seems unlikely—although not impossible—that the scattered lung clots would have killed her, especially once treatment was started, so what, if anything, was missed?

Diva meows. I realize I'm kneading her flesh like I would a lump of dough. She leaps off my lap and sashays to the bedroom. At 2:30 a.m., it's way past her bedtime. Mine too. Thank goodness I'm not working at the free clinic tomorrow.

I stare at Jasmine's medical records and wonder again why my name is on her death summary. I pull up the final progress note. I'd only given it a cursory glance before, but now my eyes widen when I see the physician name attached to it. Mine again.

How... Why?...

No way could I have been careless enough to leave myself logged in twice, and no way could this resident, Kimberly, have twice made the mistake of entering data under my name.

And then it hits me.

Kimberly Baker. The name seemed generic at first, and I was too focused on Jasmine's case to consider it, so I wrote it off as belonging to one of the dozens of internal medicine residents Boston General employs, or even the family practice or surgical residents who rotate through. But now I remember. *Baker* was Kim Lombardi's married name, and she preferred *Kimberly* to *Kim* back then. Quiet, dull Kim Lombardi had briefly been a wife. She started residency with her married name but went back to her maiden name a short time later. I believe her husband died of a heart attack while she was in med school. If I recall, he was quite a bit older than her.

Why in the world did Kimberly—Kim—sign off on two patient notes under my name? Especially since I was only on call and not on her service? It had to be an accident. Otherwise it meant she'd had my login password. How? Had she watched me sign in at some point?

More importantly, why the fuck would she?

Suddenly, I'm shivering, my cotton pajamas too thin for the loft's central air. Something is off. Way off.

My mind flashes back to the strange call from Michael two nights ago. How he was trying to tell me something, but I didn't understand.

Achhhhe, he said. *Accchhheerrr.*

I thought maybe he was in pain. That he needed more morphine.

But then it comes to me, and I leap out of my chair. It clatters backward on the hardwood floor, and Diva darts out from the bedroom.

I stare at her, my eyes blinking rapidly.

Michael wasn't saying *ache or acher*, as if in pain. He was saying *Baker*. That means he recognized that his doctor, Kim Lombardi, was a former resident he remembered as Kimberly Baker.

The same doctor who took care of his wife.

24

I right the chair I just toppled and sit back down in front of my computer screen. From the street ten stories below, a siren wails, but in the dead of night the city noises have otherwise quieted.

Dark thoughts about Kim cloud my brain, thoughts that are ridiculously premature but thoughts that surface nonetheless. Had she been reckless with Jasmine's care? Realized her mistake and then submitted the hospital documentation in my name to distance herself from any negligence?

I think back to our residency days. Kim was competent. Not the most ambitious resident Boston General has ever seen, but certainly capable.

My mind takes another giant leap it shouldn't. I recall my fifty-two-year-old patient, Ted Orenson, who died last year from a sudden cardiac arrest while hospitalized with pancreatitis. His unexpected death weighed on me. Before having the bad luck of developing infection-related pancreatitis, he was a healthy, fit guy. After he died, I worried I missed something on his heart exam during his prior clinic visits. Fretted that I should have done an EKG at his last physical, even though he had shown no signs of heart disease and his screening EKG a couple of years earlier had been normal.

As one of the hospitalists, Kim was involved in his care, but other hospitalists were too, including Dan Knudson. Ted had been hospitalized for a week before he died, and with his severe pancreatitis, he had seen a gastroenterologist as well. So why am I throwing Kim under the bus? I don't remember which hospitalist was working the night Ted died.

There's only one way to find out.

My fingers hover over the keyboard. Ted was my clinic patient, so accessing his chart shouldn't raise any flags.

After asking myself if my tired brain is creating late-night drama where there is none, I type in Ted's name and open his chart. I scan through his admission history and physical. Severe upper abdominal pain, vomiting, nausea—all symptoms compatible with pancreatitis. No mention of chest pain or palpitations. Normal cardiac exam.

I flip through some of his earlier office visits with me. General physicals, everything normal. Good cholesterol levels, one appointment for shoulder pain, another for pre-travel immunizations. Despite the low probability, he had won a million dollars on a scratch-off ticket and was thrilled to be taking his wife and grown kids on a trip to Asia.

Closing my eyes, I can see his amiable face, his excitement over his good fortune, his genuine joy when he told me that even without the money, he was the luckiest man in the world. He had people in his life who made him feel loved. Indeed, his *joie de vivre* and gratitude made me think humanity might still have a shot.

And then he died from a sudden cardiac arrest, even as his pancreatitis was improving. A perusal of his autopsy report now confirms it. The pathologist suspected a sudden arrhythmia was the culprit because she found only partial blockage of a coronary artery.

No trip to Asia. No more family he adored. No more lucky scratch tickets. Just eternal darkness.

My brain fills with images of my parents and Manuel. I can't help but picture their bodies buried in the ground forever, bugs and worms burrowing into their coffins. I push the morbid thoughts away. I can't go there right now. Grief is clingy enough by day. In the middle of the night, it's a two-ton pillar crushing my chest.

I click open Ted Orenson's final note. The hospitalist who signed off on it was neither Kim nor Dan. It was a fellow completing her academic hospital medicine training, a new program at Boston General in the last few years.

Still, considering the patient died, an attending physician should have made a notation as well. An oversight, maybe, since Ted died during the wee hours. Preferring the overnight shift, Kim is the most frequent nocturnist, but maybe with the fellow in-house, she only had to take calls from home if needed.

I rub my arms for warmth, my thoughts returning to a dark place. Just because Kim enjoys the graveyard shift doesn't mean she's…she's what? A killer?

Jeez, Hope, get a grip.

I move on to the nursing notes from the night Ted died and scan through them. On the final one, I pause.

The nurse, Polly Germaine, a sweet woman I worked with only a few times during my residency, reported that Ted's heart monitor had alarmed with a rhythm of V-fib. When she ran into the room, Dr. Kim Lombardi was already coding the patient. Despite rounds of cardiac meds and defibrillation, Ted couldn't be revived. He was pronounced dead at 4:07 a.m.

I absorb this new information, my loft a silent crypt around me. At some point, my own heart starts racing.

Six years ago Kim was the resident taking care of Jasmine Bonnet, Michael's wife, a woman who died from pulmonary embolisms, embolisms that weren't particularly large, at least according to the autopsy report.

One year ago, Kim was coding my patient, Ted, who died of a sudden cardiac arrest, a patient whose ticker seemed healthier than mine.

Neither time was her name on the final physician note, first using mine with Jasmine back in residency, then possibly using a fellow's with Ted a year ago.

It could mean nothing.

Probably means nothing.

But it could mean something…

Shivering, I glance at my mobile on my glass coffee table. My brain is saying *stop being such a drama queen* while my gut is screaming *you need to warn him.*

My gut wins.

I scurry over to my phone and call the hospital operator. After identifying myself as a doctor—it is the middle of the night, after all—I ask her to ring Michael Yerli's room.

I pray that he answers.

25

Pacing my hardwood floor in my fuzzy slippers, I listen to one, two, three rings of Michael's bedside hospital phone. Middle-of-the-night phone calls in a patient's room are no doubt a rarity, and this one will likely surprise the nursing staff as much as the patient.

Answer answer answer! my brain hollers.

On the fourth ring I lose hope that he will, but to my relief he picks up, his raspy breathing the only confirmation I need that it's him. As I imagine him trying to shake off the fog of a sedating narcotic, panic grips me. What should I say? How am I going to relay my concerns to him without sounding like a psycho?

I start with a simple, "Michael?"

His strident breaths pause.

"It's Hope. Hope Sullivan."

The rasping returns as a rabid croaking. It's as if he has a thousand things he wants to say but can't, his crushed vocal cords still refusing to cooperate.

I interrupt him. "You don't have to talk. Just listen. I understand what you were trying to tell me the other night.

You said *Acher*, but I think you meant *Baker*. As in Kimberly Baker. Grunt once for yes."

He grunts once.

"She was involved in your wife's care and is your doctor now too, correct?"

Another single grunt.

"Your wife's name was Jasmine Bonnet."

An emphatic single grunt.

"Look." I feel an inexplicable urge to hurry but am unsure how to proceed. "I'm truly sorry for your loss. I reviewed your wife's medical records and found some discrepancies, not necessarily with *how* she died. It could have been the pulmonary embolisms that—"

An angry burst of double grunting cuts me off. I imagine Michael's face flushed red, his hand gripping the phone, his heart-rate monitor ticking up.

"Wait, let me finish," I say. "I agree it's odd that, according to the autopsy report, Jasmine's pulmonary embolisms weren't all that large and yet she still died. *But*," I stress, "it's not impossible. She had several areas of lung infarction and could have had other issues going on that weren't detected."

More agitated double grunting.

"The other discrepancy I found was that your wife's hospital summary was entered into the EMR under my name. That's no doubt why you…why you felt I was responsible. But it wasn't me who submitted that note. I wasn't there when your wife died. You have to believe me. I was back in my rheumatology rotation the next day. When I finished my call shift in the morning, your wife was still stable."

I pause. Michael's coarse breathing comes through but no more grunting, as if he's waiting for me to go on.

"So if anyone might know more about it, it would be Kim Lombardi. Her married name was *Baker*, but she changed it back to *Lombardi* before her second year of residency. While I can't believe she did anything intentional to hurt your wife—"

A loud grunt of protest from Michael drowns out my response.

"Please, Michael."

"Sheee kiii errr."

Although his words are forced out in wheezy rasps, I understand what he's trying to say.

"If you knew Kim," I reply, "you'd understand how bizarre it is to think she's capable of something like that, not on purpose anyway. She's too…well, she's…"

She's what? Too dull? Too bland? Too common?

I picture the Kim Lombardi I know. Toffee-blond hair, turned-up nose, heart-shaped face. Cute but plain, nice figure but never shows it, competent but not exceptional, able to hold up her end of a conversation but not a riveting orator. Flat expression, except when someone praises her accomplished siblings and parents. Then her nose twinges in irritation or her jaw muscles contract.

Michael starts rasping out words again. "Heppp meee prooo," or something to that effect.

I'm pretty sure I understand. "Help you prove it?"

He grunts once for yes.

"I promise you I'll look into it."

The irony of me helping the man who clobbered my coworker, drugged and abducted me, and tied me to a chair almost knocks me over with its absurdity.

"I'll check out some of her other patient complications." Even as I say it I'm wondering how in the world I will be able to do that. "But it's mostly to reassure you. No doubt we're both overreacting."

Are we? If that's the case, then why am I calling him? Why does my gut tell me he shouldn't be alone in the hospital?

I replay Michael's phone call to me two days ago. I remember how Kim intercepted his call but didn't offer to help him communicate. In retrospect, it's good she didn't, since he was trying to warn me about *her*, but isn't it odd she didn't offer her assistance? Attempt to speak to the caller for him? Then again, Kim's bedside manner has always been lukewarm. Tepid even.

Still...

I try to sound casual. "Do you have someone who could stay with you while you're in the hospital?" I already know the answer. If Michael had a supportive network, his grief probably wouldn't have led him to stalking and abducting me. "Maybe it's best you're not alone."

He grunts twice. A loud and clear *no*.

Like me, he has no one. Maybe he *is* me, at least me in the future. The ghost of Hope Yet to Come. We hold it together until suddenly...we don't. Will I be him in six months? Six weeks? Six days? After all, look what I did to the barista.

Before I can stop myself, I blurt out, "I'm coming to stay with you."

No response beyond his breathing. Whether that is agreement or surprise, I don't know, but clearly, he no longer sees me as a threat.

"I'll make up an excuse to the staff," I add. "I'll stay until you're discharged." *What the living shit am I saying?* "Then together we'll look into Dr. Lombardi. I'll help you, I promise. We'll make sure—"

I silence myself. Michael's breathing has grown distant, as if he's no longer the one holding the phone. If so, how much of what I said was overheard?

Before I can say anything else, a muffled shuffling occurs. It's as if the receiver has been dropped onto the bedding and Michael is fumbling to retrieve it.

Or... *struggling* to retrieve it.

The call cuts off. I wait for a call back but don't get one. In that dead air, in that strange disconnection, my imagination runs wild. Someone purposely ended our conversation.

Maybe Michael's doctor, Kim Lombardi, formerly Kimberly Baker.

Michael recognized Kim as the doctor who took care of his wife. What if Kim, too, has made that connection? If she *did* have something to do with Jasmine's death, whether out of simple medical negligence or cold-blooded murder, then recognizing the woman's husband could put that husband at risk.

High risk.

I hurry to my bedroom and tug on jeans, a form-fitting tee, and a hoodie, well aware that it's three thirty in the morning. Then I stuff an overnight bag with a change of clothes and basic toiletries.

When I finish, I fill three bowls to the brim with dry cat food and six bowls with water. Diva may snub her nose at the dry stuff, but she'll eat it if that's her only option. I'll lavish her with an apology of treats and catnip later. These provisions will hold her over should I need to be gone a couple of days, and I can always call Nathan to check in on her. He can come to the hospital to pick up my key. I think he would do that for me.

Overnight bag in hand, I flee my loft and race to Boston General.

26

HIM

In the dimly lit hospital room, Michael sees Dr. Lombardi watching him, her mask lowered around her neck, her mouth a flat line of unreadability. A sterile scent wafts from her rumpled white coat, as if she's just finished performing a procedure on another patient. The phone receiver is back on its cradle. They wrestled for it after she snatched it away and put it to her ear. In his weakened state, she won the battle.

"That sounded like Hope Sullivan," the doctor says. "Why would you be talking to Dr. Sullivan?"

Michael doesn't say anything. *Can't* say anything, both because of his damaged vocal cords and his growing fear. He wonders how much of the conversation Dr. Lombardi heard, a doctor he is now one hundred percent sure killed his wife. The last thing Michael caught Hope Sullivan say was that she was coming to stay with him. That must mean she fears he's in danger.

Am I?

That Hope would help him, after what he did to her, after he assaulted her colleague and drugged and restrained her, fills him with a flurry of emotions. Shock. Gratitude. Anxiety. Shame.

Dr. Lombardi crosses the room to the chair near the window, on top of which sit Michael's clothes in a paper bag. She digs through his pockets and finds the cell phone that hasn't left his pants since the paramedics picked him up at his place. She moves to his bedside, and when he reaches up to grab his cell phone, wondering why she is giving it to him, she uses his face to open it and steps back again.

She begins scrolling. Taps the screen a few times and then plays a video.

He grinds his teeth and tries to sit up so he can snatch his phone away, but the motion makes his head spin. He's too weak to stand let alone walk. He still requires the plastic urine bottle. His face heats in embarrassment every time the nurse comes to empty it.

He makes a raspy, incoherent attempt of telling Dr. Lombardi to get off his phone, but she ignores him. Instead, she approaches the bed again. The light from the hallway reveals a rare flicker of animation on her face.

"This is quite the video you've recorded here."

She lifts her own phone next to his. Seconds later the tone of an AirDrop swishes.

"Who would've thought Hope capable of such a thing?" The doctor stares at Michael, lips parted, eyebrows raised, as if she can't quite believe what she has watched. "At first, I didn't know who the woman was, but then I recognized her voice. That wig too. She used it for a faculty roast back in residency."

Michael remains quiet.

Dr. Lombardi must take his silence as confirmation that it's Hope Sullivan in the video. "Are you blackmailing her? Is that what this is all about?" She shakes her head, as if she still can't believe what she has discovered. "Forcing her to help you look into me? That's what I heard her say on the phone. That the two of you were going to *look into* me."

Michael's gaze travels from Dr. Lombardi to the plastic

remote hanging over his guard rail, the one with the red call button.

"What, exactly, is it you think I've done?" She tosses his phone back on the vinyl-cushioned chair and sits on the edge of his bed.

Once again Michael finds her nearness unnerving. So, too, is her newfound buoyancy. Until now she has shown no personality in her interactions with him. No humor or anecdotes. Just stale rounds that offer simple progress updates.

"Hmm?" she asks. "Do you think I'm guilty of something?"

He rasps nothing in reply, unsure if it's a trap or not. Wonders, too, if he has it all wrong. He was wrong about Dr. Sullivan. What if he's wrong about this doctor too? What if his wife's death really was unpreventable? What if his obsessive quest to right an injustice stems only from his inability to accept the fact that Jasmine is gone?

"You recognized me, didn't you?" Dr. Lombardi says. "I saw it in your eyes the other night when you woke up from your coma. You think I killed your wife."

Michael startles at her bluntness. His doubts from a second ago vanish. Now he is convinced she's a killer because no innocent person would say such a thing.

His face ignites, and he croaks out a definitive *yesss* but then immediately realizes his mistake. He should have appeared shocked. Now she knows he's on to her. He's never been good at controlling his emotions. They dance off his face and body like imps.

Fearful now, he slides his hand over the starched sheets and up toward the plastic guardrail, the tubing from his IV line dangling from the crook of his elbow. He reaches for the nurse call button, but before he can press it, Dr. Lombardi snatches the remote away. She holds it behind her, the cord stretched taut over the blanket.

Michael manages a hoarse cry, but it's too muted for anyone at the central desk to hear. He tugs at the cord and tries to grab the remote back from the doctor. Then she says something that stops him cold. An ugly, vicious thing.

"Whaaa diii uuu saaay?" he croaks out, the effort stabbing his throat. He swallows and tastes the metallic tang of blood.

"I said the babies weren't yours."

Her voice is low, barely registering above the hum of his pump, but Michael heard her all the same. He is stunned into silence.

"Your wife told me so," the doctor adds.

Michael lays rigid on the hospital mattress, the bedding damp from perspiration. Dr. Lombardi stays perched on the edge of the bed. The hallway light illuminates her body, but her face remains shadowy.

"I told your wife—Jasmine, wasn't it?—that we'd be checking her blood type in case she needed a transfusion. Just a standard precaution. That worried her though. You know why?"

Michael glances at the open doorway and wonders how he can get to it. Dr. Lombardi must read his mind because she rises, places the remote with the nurse call button on the floor far from Michael's reach, and closes the door.

She returns to his bed and flips on the recessed lighting behind it. Then she winds the remote's cord around the infusion pump. He tugs the cord anyway, trying to get the call button back within reach. The IV machine tilts precariously. Dr. Lombardi rights it before it falls and then pushes the button on Michael's PCA pump. A dose of morphine he didn't ask for slips into his blood.

Dr. Lombardi sits back down on the bed, her features stony. Michael is aware she is going to kill him, but he's too paralyzed by her words to process it. Not his babies? Impossible.

"See, when I told your wife we'd check her blood type in the rare event we would need to transfuse her, she got worried. She confided in me that she was pregnant and wanted to know if a transfusion would hurt her twin babies. To better answer her question, I asked about your blood type. She became even more upset and confessed to me the babies she was carrying weren't yours. Of course, I never mentioned any of this in the chart, and I was the only one who knew she was pregnant until the autopsy."

Michael feels as if he's been kicked in the throat all over again.

Of course the babies were mine.

His anger returns, and he opens his mouth to grunt something, but Dr. Lombardi answers for him. "Bullshit? Is that what you want to say?"

When Michael nods, the doctor drones on. "I'm not lying, Mr. Yerli. Why would I?"

Her words hang in the sterile air. Deep inside them lies the subtext that she has no reason to lie—because she is going to kill him.

"She told me you two tried something fierce to get pregnant, but nothing took root. She worried she was too old. Then she went out of town, some sort of legal conference, I think."

Michael remembers the week his wife went to Washington, DC, for a law meeting because it was a few weeks later she told him she thought she was pregnant.

"She met up with some guy there. An old law school buddy of hers."

No. Michael doesn't want to hear it. Can't hear it. He and Jasmine had sex the night she returned, so he never questioned the twins might not be his. Why would he? She would never cheat on him.

"And, well, you know how it is, one drink led to another, and your wife started to think, 'Maybe it's not me who can't make babies. Maybe it's Michael.'" Dr. Lombardi holds up her hands. "I'm paraphrasing, of course, but you get the gist. I guess one encounter was all it took, because a short time later she realized she was pregnant."

Wetness trickles down Michael's face. Crying isn't a new thing for him. Over the past six years his grief has taken him from sobbing, to shattering the china he and Jasmine once owned, to stalking the doctor he thought killed his wife. But tonight, in the hospital room with Dr. Lombardi, his body drugged and weakened, the knowledge that his wife cheated on him turns the tears to acid.

"So see?" Dr. Lombardi's voice is the warmest Michael has heard from her, childlike almost. "I did you a favor. Your wife had everything. A successful career, awards in her field, a husband who adored her. I remember how you sat rooted to her side that night in the hospital, stroking her hand, promising her everything would be okay. And yet she threw it all away. Do you know what people would give to be in her shoes?"

Michael shakes his head, wants to say that the doctor doesn't understand, that Jasmine had lots of struggles too. How could she not? But he only manages nonsensical rasping, his shock over his wife's infidelity too great.

The doctor is lying. She has to be.

Then he remembers Jasmine's distraction when she returned from her conference. Remembers her excitement over the news of the babies but her hesitation too. He assumed her hesitancy was because they learned they were having twins, but now he understands it could just as easily have been from the weight of her secret.

Dr. Lombardi reaches for the PCA pump and releases another dose of morphine into Michael's line. She lowers the head of the bed from its angled position and strokes his hair. He jerks his head back, but it has nowhere to go but deeper into his pillow.

"Some of us never get the chance to shine." Her fingertips now trace his thick eyebrows. "Some of us work hard to be noticed, to be respected, even become doctors and professors and engineers, and yet we never rise above mediocre. There is always somebody better, somebody who steals the spotlight, people like my parents and my siblings, me nothing but an underachieving afterthought."

She offers a sad smile, her cold fingers still on Michael's forehead, and for a morphine-confused moment, he thinks she's the Grim Reaper in the flesh. He's so tired now. Has to fight to keep his eyelids open.

"So when people who have everything don't appreciate their good fortune," she continues, "I have to teach them a final lesson. Show them how quickly it can be taken away." Dr. Lombardi's icy fingertips slide down to Michael's wet cheeks. She makes a clucking sound that's probably meant to be soothing but is anything but. "I suspect you're like me, Michael. One of those adequate but forgettable people who disappear into the room, no matter how hard we try to be important. You were lucky to get someone like Jasmine, weren't you? She was too good for you."

Michael nods. He blinks his tired eyes. Hot tears bite his cheeks.

"You and I are alike," the doctor whispers. "Too bad it has to end like this."

Michael knows he needs to fight. As much as he is ready to die, he refuses to let it be at this woman's hands. Dr. Sullivan will be here soon. She'll help him.

He flexes his weakened muscles. A week in a coma and veins full of morphine keep them sluggish, but he forces them to move. He reaches for the doctor. Tries to scratch at her face, her neck, anything to keep her from doing what she's about to do.

His efforts are nothing but a puff of air in the wind. She stands up from the bed, her hand in her white coat's pocket.

Outside the closed door, the only sound is a distant beeping from another patient's room.

"I'm sorry. I wish you hadn't figured out what happened to your wife. You don't deserve this, but I can't have you working with Dr. Sullivan to 'look into' me, can I?"

Hope. Hope is my only hope now. In Michael's drugged-up fog, he almost smiles at both the pun and the irony.

Dr. Lombardi's hand reappears from her coat pocket. In it lies a syringe.

Fight for me, he says in his mind to Hope Sullivan. A doctor who throat kicks is a doctor who can stop this sociopath. *Fight for my Jasmine.*

Dr. Lombardi approaches Michael's PICC-line port. "I've been carrying this around for a while now." She raises the syringe. "Ever since you recognized me, I've been hoping I wouldn't have to use it, but I kept it close just in case. Funny how our paths crossed again, isn't it? What a small world." She sighs, as if pained. "I'm not happy it's come to this, though."

She raises her surgical mask back over her mouth and nose.

Michael fights to keep his eyes open. So tired. The syringe's needle pokes into his access port. A sob bubbles in his throat. He feels it more than he hears it.

Can't fight back, Jasmine. Too weak.

He wishes he believed in God. Maybe he would see his wife again if he did. He still loves her. He forgives her. They could live in a heaven free of pain. Free of cruel people and grief.

Is it too late to believe?

A sudden pain cinches his heart, a pain the morphine doesn't touch. His eyes snap open in agony. He can't breathe. Can't get any air. Can't swallow.

His chest flails. An alarm beeps beside his bed. Dr. Lombardi stands next to him, holding what looks like an oxygen bag, as if ready to resuscitate him but not until forced to.

The last thing Michael sees, the last thing he will ever see, is the door bursting open and Dr. Lombardi quickly putting an oxygen mask over his face.

He gives in to the darkness.

27

The elevator pings open on the internal medicine ward, and I run toward the central desk, its lighting a beacon against the darkened hallway. My overnight bag thumps my shoulder, and the strings of my hoodie flap against my torso.

I wish I'd left earlier. Wish I hadn't taken the time to pack an extra change of clothes. My intuition warns me time is not to be wasted. At least the Uber arrived promptly. It seemed unsafe to walk to the hospital in the middle of the night, and I didn't want to have to park my car since I'm not sure how long I'll be here.

When I reach the counter, I find no one. From the far corner of the ward, voices converse in a low tone.

Tightening my mask around my nose (Boston General still encourages them for inpatient units), I head in that direction, passing darkened rooms with blipping monitors and humming infusion pumps. As a resident, I enjoyed the quiet of the hospital after midnight, at least when the number of admissions were few, but right now I feel nothing but a rumbling dread.

I spot Kim Lombardi talking to Polly inside a patient's room, the door wide open and the lights bright. Instinct tells me it's Michael's room. Just as quickly, common sense tells me I'm being dramatic. It could be anyone's room.

As I approach the door, the two masked women turn to me. Kim's eyebrows are furrowed, while Polly's are raised in surprise.

"Dr. Sullivan," the nurse says. "What are you doing here so early? Did we admit one of your patients last night?"

"I'm here to see Michael Yerli."

"Why is that?" Kim asks.

It might be my drama again, but I swear there is a challenge in the hospitalist's tone.

"I'm...he's a patient of mine."

"Really," Kim says flatly. She eyes the carryall over my shoulder but says nothing.

"Really," I reply.

Polly makes a sound of sympathy. "I'm so sorry, Dr. Sullivan, but..."

Her gaze travels from me to the bed behind her, and when she steps away to let me enter the room, I inhale a sharp rush of air.

Michael is lying there, eyes staring up at the ceiling, gown pulled down, boxers exposed. Burn marks on his hastily shaved chest form two pink rectangles in an otherwise dark forest of hair. Aside from the beard he now sports from his prolonged hospitalization, he is the same man I saw in his basement apartment—except now he doesn't blink. His chest doesn't rise. His muscles don't twitch.

The bed's top sheet and blanket have been yanked all the way down to the foot of the mattress, and a defibrillator and crash cart stand nearby. Although a pulse oximeter probe still hugs his finger and his IV line still dangles from the crook of his elbow, his infusion pump and cardiac monitor have been turned off.

I struggle to process the scene.

"We tried everything." Polly seems shy to make eye contact with me. "The whole team was here."

Stepping up to the bed, I let my overnight bag drop to the floor. I take Michael's still-warm hand and squeeze it, as if expecting him to squeeze back. How is it I feel such sudden and unexpected sorrow for a man who could have killed Bo and might have done the same to me had I not fought back?

"What happened?" I whisper. I'm not sure the other two women hear me, so I raise my voice and repeat the question.

Kim approaches the other side of the bed. I struggle not to glare at her. I don't know anything yet. Michael was badly injured. He was in a coma. Kim might not have had anything to do with his death. *Most likely* didn't have anything to do with his death.

Of course, that means I'm the one who killed him then. Maybe not this morning, but my actions are what landed him in the hospital.

I steel my jaw, determined to show as little emotion as Kim. Usually that would be easy for me. Right now, it feels impossible.

"He went into sudden cardiac arrest," Kim says. "A fatal arrhythmia. I was finishing an assessment on him, so I was luckily close by, but we couldn't bring him back. He's been throwing strange rhythms for the past week, so it's not a complete surprise." Kim glances at Polly. "Would you mind grabbing my tablet from the counter? I'll show Dr. Sullivan some of Mr. Yerli's tracings."

Polly obliges, and when she returns with the tablet, Kim scrolls through Michael's telemetry. "See? At first some brady-cardia, then SVT throughout the week. Even some short runs of V-tach."

When I lean in for a closer look at tonight's arrhythmia pattern—the one that proved fatal—Kim hands the tablet back to Polly before I'm able to read much of it. With another timid glance in my direction, the petite nurse exits the room and patters off down the hallway. It's unclear why she seems bashful in my presence, but I don't have time to ponder it.

"Did you have him on a beta blocker?" I ask Kim, studying Michael's lifeless face. "What do his labs show?"

I try to keep my tone clinical, non-accusatory, but despite the absurdity of my suspicion, what I want most to ask is if Kim injected something lethal and then held off resuscitating Michael until someone else came into the room. That would give the appearance she had been helping him all along. Something lethal like a potassium chloride overdose. That drug wouldn't show up on autopsy. Both components are normal electrolytes in blood. Other medications come to mind too.

It's critical I hide my mistrust, though. First, because my theory might be pure fantasy and I could lose all professional credibility. Second, because I don't want to show my hand. If Michael flashed Kim his I-think-you-murdered-my-wife cards, a push of potassium chloride might have very well been the next card *she* flashed.

Kim answers my question about Michael's lab tests. "They're still pending, but they'll probably be normal." She stares hard at me. "He was badly injured. Beaten up. The police tried to get him to write out what happened to him, but all he did was scribble that he was drunk and fell. The police didn't believe him"—she points to Michael's battered body —"there's no way he could have done this to himself, but he refused to admit to any assault, and without a name, what can they do?" Here she pauses and raises an eyebrow. "Seems he's protecting someone."

Yeah, me, but why? Especially after what I did to him.

I realize I'm still gripping Michael's hand. I drop it, but my body burns, and I want to lash out at something. Not wanting Kim to see my growing emotion, I shift away and move to the window. Near it, I spot Michael's phone on the chair—a phone that probably contains his emails to me. Or worse.

"What are you *really* doing here?" Kim asks, interrupting my thoughts.

She eyes my overnight bag near Michael's bed and nudges the fabric with her loafer. With her attention diverted, I swipe Michael's phone off the chair and slip it into my hoodie pocket.

"And how did you know Mr. Yerli was in the hospital?" Kim eyes me again. "None of us called you. We didn't know he was…your patient. You haven't stopped by the entire time he's been here."

Her tone is always impossible to read, but I sense she is trying to trap me in a lie. What can I say? No doctor would bring an overnight bag to stay with his or her hospitalized patient. I step forward and pick up the carryall.

"Michael and I…" I pause, forming my thoughts. "We've been seeing each other." Although this lie could land me in deeper trouble with the Medical Board, Kim can't dispute it. "I'm not proud of it, and I hope you'll be discreet, but I only saw him once as a patient."

"Oh," Kim says, leaving me unsure as to whether she believes me or not. "Was it you on the phone tonight?" She glances at the clock hanging near the wall-mounted TV. "Guess I should say this morning, huh?"

Again, I feel like she's setting a trap. Does she already know I'm the one who called him? Was she the one who ended our conversation? If I lie, it will only add to her suspicion.

"Yes," I finally say. I pray she doesn't notice that the chair next to me no longer holds Michael's phone.

"Why?"

"He was lonely. Maybe even scared."

"What did he have to be scared of?"

The two of us stare at each other. If Kim is playing games with me, it's impossible to tell. She has always been impassive, and her surgical mask makes the guessing game harder. Sometimes, back when we were residents, her passivity—her sloth-like indifference, even—annoyed the heck out of me. But mostly she was just…there. Bland, predictable, forgettable.

Now though, as we blink at each other, Michael growing cold by our sides with no one but me to grieve for him, I wonder if Kim has fooled us all.

I told myself that after my revenge on the barista, I would put a halt to my tune-ups. That I was crossing a line that might turn me into a monster.

But now?

I tear my gaze from Kim and lower it to Michael. His bearded face wears the ugly grimace of death, and in it I see fear and uncertainty. His rage is gone.

That's okay. I'll carry it for him.

I close his eyelids and bend down to kiss his forehead. Feelings I don't understand stab my heart.

If Kim did this to you, I silently promise him, *if she killed Jasmine, others too, I will find out. And I will make her pay.*

28

At nearly 5:00 a.m., I stumble out of Boston General's main entrance and spill into the Uber I summoned. The area is still dark and mostly deserted, but instead of wondering about the trustworthiness of the hirsute driver behind the wheel, my mind struggles to process Michael Yerli's death. Was it truly natural? An arrhythmia as Kim said? Or did she play a role in his cardiac arrest?

Either way, had I not fought him so aggressively in his basement apartment, he'd still be alive. That thought is a kick to my own throat. No new-agey affirmation in the world will bring me peace knowing that.

I rest my head against the backseat of the Nissan and try to breathe away my guilt. Sleep is what I want. It's what I need. But I'm not going home to sleep. I'm going home to retrieve my car and drive to Michael's place. I want to learn more about him, not only because of our perverse connection but because he might have incriminating evidence against me. If I'm arrested for my extracurricular activities, I won't be able to avenge anyone, let alone him.

Although I am relieved to have his phone in my pocket, I hope no one looked through it before I snatched it off the chair in his room. If they did, they might have found the video he claimed he took of me while I tuned up the wife beater. I haven't had the chance to check yet, and I'll need his face or passcode to open it.

Kim mentioned the police haven't yet done an investigation, that Michael refused to name any attacker or press charges, but now that he's dead, that changes things, doesn't it? Overworked police department or not, the assault on Michael could be upgraded to a homicide. Once the detectives start detecting, how hard will it be to follow the breadcrumbs back to me? I need to get to his apartment before they do.

If I'm lucky, his door will still be unlocked, the paramedics not taking the time to secure it after wheeling him into the ambulance. If it isn't, or if the landlord got wind of what happened to Michael and stopped by to lock the door, I'll have to create a plan B.

On the other hand, it's possible Kim won't call the police. If she killed Michael, she won't want them sniffing around any more than I do. She'll simply go through the usual channels for a patient death. Polly might call them, though, and I still have zero proof Kim murdered Michael. Until I do, I have to assume Michael's death will be investigated.

The Uber driver drops me off at my building. I hurry inside and speed walk through the lobby, relieved the door attendant isn't behind the desk at the moment. I'm not in the mood for small talk. I also don't want to risk an encounter with Nathan, so I enter the parking garage directly instead of going up to my loft. It wouldn't be the first time my hypochondriac neighbor caught me at dawn on a Saturday.

Antsy with adrenaline, I climb into my SUV and input Michael's address into the GPS. Twice I have to retype the street name because my fingers are so jittery I keep punching the wrong letters. Finally, with the address correctly entered, I back out of my too-tight parking space and weave my way to the exit. Anxious to get there, I drive to South Boston where Michael lives—lived—in a neighborhood that is probably safe for a daytime stroll but no place I'd want to be caught alone after dark.

It's almost five thirty now, and the sun is starting its ascent. By the time I reach the brownstone that houses Michael's basement apartment, the traffic has picked up, and there's enough daylight to feel more secure.

I drive around a two-block radius in search of a parking spot. In this residential neighborhood, all seem to be taken. Each pass reveals treeless, shabby sidewalks and porches with terracotta pots housing wilted plants. On the fourth drive-around, a pickup truck vacates a spot, and I pull into it.

I wait a few minutes in my SUV to steady my nerves. At 6:00 a.m., just after the first dog-walker and one other person exit their brownstones, I put on my sunglasses, climb out of the Highlander, and stroll the block and half toward Michael's place. Thinking it might be better to disguise myself, I slip my hood over my head but then remove it again. It will only make me look more suspicious.

As I approach the side stairwell leading down to Michael's place, my heart rate climbs higher. I've performed far riskier and illegal tasks than this during my tune-ups, so why am I suddenly a quaking Cathy?

Keeping my head up as if I belong there, I trot down the concrete stairs. I have no idea who lives above Michael or in the unit on the other side, but hopefully they're not nosy.

With the carryall over my shoulder, its contents (save for two bobby pins from my makeup bag) unloaded in my vehicle in case I need an empty bag, I wonder if I'll have to pick the lock. I've only done it once, back in college when I had to help a drunk friend get into her apartment after she'd left her keys at the bar. It took a while, but two bobby pins and some jimmying later, we were in. Judging by the old doorknob on Michael's entrance, I might be able to do the same here.

I slip on a pair of gloves and turn the knob. It opens easily. My earlier assumption about the paramedics rushing out with their injured party and not taking the time to find Michael's key to lock the place back up was correct. I inhale deeply and step inside the mildew-scented cave, locking the door behind me.

To my left lies the kitchen. The empty beer bottles and takeout containers remain scattered on the laminate counter-top. The beige appliances must be at least forty years old, and the cheap table is scuffed, but nothing seems out of place. The sagging sofa appears the same, as does the desk in the corner with the computer equipment. Everything suggests the police haven't been here yet. Why would they? Michael gave them nothing to pursue.

Until now, anyway. Now his death might give them plenty to pursue.

That thought gets me moving. The apartment is small, and I act quickly. Even though all I'm interested in is the desk with the computer equipment, I want to make sure the place shows no other evidence of me. When I pull open the kitchen drawers, one falls off its slider and takes three attempts to right again. Wooden spoons, mismatched silverware, and a few warped lids lay inside. There's nothing of interest in the cabinets either.

I move on to the bedroom, but the sadness of it makes me slow my pace. There's a twin bed with no headboard, a plastic dresser—most likely from a big-box store, and a closet with a broken sliding door. Inside hang jeans, sweatshirts, and one suit.

Was that the suit he wore to Jasmine's funeral? Did he have to sell their nicer belongings because he couldn't hold a steady job?

A search of his clothing pockets, the plastic dresser draw-ers, and his tiny bathroom nets me nothing but a knot of sympathy in my gut. In different circumstances, I could have been him. He didn't inherit money. He couldn't throw himself into his work as a doctor. He couldn't disguise his grief from those in his circle because, unlike me, he didn't find an outlet to unleash it.

Yes, I could have been Michael. Could *still* be Michael if I'm not careful.

The living room remains the last place to search, and in here the desk is the only thing of interest. The couch and the empty television stand hide nothing.

The desk is really just a sturdy plastic table, the computer equipment the only thing of value. It sits near a hopper window and catches a thin ray of sunlight that squeezes its way in. A portion of the sidewalk and street are visible, and when a couple in shorts and T-shirts pass by, perhaps on an early morning stroll, their voices come through remarkably well. Traffic, too, rolls by, and something thumps from the unit above me, a tenant maybe getting up.

The table holds both a desktop computer and a laptop, as well as a printer, a speaker, and a microphone headset. Michael mentioned something about working in IT at one time, but then he'd been forced to freelance because he couldn't keep a job. Judging by his feeble apartment, decent-paying work didn't come often.

I study the desktop computer. There's no way I can lug it out without looking suspicious. Instead, I power it on and pull over one of the table chairs.

Footsteps stomp above me now, and I picture the tenant getting ready for work. One person? Two? Would they think it suspicious to find me here?

I double down on my efforts to be quiet, but an audible groan escapes me when a password box pops up on the computer screen.

Crap.

I blink at the screen. It undulates back at me. All I can do is try the most obvious.

I type in the name *Jasmine* and hold my breath.

Nothing.

I stare out the window and try to remember Jasmine's date of birth. Can't. But after reviewing her medical records, I do remember her date of death.

I try it.

Nothing.

This is pointless. A guy who worked with computers would use a solid password.

I try another one, this time combining Jasmine's name and date of death. Of course, nothing happens.

A sense of urgency throbs inside me. How many tries will the desktop computer allow before it locks out? I remember something about five. Or is it ten?

More footsteps above, more climbing of my heart rate. I need to hurry, but how?

In my mounting stress, I knock the keyboard sideways. When I do, a slip of paper pokes out beneath it. Lifting the keyboard, I find a password cheat-sheet taped to the table.

The index card's writing is tiny and cramped with at least three dozen passwords scribbled on it. Squinting, I search for one that will unlock the desktop. Nothing is labeled specifically, but there is one for *Microsoft*. Seeing what Michael has chosen for it, I stifle a cry of surprise. Or maybe, no surprise at all.

HopeSullivan1003.

My name and condo number.

With trembling fingers, I type in the password.

The desktop computer unlocks.

An exhale of relief pours out of me, and I start perusing Michael's files. I work as quickly as I can, which, thanks to his digital organization, is easy to do. Every folder I open appears to be work-related. Former clients maybe. Old jobs he wasn't ready to delete.

A sudden noise outside the window makes me jump. It sounds like a police radio.

I whip my head toward the window, and to my horror I realize that's exactly what it is. A man in gray pants and a button-down shirt is exiting a sedan. As soon as he shuts the car door, the radio noise disappears.

A detective? Here already? Both his sober sedan and sober expression scream that must be the case.

Praying there's nothing on the desktop PC that will incriminate me, I power the thing off and dart off the chair, but not before ripping the password cheat-sheet off the table and stuffing it in my pocket. If the police discover what Michael's password is, a nine-year-old sleuth could connect him to me. Even without it they might still be able to, but hopefully the girlfriend defense will stick. I'll explain my lack of hospital visits as not wanting to advertise I was dating a former patient.

The doorbell to the brownstone complex rings, but from my subterranean position it's merely a distant buzz. Thank God the detective didn't start with the basement. Maybe he didn't realize it's a separate unit with a side entrance.

You don't know he's a detective yet. Could be a visitor.

Yeah, with a police radio in his car?

Footsteps upstairs again, the tenant no doubt wondering who is ringing his or her bell at six fifty on a Saturday morning.

I grab my bag and start to leave, but then halt. The desktop unit might be free of info on me, but that doesn't mean the laptop is, especially if Michael transferred anything over from his phone.

I rush back to the desk and grab the laptop. I yank on the charger, too, to avoid leaving evidence of a laptop behind. When it tangles with another cord, my heart jumps somewhere between my ears.

Muffled voices above me. There's still time for escape.

A final tug releases the cord, and I jam it into my carryall with the laptop. I race to the doorway. As soon as I open it, a door closes above me. The detective, if that's indeed who he is, will be rounding the brownstone to the side entrance now.

I sprint up the outdoor stairwell, grateful for my soft-soled Skechers, and take off down the narrow pathway that separates Michael's brownstone from the next. I run the opposite direction from the detective's sedan. As soon as I hit the paralleling street, I take a sharp left.

No voice calls after me. No footsteps jog down the path I just vacated. No neighbors holler out, "Over here, she's over here!"

I exhale a thousand pounds of relief and dare a peek down the pathway. A head disappears down Michael's stairwell, the detective unaware of my escape.

I clench the lumpy bag to my side. Once I will my shaky legs to move again, I hurry off to my car.

29

After six hours of restless daytime sleep, I sit at the back of a small pub near Boylston Street, my draft beer untouched. I've asked one of my patients to meet me here, something I've never done before, but I have nowhere else to turn. Proving Dr. Kim Lombardi is a killer requires a kickstart from someone more tech savvy than me.

My fingers drum the sticky tabletop, and my knees bounce up and down on the stool. Every time I quiet them, they start up again. The place smells like spilled beer and fried food, and the sunburned man in bike shorts at the table next to me reeks of a day spent cycling.

The pub's door opens, and the little bell above it rings. Janelle walks in. I still my fidgeting and give her a wave. She spots me in my recessed corner and heads over, her cut-off jean shorts and white tank top more laid-back than my summer pants and linen tee. Her strong arms and quads suggest hours spent at the gym, but her neutral expression tells me nothing about how she feels about my earlier call.

I pray I've done the right thing. Pray it won't come back to bite either Janelle or me. Just because I diagnosed her chronic lead poisoning doesn't mean she owes me a favor, especially one that, although technically not illegal for her since she works in the hospital's IT department, could raise eyebrows.

You ever need anything, Dr. Sullivan, you give me a call, she said when I last saw her in clinic. Bet she never thought I'd take her up on it.

As soon as she sits down across from me, the waiter approaches. Janelle orders the featured ale of the week, a fruity blend, and when he departs, her deadpan face finally shows movement. A curl of a lip on the left and a raise of an eyebrow on the right.

"Not gonna lie, Doc, I was awfully surprised to get your call this afternoon. Even more surprised by what you wanted."

The smelly biker guy is checking Janelle out, so I lean in closer to the table and say, "I'm sorry. I don't want to cause any trouble for you. If anyone asks, I'll leave your name out of it, but I can't access a list like that by myself. The physician EMR privileges don't include those search functions."

The waiter delivers Janelle's frothy ale. She drinks a quarter of it and then wipes the foam from her lips. "Don't worry, you're not going to get me in trouble. In IT we're always tweaking things. For me, it's just another test run of the search system. But for you?" She angles her head, her ebony hair adorned with a colorful headband. "If you start poking around in the EMR for these names, that could spell HIPAA violations for you. I don't have to tell you that."

"So you have the list then?"

"I do."

I lean back on my stool and finally gulp a swallow of my beer. When I called Janelle this afternoon, I asked for a list of Kim's patients who have died since Kim has been at Boston General, first as a resident and then as a hospitalist. Seven years in total.

"Are you going to tell me why you want it?" Janelle asks.

"I'm guessing it's because you're worried she might be responsible for their—"

I raise my hand to keep her from saying anything else. Once again, I hope I made the right decision in calling her. Ever since I saw Michael lying dead in the hospital room fourteen hours ago, my brain has been all over the place. His lifeless eyes staring up at the ceiling and his scorched chest from the electrical paddles are all I see.

"I…it's best I don't get you further involved," I say. "It was unethical of me to ask you in the first place, and believe me, I wouldn't have if I knew what else to do."

My face must reveal the pain that won't leave my heart, because Janelle puts her glass down and says, "Hey, it's okay. I'm not going to rat you out, but could you at least tell me if you're worried the deaths are…accidental or intentional?"

My lack of response must tip her off it's the latter because her lined eyes widen. "What have you gotten yourself mixed up in, Dr. Sullivan? Maybe you better involve someone higher up on the hospital food chain. You might be a little too—no offense—pure for this kind of thing. You're more Snow White than Lisbeth Salander, you know what I mean?"

Oh Janelle, if only you knew…

It's actually a relief to see I've got everyone fooled. Like Kim, I suppose, which is a similarity that doesn't please me.

I drink more beer, and it's like clay pouring down my throat. How can I be sure Janelle won't talk? At least until I can sort everything out?

But what other choice do I have? My EMR access can't generate a list like that, and it's not like I have a string of hackers on speed dial. I'm not a detective either. I'm simply a woman who hopes my suspicions about Kim are wrong.

I clear my throat. "All I can say is I'm worried about something. It might be nothing. It's probably nothing, so I need to trust that you'll keep this between you and me. But if it is something…"

"Then it's better to stop her ass now."

"Exactly."

"All right. I hear you." Janelle reaches into her gray satchel and pulls out two folded pieces of paper. "These are the names I found. Seems like a lot of deaths if you ask me."

I shrug. "For a hospitalist, and before that a resident who rotated through the ICU, maybe not."

"How do you plan on looking into them? Your snooping around in all these charts could be a problem for you." She hands me the list. "And, well, I'd hate to see anything happen to you."

"I appreciate your concern, I really do, but you let me worry about that. I'll figure it out." *Will I?* I slip the list into my laptop bag. "I can't thank you enough, and again, I'm sorry to involve you."

We lock eyes for a hard beat, and then she polishes off her last swallow of beer and rises from the table. "Don't worry about it. When this is all over, you can take me out for a drink and tell me about your heroic deeds."

To my surprise, she winks suggestively before strolling out of the bar.

I'm not sure what kind of unspoken agreement we've just made, but if these two pieces of paper she gave me get me closer to learning if Kim Lombardi is a killer, then I figure it's probably worth it.

Sitting in Starbucks on Sunday morning, using public Wi-Fi with an IP address different from my own, I open my laptop. Figuring out how to access the medical records of the deceased patients from Janelle's list without getting fired wasn't easy, and my plan is far from foolproof, but it's the best I could come up with in my disconcerted and restless state. I'll have to report my computer as stolen.

This is actually my second trip in fourteen hours to Starbucks. After I left the pub last night, I stopped at a different Starbucks to snoop through the laptop I took from Michael's apartment. According to his cheat-sheet, his Mac's password was the same as his desktop PC's: *HopeSullivan1003.*

After scouring the Mac for any evidence of me, the only things I found were copies of his wife's medical records bearing my name on a note I never transcribed and the video he made of me through the cracked wall of my barn. I'd already seen the clip on his phone. His passcode for that was *1003*—no surprise there. For once, his obsession with me came in handy.

That video could land me in jail, especially the nifty little parts where I squeeze the wife beater's chest with pliers and stab him in the thigh. How hard would it be for the police to see through my auburn wig and makeup?

Needless to say, I deleted the video from Michael's phone. I also deleted it from his iCloud account. As for the file he saved to his laptop, I got rid of that with a file-shredding application so that it can't be recovered from the hard drive. At least that's what Google tells me. Unlike my patient Janelle, I'm no tech expert.

As I sip my apple-cinnamon tea in this Starbucks, Michael's lifeless body swarms my brain. Like clockwork, Manny and my parents follow, and then—the pièce de resistance—my baby. Doesn't matter that my fetus was nothing more than a clot of cells in my blood-soaked sheets. He or she was still my child. A child I'll never know. One who would be turning two soon.

The tea clogs my throat. I blink the images away and push Michael back to the surface.

Less than two days ago he was alive, and while not well, he was on the road to recovery. With every passing second, I grow more convinced Kim had something to do with his demise. She knew he was on to her, and she had to eliminate him as a result. How convenient for her he happened to have had some earlier arrhythmias. A killer's stroke of luck.

Your luck's about to run out, Kimmy dear.

And you, Hope darling, I imagine her retorting, *have no proof.*

Using anger to help me find that proof, I bury my bleak mood and return to my laptop, where I log in to Boston General's EMR system. If only I could access the site from Michael's computer. That would make it more convincing someone hacked my username and password and entered the site as me. But it's impossible. Using the EMR remotely requires a secure VPN and software installation on a hospital-approved device, which, of course, Michael doesn't have.

I can't ask Janelle to set it up for me. I refuse to implicate her beyond what I already have. The best I can do is report my laptop as stolen. Hopefully, with my Snow White exterior (to quote Janelle), I'll be able to convince IT that someone snatched my laptop and accessed the EMR as me. Maybe even make them suspect Kim Lombardi herself since it's her patients I'll be looking at. In that regard, it might help my case along.

On the other hand, my unethical activities might get my license revoked faster than the Medical Board can say "*J'accuse.*" Honestly, I'm so bent on retribution at the moment that I'm not sure I still care.

Hey now, Hoppy, I hear Manuel say. *That's sleep deprivation talking. You love being a doctor.*

I shrug, as if my fiancé is sitting across from me instead of decomposing in the ground.

Getting down to business, I open Janelle's list of names of patients who died under Kim's watch. I ignore the sense of defeat its length gives me and instead position my legal pad and pen at the ready.

With each patient, I head straight to the death summary in their EMR documents, along with their final progress report.

If Kim's name is nowhere in sight near the time of their deaths, I move on. The charts where she pops up as the treating physician in their last hours I peruse in more detail. In these, I scan the notes for my own name too. She used my account to submit Jasmine Bonnet's final record—what's to say she hasn't done the same with other patients as well? Or with other doctors, like I suspect she did in Ted Orenson's case, my patient with pancreatitis. A training fellow's name was on his final note. Would be a risky thing to repeat too often, though. Most likely she's kept the forgeries to a minimum.

Halfway through the list, I pack up my laptop and head to a different coffee chain a few blocks away. I don't want to stick out in someone's mind. An employee might remember the woman who sat for hours in the corner, pecking away on her laptop.

Inside the new coffee shop, I order another cup of tea and an almond tart. I ignore the brown card next to it that tells me the baked good contains six hundred and twenty calories. I feel I've earned them.

The new location is equally crowded, and I'm forced to take a seat at the window bar. At least it's near the wall so I can lean back and angle my laptop away from prying eyes. A man at a nearby table barks at his wife about their home repairs and why she should have picked a different contractor. At another table, a child sniffles and coughs repeatedly.

I close my eyes and channel my concentration, hoping to tune out the chaos. Once I do, I resume my chart searches, and an hour later I finish with the last name on Janelle's list.

I study my jotted notes on the legal pad. In Kim's eight years at the hospital, first as Kimberly Baker, a resident, and then as Kim Lombardi, a hospitalist, six patient deaths seem suspicious to me. Seven counting Ted Orenson, but I didn't reopen his chart. Michael's wife is of course among them. So is he, but I didn't access his chart either. The less links between us the better.

Three men, four women, their ages ranging from thirty-three to sixty-four. Like my pancreatitis patient, none were terminally ill, and even those with more serious illnesses seemed to be improving—or at least stable—before their demise.

The cause of death listed for everyone was cardiac arrest (just like Michael), and all had co-diagnoses that clouded the picture. Things like pulmonary embolism (Jasmine), pancreatitis (Ted), sepsis, and Covid-19. All of those conditions could indeed lead to cardiac arrest, so an injection of potassium chloride by a demented doctor would easily be missed.

So what makes me suspicious of Kim's hand in their deaths? I tap my pen against the legal pad and ponder the question. The blowhard husband and his wife have left, replaced by a soft-spoken older couple, and the nose-sniffing cougher is long gone.

Mostly it's the timing of their deaths and the fact that none showed signs of deterioration before their hearts stopped. Of course, that is the very definition of sudden cardiac arrest, but even the Covid patient was off the ventilator, and her heart ultrasound showed little residual damage.

I can't define my suspicions beyond that, and if I voiced my doubts to another health-care provider, they would probably counter each one. It's more a gut feeling I have, based on my training and my practice thus far. Something smells off, and Kim seems at the core of it.

The question is why? What is her motive? Even if it's an illogical one, a motive the rest of us wouldn't understand, she must still have one.

The only common thread I can find among the patients is that their personal histories, the bits that were recorded anyway, seemed quite fortunate. Not all wealthy but all successful, and from what I could glean from the nursing notes, all had a wonderful support system of family and friends.

So again, the two big questions are, why is she doing this and how can I prove it?

The even bigger question is, how can I stop it?

30

———————

My Fourth of July has been about as festive as a coma. I've been sitting at my desk and staring out my living room window for the better part of the day.

The harbor below is a literal sea of nautical activity, and the blue sky with its marshmallow clouds provides the perfect backdrop for the Independence Day celebrations. The holiday, the weather, the laughing people—they all clash with my addled mood. It's as if an anchor from one of those boats has fallen on my chest. My role in Michael's death is suffocating me.

Why did I kick his throat so hard? I had a right to defend myself, sure, but I didn't need to be so merciless. And why did I steal precious seconds to pack a bag to stay with him at the hospital instead of racing there straight away? Had I gotten to the hospital a few minutes earlier, he might still be alive.

Accompanying this anguish is a shooting pain in my jaw, probably from clenching and grinding it over thoughts of Kim Lombardi killing Michael, along with his wife six years ago.

Maybe, Hope, maybe. You have no proof she did.

Diva mews at me and jumps into my lap. Her loose hair sticks to my leggings, but I don't bother wiping it off. Nor do I bother eating or showering or exercising or doing any of the other things I should be doing. The only thing I want to do is make Kim pay for what she's done.

If she's done it, that is.

This morning, hoping to learn about Michael's funeral arrangements, I called the general medicine ward and spoke to Polly, the nurse saddled with the Fourth of July shift. She said Michael's body was sent to Macaby Funeral Home in South Boston. She was able to track down his estranged father in New Jersey, who, according to Polly, claims to be destitute himself, with little means to pay for a burial or cremation. He agreed to take care of things nonetheless.

I was about to ask the nurse how she found Michael's father, but a patient crisis called her away. Maybe the police gave her his name, but if the detective who showed up at Michael's apartment was still investigating the assault that landed Michael in the hospital, the body wouldn't have been released to the funeral home. It would have been sent to the medical examiner's office for autopsy instead.

Maybe the cop only stopped by Michael's to see if there were any loved ones to notify. Maybe Michael's passing is being written off as an unfortunate but routine patient death, and now with him gone, not to mention his previous claims of self-injury from a fall, what benefit would it be to the police to devote man-hours to a suspect-less assault that might not have even happened? That spells good news for me.

Even with Michael's younger age, a fatal arrhythmia is a clear-cut cause of death and might not prompt an autopsy, especially if his father refuses one. An autopsy would be costly for a man of limited means. It also wouldn't rule out Kim being a murderer, not if she used something like potassium chloride to stop Michael's heart.

I summon the energy to rise from the desk and retrieve my phone from the granite island. With my trek to the kitchen, Diva assumes it's dinnertime, and a glance at the microwave's digital clock tells me it's close enough. After scooping out Monday's offering—a pungent chicken blob—onto a clean dish and refreshing her water bowl, I stroke her behind the ear and then return to my place by the window, phone in hand. The din of the Fourth of July revelers ten stories below shows no sign of slowing down.

I Google the number for Macaby Funeral Home. When I call it, someone named Cynthia answers, and when I ask about Michael Yerli, she informs me there will be a private cremation ceremony on Wednesday, family only. I assume that means Michael's father will be the only guest, and the thought of such a meager showing presses that anchor deeper into my chest. Like me, Michael must not have any siblings.

I would like to pay my respects at the funeral home, but I shouldn't connect myself to him any more than I already have. Although I feel fairly confident the police are no longer involved, it's not a given. No need to offer them any ammunition against me. Besides, a better tribute to Michael would be proving Kim is his killer. She is a far more valuable jewel to hand over to the police than me.

Whether from guilt or pity—maybe both—I give Cynthia from Macaby Funeral Home my credit card number. "Charge everything to me," I say, "including whatever keepsakes Michael's father wants to purchase. A ring containing some of his son's ashes maybe? You guys do things like that, don't you?"

She assures me they do.

"Or a memory book, or an engraved plaque with his picture. Whatever Mr. Yerli wants." I stare down at a speedboat leaving a sailboat in a wake of turbulent waves. "Oh, and a nice urn. Marble, bronze, whatever Mr. Yerli selects."

Cynthia says, "Of course."

I appreciate her discretion and lack of questions. Funeral professionals seem especially skilled at that.

After I end the call, I stare across the room at my spotless kitchen. Did I eat lunch? Breakfast? I can't remember. Most of my day—all of my day—has been spent stewing over Michael, Kim, and the six other patients she might have killed, including my patient Ted Orenson.

I can't reenter their charts. I already left a message with IT that my laptop was stolen. When I buy a new one, they'll set me up with a secure portal, and that will be that. Until then, I have no outside access to the EMR. Whether my chart searches in the coffee shops yesterday will trigger a flag, I don't know, but if they do, IT will think whoever stole my laptop is the culprit.

Then again, maybe the fear of HIPAA has been so ingrained in me that I'm overestimating the response. For all I know, the chart accesses and stolen laptop will be a mere snowflake in an IT blizzard, but just in case, I need deniability.

From near the bedroom door, Diva rubs her whiskers clean of chicken dinner and stares at me.

"Is my angst boring you?" I ask. "Are you—"

A knock on the door cuts me off. My heart rate soars. I check my phone for a missed call from Tony, the doorman, about a visitor. Nothing.

Should I answer it?

Dear God, is it the police?

Knowing I'm overreacting, I force myself to relax and go check the peephole. My neighbor, Nathan, is on the other side. What ailment will require my attention today?

I swing open the door. "Hey, Nathan, what's up?"

To my surprise, he holds out a piece of shortcake smothered in blueberries and strawberries and served on a colorful paper plate. A mound of whipped cream tops it all.

Eyes cast downward, he adjusts his glasses with his free hand. "Red, white, and blue. You know I don't indulge much, but it's a holiday. The whipped cream is the white. No white fruits that I know of. Well, I'm sure there are somewhere, maybe in a more tropical—"

"Thank you, Nathan." I accept the proffered cake. "That's really thoughtful of you." Something warm and positive wants to sliver its way into my psyche, but my unsettled anger won't let it.

"It's nothing." He shrugs and plants his hands in his chino pockets. Diva comes to sniff him out, and he bends over to give her a pet.

Expecting now to hear about a new skin lesion, or a click in his knee, or a scratch in his throat, Nathan surprises me all over again by asking, "Are you okay?"

"Of course," I say, probably too quickly. "Why do you ask?"

"It's just, well, I called out to you yesterday when you were leaving, and you didn't respond. Just got on the elevator." He digs the toe of his sneaker against the hallway carpet. "Your face was all pinched. I thought you were mad at me."

"Oh gosh, I'm sorry. I didn't hear you." Was that when I headed out to Starbucks with my laptop and Janelle's list? "Of course I'm not mad at you. Why would I be?"

"And now, before I knocked to give you this cake, I thought I heard you talking to yourself."

I laugh, and the genuineness of it lightens my mood for a precious second. "I was talking to Diva."

Nathan doesn't laugh back. He peeks at me, first shyly and then more boldly, his narrow face etched with concern. It dawns on me what he must see. I'm covered in cat fur. I haven't combed my hair since my attempt at yoga this morning. Haven't showered. Haven't put on a hint of makeup.

Self-conscious now, I set the cake on the kitchen island and smooth my hair. "I'm sorry. I was exercising."

"Oh, sure, sure," he says.

I can tell he doesn't believe my lie. I force a smile. "Would you like to come in? I can make some tea to go with the cake."

He hesitates, and the fact his hesitation seems more out of worry for me and less from his social anxiety embarrasses me. Do I look that discombobulated? That crazed?

"I think you could use some rest," he says. "So maybe another time."

Rejected by Nathan. Wow. I really must be a mess.

With a final goodbye, he shuffles back to his apartment.

After I shut my door, I scoop up Diva. "So it's come to this, has it? Nathan feeling sorry for *me*." I lower my voice, scared he might hear me again. "Guess a shower's a good start, huh?"

Cat in arms, I make my way to the bedroom and vow to get it together.

The next day and a half in clinic prove I haven't exactly gotten it "together." Learning one of your hospital colleagues might be a killer does a real number on the brain. It's as if all the emotions I buried two years ago have resurfaced a thousand times greater.

Yesterday, I ordered the wrong labs for a patient. Then I called another one to tell her she had an abnormality on her chest x-ray, only to realize it was a year-old study and not the most recent one. After I hung up, I spilled a full cup of coffee all over my counter. The coffee was brewed in the clinic. I'm not yet ready to face the barista, even though with each passing day I'm confident I'll never be identified as her assailant. Today, I'm so far behind on my schedule that I worked through the lunch hour and am just now seeing my last patient of the morning at one-ten in the afternoon.

While our nurse Alice runs an EKG on the woman, I wolf down a yogurt and banana at my workstation. Terrence approaches me, his white coat starched and his tie a swirl of blue and red smiling skulls.

"What's going on?" he asks, not wasting time on niceties. His expression is all doctorly concern. "You're all over the place, and not in a good way. Are you sick? Want me to check a CBC on you?" He inspects me more closely. "You're looking a little sallow too. I better add chemistries."

"Okay, okay, Dr. House, quit diagnosing me. I'm fine." I try to make light, smile hard enough that it reaches my eyes, but all I can think about is whether Michael's body has been cremated yet and if a once troubled man is now nothing but a pile of ash.

A strangled sound escapes my throat. I cover it with a cough and thump my chest. "Excuse me. Swallowed my banana wrong."

Terrence seems unconvinced. He appears about to push harder, but Alice returns with my patient's EKG and gives me an out.

I scan the heart tracing, and as I leave my workstation to enter the patient's room, I thank Terrence for his concern. "I'm fine, really. If I look tired, it's only because my new cat hogs my bed." At least part of that is true. Diva takes up a hundred times her body size in space.

I manage to work through my next few patients without much distraction. Thanks to a no-show, which would normally make me bristle, I even manage to catch up. The brief respite allows me a chance to sort through the snail mail our receptionist has dropped off at my counter.

While rummaging through it, a sense of normalcy returns, and I cling to the feeling. Maybe I just needed some time to get my head back in the right place. I could invite Terrence and his family out for dinner. Ask how his book is going. Talk about normal people stuff. That might help too.

One after the other, I slit open envelopes with the letter opener Frank Goldberg gave me when I joined the practice. Most of it is junk mail. A few pharma-company fliers. A couple of "welcome our newest doctor to the hospital" postcards. When I pick up the second-to-last envelope, my hand freezes.

It's a certified letter from the Medical Board, signed for by our receptionist.

I haven't spoken with Martin Hernandez in two weeks, not since he reassured me the complaint against me was bogus, a complaint I now know was lodged by Michael to snare my attention. No phone call this time. Just a scary-looking letter that sits like a pile of anthrax in my palm.

Hands shaking, I slit open the envelope, barely hearing Alice tell me my next patient, an asthma check-up, is ready in room five.

Relax, I tell myself. *Probably just a letter of formal clearance.*

When I read the letter, its precise and business-like verbiage is anything but a letter of formal clearance. I sink down on my stool but miss half of it and plummet to the floor.

Frank, who's exiting one of the staff bathrooms down the hallway, rushes to me and helps me up. For a senior citizen, he's remarkably spry, and in my embarrassed stupor, I imagine that will serve him well in retirement.

"Hope, dear, are you all right?"

I don't mind that my clinic head calls me *dear*, but I do mind that he has seen me topple to the floor like an idiot. I also mind that he's now holding the letter from the Board. He scans it while I smooth my clothes with what I hope is a modicum of dignity.

"What's this?" he says. "I thought that matter with the Board was all cleared up."

"It was. I mean, it is." My voice cracks. "This is something new."

Am I about to lose my license? Two complaints in one month? Will they scrutinize me more closely now? Find my connection to Michael?

Frank peers at me above his wire frames, not out of anger or suspicion, but out of concern, like Terrence before him and like Nathan last night. I would almost prefer anger. My boss's paternal affection reminds me too much of my father.

"What's this about a drug allergy and hospitalization?" Frank flaps the letter, and the breeze carries his stale breath my way. "Why is this patient reporting you?" He must notice my chagrin because he adds, "It won't go anywhere. Drug reactions are awful, and I'm sorry he got sick, but we can't foresee these things. The Board will recognize that."

I shake my head. Mumble more to myself than him.

"What's that?" Frank asks. "Here, sit down. You're shaking. Terrence said you might be ill, and I think he's right."

"I prescribed clindamycin. The patient claims he told me about the allergy, but it didn't get added to his allergy list." I realize my comment deflects blame onto the nursing staff, so I straighten and say, "That's on me. I should have reviewed the list with him myself."

"Well," Frank hesitates, as if no longer so sure it's an open-and-shut case, "that can happen."

Yeah, to an intern, I want to say.

"Why don't you go home," Frank suggests. "Take some days off. At least until next week. You can sort this out with the Board and get some rest. An allergic reaction won't be worth their time, although you might want legal representation all the same."

"I can't do that. Go home, I mean. We're short-staffed as it is. Bo is out of the hospital, but he might not be well enough to see patients yet."

"I'll call Rishi. He's been doing better this past week. Less fatigue since his last flare. He can take over your patients on Thursday and Friday, and Terrence and I can divide up the few you have left today. It's Irene's admin day, but we can pull her out of her office if need be, and Bo already told me he's coming in Friday morning if he feels up to it."

"No, I'm fine. Really, I—"

"Go home, Hope." Like my father's, Frank's tone implies the issue isn't up for discussion.

I sense rather than see Alice lurking in the hallway behind me, and from one corridor over, Terrence pokes out his head.

"We've got this," he says. "You'd do the same for us. You *have* done the same for us. Now go home and rest. Sleep cures most everything."

It certainly cured Michael, I think. *Cured him right into an ashy, eternal rest.*

Head lowered, I collect my things. The other day I mused I no longer cared if my license got suspended. Idiotic bravado, that was. My work is everything to me. It's what tethers me. Keeps me social and selfless and allows me the tiniest sliver of belief in the greater good, the belief that humanity still outweighs inhumanity. Without this clinic to orient me, I'm left only with a desire for vengeance, and then what will I become?

As I leave the clinic via the back entry to avoid being seen by my patients in the waiting room, the exit-door pills in my nightstand call out to me. With them beckons Michael's eternal sleep.

He got out. He escaped his chains of grief. He is finally at peace.

Maybe that's my road to freedom as well.

31

Wine sloshes over my glass onto my sofa, leaving burgundy drops on the cream upholstery. I curse loudly enough to drown out the eighties' punk rock wailing from my ceiling speakers. Diva darts into the bedroom. A few moments later she peeks out at me from the door.

What in the world was I thinking making my loft a sterile study in white? All I need now is a straitjacket, and I'll be that much closer to a nine-hundred-square-foot rubber room.

I dart off to my laundry closet and rummage around the various detergents and disinfectants for the fabric cleaner. With rag in hand, I return to the living room and scrub at the discolored sofa. When the red wine fails to disappear, I flip the cushion over and pretend the last five minutes never happened. If only I could pretend this day never happened.

Outside the window, the cloudless sky is still bright at 7:00 p.m. Massachusetts Bay sparkles in the horizon, and I realize I should be going for a run instead of sulking and getting drunk. When did I turn into such a drama queen? I'm not going to lose my license for prescribing an antibiotic to an allergic patient. I'm not going to lose my job. I effed up with that patient, no doubt, and it'll go through the hospital's safety reporting system, but I have helped a lot of people overcome a lot of poor health, and that is what should be my focus.

"See?" I say to Diva, dumping the rag in the laundry basket and replacing the fabric cleaner. "I'm channeling Manny. These are the things he would say to me if his blood hadn't been replaced by malignant cells."

If only I could believe like Manny did. It's one thing to read daily affirmations and say positive mantras. It's another thing to have faith in them. To truly feel them.

At least the wine helps. I polish off the rest in one long swallow. Then I pour another glass and move to the kitchen island in case I spill again. Soon, my brain glides into the lovely escape of inebriation.

Knowing I should eat something—my last meal was the yogurt and banana at lunch—I stand unsteadily and totter to the freezer. There must be some frozen dinners in there. Before I manage to pull the drawer open, my phone chortles the trio of notes that indicates a call from the doorman.

A package delivery? In the evening? No, that would be left in the mail room. I'm not expecting anything from Door Dash either. I'm not so drunk that I would forget ordering. Not yet, anyway.

So the phone alert can only mean one thing. Someone is here to see me.

My first thought is Connor Cocky Casey, but after our hook up last Friday he mentioned he was going on vacation the week of the Fourth of July. He would still be out of town. Besides, I made it clear our romp was a one-night thing.

A more alarming idea comes to mind. *Is it Kim? Could she know I'm on to her?*

I pad uneasily to my phone on the coffee table and take the call. "Yes, Tony?"

"Good evening, Dr. Sullivan. You have a visitor."

"But I'm not expecting—"

"Says he's Bo Linton, a doctor you work with. Should I send him up?"

Whoa. Did not see that coming. What could Bo want?

My wariness shifts to curiosity and then back to wariness. Has Bo's memory of the assault returned? Does he remember I was in the clinic the night Michael clobbered him? If so, questions will be asked that I'm not prepared to answer. Ken Doll or not, Bo isn't stupid. He'll see through my lies.

But Michael is *my* secret. Proof of his murder is mine to find, and now that he's gone, his vengeance against Kim is mine to take.

"Um, Dr. Sullivan?"

"Oh, sorry," I say to Tony. "Yes, thank you. Send him up."

I cross to the decorative mirror hanging between my door and the laundry closet. After smoothing my hair, I rub smeared liner from my upper lids. I'm still dressed in my clinic clothes, so at least I'm more respectable than I was for Nathan the other night in my cat-hair leggings, but the wine has made me glassy-eyed, and my complexion is dulled from lack of sleep.

From inside the loft, I hear the muted ding of the elevator down the corridor. Bo will be here any second. I plant my eye against the peephole, and as soon as his warped figure appears in front of the lens, I open the door. Across from me, Nathan does the same, but when he sees I have a male visitor, he jolts and retreats back inside his loft. Doesn't even give me a chance to greet him or thank him for his patriotic shortcake, which was something I actually did enjoy.

I wave Bo in. "I gotta admit, you've caught me by surprise. How did you know where I live?"

"Frank told me. He mentioned you had a rough day. I'm…I'm sorry to hear that."

The tenseness in Bo's angled jaw makes me want to shoo

him back out before he broaches a subject I don't want to talk about.

"You came to my condo to tell me that?" My tone is harsher than I'd intended.

He runs a hand through his hair. Winces as his fingers brush the contusion from Michael's blow two weeks ago.

If he has come to find answers about the assault, he'll be disappointed. If he has come to ask me out, he'll be equally disappointed. He could never match my Manny.

"Can I get you a drink?" I point to my full wine glass on the island and pull out a stool for him. "That's my third, so I apologize if my words are fuzzy."

"No, no," he says quickly, and I only now remember that Terrence mentioned Bo is an alcoholic.

Eager to correct my misstep, I offer him water instead. "It's infused. Oranges and lemons in it. Want that?"

His face relaxes a degree. "Yeah, that would be great. Thanks."

I pour him a glass from the pitcher in the fridge and slide it over the granite toward him. We're dancing around the issue he wishes to discuss. If only I knew what that issue was.

Leaving one stool between us—there are only three at the curved island—I sit and take a drink of wine. When I can't take his silence anymore, I ask, "Why are you here, Bo?"

He rubs his hands over his jeans and tugs at the collar of his cotton shirt. "I, uh…" He drains half the glass of infused water. "Man, this is really hard."

His obvious anxiety ratchets up mine. His flushed coloring and restless fidgeting suggest he is not here to ask me out. An attractive doctor in his forties can't be that awkward around women. His reaction also seems out of proportion to a surfaced memory from the night he was attacked in the clinic. So, what exactly does he know about me?

My fingers tremble against the stem of my wine glass. He must have discovered my revenge acts. But how? I'm always so careful, so well disguised. I take great care to avoid being seen or followed.

And yet, Michael discovered my double life, didn't he? Maybe I'm not so skilled after all.

I drain my wine in three swallows and brace myself for what Bo has to say.

I refill my wine glass a fourth time, which empties the bottle. If I don't eat something soon, there will be two Bo's in front of me instead of one. Then again, I don't need clear vision to spot his anxiety.

"Hope, there's…uh…something I need to tell you."

"Just say it. Please. You're freaking me out."

He polishes off the rest of his water. Diva enters the room and weaves around our stools. Bo stares at her but doesn't seem to register her presence.

"I know you lost your parents," he finally spits out.

Once again he's caught me off guard. "Yes," I say slowly. "About three and a half years ago. It was a—"

"Car accident."

My speech slows even more. "Yeeess, a hit-and-run. And you know this how?"

"Because…because…" Bo makes a guttural sound and buries his face in his hands. "Because I'm the one who hit them."

I freeze. In the instant of that muffled confession, time stops. Completely. No gravity. No sound. Only the blood rushing behind my eardrums. The wine glass in front of me swells and shrinks, and every molecule in my body separates from its neighbor.

"Hope. Say something."

Through my blurry fog of shock, Bo stares at me. One of him, then two of him, then one again. His eyes are moist with tears.

"I'm so sorry," he moans. "Let me explain. I never meant to hurt anyone that night. I—"

"How...?" I stammer. "What...?" None of this makes sense. I'm drunk. I misunderstood him. For all I know, he's not even really here.

I reach out to touch him, see if I've only conjured his visit in my mind, but not only do I feel the firm flesh of his forearm, I realize he's misinterpreted my gesture.

He grabs my hand in his own. "I've wanted to say something for so long. My life has been a living hell since that horrible night. At first, I thought maybe it didn't even happen. That I had imagined it. I was in an alcoholic fugue for twenty-four hours, a bender that nearly killed me."

Bo killed my parents?

This tall, blond man in a short-sleeved shirt drinking my infused water at my kitchen island killed my parents?

"But then I sobered up, saw what all the local news channels were reporting, found the dents in my Volkswagen, and bits and pieces of the crash came back to me. Not much—most of it was a blackout. Is still a blackout. But I traveled that same road as your parents at the same time of night, and with the damage to my car, I had to assume it was me."

Like a mute, I stare at him. His lips disconnect from his face, two pink worms spewing nonsense into the air. My throat collapses. I'm not even sure I'm breathing.

Bo keeps spouting his bloodbath, but his own sorrow does nothing to cushion the blow.

"I went to their memorial service. Found the date and time online. I was at the cemetery when you buried them. Stood

way back out of the way. When I discovered who you were—
that you were a doctor in the same field as me—well, I guess I
kind of became obsessed with you." He holds up a hand, his
fingernails chewed to the quick. "Not creepy obsessed, I don't
mean that, nothing improper. But I kept tabs on you. Made
sure you were"—he swallows a sob—"made sure you were
okay. When a locum-tenens job at Congress Medical opened
up, I knew I had to apply. I won't stay there if you don't want
me to, and of course, why would you? But I wanted you to at
least get to know me first. See that I've changed. See that I'm
no longer that drunk asshole. That I'd give everything I own,
every second of my time, every last one of my living cells if I
could take that awful night back."

His voice chokes off, and he requests more water. I don't
move from my stool. Can't.

He drops my hand and rises. Refills his glass, this time
from the tap instead of the pitcher of infused water, as if realizing he's no longer worthy of anything more. He drains the
glass and puts it next to my sink.

Still standing there, he says, "That day you buried them
was the last day I ever took a drink. Before that, I was what
you might call a functioning alcoholic—still able to go to work
every day, although God knows I wasn't the best doctor in my
hungover state. But at night? On the weekend? I was a
blackout drunk. I was despicable." He spits the words out, and
when he grabs his stomach, he looks like he's about to puke on
my floor.

I don't care. My molecules have not yet reassembled. They
float and shimmer around me, and a gray veil shrouds the
entire loft.

"I quit my job, checked myself into treatment, went to
every AA meeting I could find. Then I started working locums
so I could volunteer in places of need, helped out at youth
shelters, did everything I could think of to do to repent.
But…"

His voice strangles off again, and he sobs. For sixty seconds? Sixty minutes? Sixty years? I don't know.

Bo finds my paper towel roll hanging next to the gas range. He yanks off a piece and blows his nose. All the handsomeness has left his face. He looks like a pink troll with bruised eyes and a fat nose.

"I made amends, Hope. To everyone I hurt. My wife, who divorced me well before the night of the accident. My brother —so many vile things I said to him during my drunken flights. My parents, whose hearts I broke. Friends who kicked me out of their lives for their own sanity. Most have forgiven me now for how I treated them. Some haven't. But there's only one person I haven't made amends to." He honks his nose in another one of my paper towels, the used one crushed in his palm. "And I can't tell you how much it means to me that you're hearing me out, that you're allowing me this chance to ask—no, *beg*—for your forgiveness."

Jesus. Does he take my silence as a gift to him? A gift to let him have his say?

Because of him, two of the kindest, most generous people in the world are dead. As if I'd *ever* consider forgiving him. I'm not even sure I'll let him leave here alive.

My hands form fists against my lavender pants. My molecules finally start fusing back together.

"If you want to call the police, I'll understand." Bo sniffles. "I won't fight it. I'll spend a decade in prison if that's what they stick me with."

My mouth opens. I work my tongue, try to form words.

"But I had to come clean with you. Not just for me, but for you too."

A heat creeps through my body, starting from my bare toes and rising up to my gut, my chest, my face. I start to speak, but my croaky whisper doesn't carry over Bo's pleas.

"You deserve to know the truth," he says. "You deserve to

have answers, and while I know my telling you won't bring them back and will only reopen your wounds, I hope someday it can at least bring you some peace. Five months before I…killed your parents, I lost my twin sister to cancer. It was like losing half of myself." His face pinches in pain. "I'm not making excuses, but her death took my drinking to a whole new level. I spiraled deeper and deeper into a booze-filled hole, and I couldn't climb out of it. So I can only imagine your own suffering. How not knowing who killed your parents must have tortured you all this time." He hiccups. "And then to lose your boyfriend—Manuel wasn't it?—so shortly after, well, I can't even imagine—"

At the mention of Manny, I shoot up from my stool. Every one of my muscle fibers ignites into flames, and I no longer control my body.

"Don't you dare say his name!" I shriek. "I'll kill you!" I run toward the knife block near the range, on the other side of Bo and my paper towel holder. "I'll fucking kill you, you asshole!"

Bo's troll face opens wide with surprise, and just as I grab the biggest knife in my set, he leaps out of the way and rounds to the other side of the island.

He holds out both palms. "Hope, oh God, Hope, I know how much this must hurt."

I rage toward him, knife upraised, images of my nearly decapitated mother—her neck stitched up and hidden by a Gucci scarf in her coffin, for Christ's sake—flooding me with an unbearable pain. "Get out get out get out!" I wail.

My voice is unrecognizable to me, and in a nanosecond of lucidity, I spot Diva shoot from the sofa and disappear into the bedroom.

"Please, Hope." Bo's tears are flowing again, and his steps retreat to the door. "Put the knife down and let's—"

I emit the most ear-shattering scream any human has ever produced. I run toward him, seeing images of my father now, bruised and battered, injuries so massive even the skilled mortician couldn't hide them.

Bo grabs the doorknob. I keep shrieking. Shrieking and shrieking and wailing for him to get out before I kill him.

He bolts out the door. Nathan stands near his own open threshold, his thumbs feverishly tapping his cell phone.

Bo tears off down the hallway and stabs the elevator button hard enough to break a finger. Only when the doors close on him and he disappears from my view do I quit wailing.

Nathan is talking to someone, a 911 operator probably. "I don't know, I don't know, but he's going to get away."

I shake my head, my throat scorched and raw from my laryngeal explosion. I place my hand on Nathan's shoulder, grab his phone, and tell the operator it was just a mistake. "An ugly argument, that's all." I'm amazed I'm able to form a coherent sentence. "No, he won't hurt me, and I don't think I'll ever see him again."

Once I've convinced the operator of my safety, I hand Nathan back his phone. I blink at him. Before I can stop it, I start to cry. Within seconds I'm a torrential downpour. Nathan's face becomes a mix of helplessness, fear, and sympathy.

Regardless, he opens his arms to me. After an initial resistance, I step forward and fall into them.

Two hours later, I'm back at my place. Still drunk. Still shaking. Still a mix of rage and grief.

But at least I'm not a killer. I didn't stab Bo, even though I wanted to, so maybe there's hope for me yet. If my flame ever burns that dark, my exit-door pills should be the first thing I swallow. Just as I protect others from the world with my tune-ups—or at least I like to think I do—I need to protect the world from me.

In a sobbing display that shamed me, I poured my grief out to Nathan. There, seated on his checkered sofa, next to a bookshelf full of statistical manuals and a bust of Isaac Newton, I told him about my parents, the accident, Bo's confession, even about Manuel and the baby I lost. The only thing I didn't reveal was Bo's identity because Nathan insisted I call the police, and I'm not sure yet what I want to happen to Bo.

My hypochondriac neighbor gave me the most soothing affection and warm human touch I've had since Manny died, rocking me in his arms, assuring me that after a good night's sleep and a sunny day, my heart would be lighter. He even welcomed Diva, who had once again slipped out of my open door into his, maybe to find out if the tuna was greener on Nathan's side of the hallway.

Nathan then rambled off statistics about grief and the high likelihood of moving on once the emotions have all been processed. In spite of my state of mind, his sweetness made me laugh, to which he said, "See? It's already working."

I must admit, I saw a whole new side to Nathan, even if it was through my tears. If he held back reporting on every bodily finding, a woman might snatch him up. A nice woman. One who doesn't stab wife beaters and chain up dog abusers.

Now, back inside my own place, my tears have dried, and my fury has dulled to an angry flush. The wine glass is back in my hand, and although I know it shouldn't be, I need its contents to sedate me into an emotionless void. Feeling is too difficult.

To avoid ruminating over Bo's confession, I think about Kim instead. I think about proving she is a killer. The more wine I drink, the more convinced I am of her guilt.

I want to hurt Bo, I do. *There he is, back in my mind again.* I want him to pay for what he did, but given the way my life has been going lately, I might only get one more chance at revenge. Do I use it on him? A reformed man who likely won't hurt anyone again? Or do I use it on Kim? A woman who might very well hurt someone else.

I chug my way through the second bottle of wine, hoping to pass out. The drunker I get, the clearer things become.

Kim needs to pay.

"Giv' me m' phone," I slur to Diva, who stares at me from her designer cat tower near the window. "Shees no' gunna get away wi' this."

When the cat doesn't bring me the mobile, I wobble up from the sofa like a toddler with ataxia and snatch it off my coffee table. The phone flies from my hands and thumps onto the area rug.

"Budder fingers," I say, snorting stupidly. When I bend over to sweep the phone back up, I nearly pass out from wooziness.

With blurred vision, I open my contact list, widening my eyes to read it. When I think I spot Kim Lombardi's name and number, I press call.

She answers after one ring. I'm not sure whether she's working at the hospital tonight or is at home, but either way she sounds awake.

"I know wha' ur doin', Kim Lombarrrdi," I blurt out. "You kilt Michael." My tears threaten to return, and now, instead of my parents' dead bodies, I'm picturing Michael's ashes in the funeral home's incinerator. "I won' let you ge' away with it. I won'. I'm goin' to police."

Before she can respond, I end the call and stumble to my bed. The moment I collapse onto it, my heavy eyelids slam closed, and my phone slips from my hand.

33

———

I wake up the next morning with a head two sizes too big. Undulating waves of nausea slosh back and forth inside it.

How much did I drink last night? I remember diving deep into a second bottle. It's a wonder I woke up at all. I shoot a sideways glance at my black lacquer nightstand with the waiting bottle of pills tucked inside.

Not yet, I tell them. *I'm not quite finished.*

For a minute I lie there. Diva is perched on the end of the queen bed, my duvet bunched up around her. She licks her paw with more attitude than necessary, and I suppose it's her way of telling me she wants her breakfast.

Slowly, ever so slowly, I rise to a seated position. The fact I'm still dressed in my lavender work pants and summer blouse, both horribly wrinkled, brings a level of hangover humiliation I haven't felt since I did the walk of shame in histology class back in college. Aside from my recent bump and grind with Cocky Casey, one-night stands were never my thing.

Despite the pressure in my bladder, I hang out in my seated position a while longer, my hands pressed against the mattress, my brain trying to catch up with the events of last night.

Then, in another wave of nausea, it hits me.

Bo Linton.

Bo confessed to killing my parents.

I charged him with a knife like a crazy woman. Then I sobbed in Nathan's arms, an actuary with hypochondria who swears there is a risk assessment for everything, including my grief.

I close my eyes against the swirl of anger and embarrassment. Within seconds, they snap back open.

Oh God. Oh God oh God oh God.

Please tell me I didn't.

I scan the nightstand for my phone, but it isn't in its charger. Panicked, I flounder around the duvet and find it near Diva. My agitated motion floods my mouth with stringy saliva, the kind that comes right before you vomit.

Settling back on the bed, letting the queasiness calm down, I use my face to unlock my phone. I tap open the recent calls.

Shit.

It really happened. I called Kim Lombardi when I was rip-roaring drunk. I told her I think she's a killer.

What have I done? I have no proof she killed Michael. No real proof, anyway. What if I've created a far-fetched fantasy in my mind? A scene better suited for Terrence's spy novel than a real-life accusation against a real-life colleague.

More acid floods my mouth, and this time I can't settle it. I leap off the bed and race to my en suite bathroom. Dropping to my knees, I slam the toilet lid up and puke my guts out.

When nothing remains but rank humility, I rise like a ninety-year-old woman, relieve my bladder, and rinse my mouth with Listerine. After I stumble my way back to the bed, I check the time of my call to Kim.

12:08 a.m.

It's now after 1:00 p.m.

What must she be thinking? Not only have I overplayed my hand, accusing her before I could prove it, I've given her ample time for a countermove, a way to cover her tracks. At least she can't tamper with the EMR. Medical notes are unalterable without a dated addendum. That at least affords me some comfort.

But by showing her my cards and then promptly passing out, I've given her the opportunity to mount a defense. She won't be caught off guard. She will deny everything and point to me, her accuser, with a raised eyebrow in her otherwise impassive face. "You're going to take this woman's word against mine?" she will say. "A woman who's been reported to the Medical Board twice and almost killed a patient by prescribing the wrong medication? She obviously still has mental issues from losing her parents and fiancé."

I close my eyes. I have to fix this. I have to call her and tell her I was drunk. Just pulling a prank, that's all. "And hey, while I have you on the line, let's do lunch sometime."

Yeah, right.

But I at least have to try.

I open my contacts. As I'm about to call her, my phone buzzes, and a cold fear washes over me.

Kim is calling me.

34

———

The phone keeps buzzing, my palm gripped around it. Kim's name lights up my screen. She's FaceTiming me, no less.

Maybe I shouldn't answer. Maybe I should clean myself up, gather the patient information I've collected, and take it to the police. Maybe I have enough for at least their consideration.

But how can I do that without implicating myself? I broke HIPAA rules to access the charts. I lied and claimed my laptop was stolen. I swiped Michael's computer and phone and deleted the video of me torturing a wife beater. What's to say he doesn't have a backup copy someplace? Kim is aware I know Michael. I brought a sleepover bag to his hospital room, for God's sake. That will raise questions.

I have no choice but to answer her.

As soon as I do, Kim appears on my screen. She wears a white blouse, and her hair is pinned back. Her face lacks both makeup and expression.

I flip my camera orientation around so the only thing it will show her is the wall across from my bed. She doesn't need to see me like this. For all I know, I have dried vomit in my hair. It will be audio only from my end.

Kim doesn't bother with a greeting. "You'll never believe who I ran into, Hope."

A sunny kitchen surrounds her, its curtains the color of her blondish-brown hair and its fridge smothered with photographs. A crocheted cozy covers a teapot on an old-fashioned range, and a plate of cookies sits on the counter, just to the left of Kim's shoulder. She must be seated at a table, but this kitchen with white appliances and striped-yellow wallpaper doesn't match the kitchen in Kim's home. I know because I checked her place out on Zillow when she bought it a few years back.

When I don't answer, she resumes talking. "There I was, walking past a pharmacy in Dorchester when I saw her leaving the place."

Dorchester. That's south of Boston proper. Kim lives in Brighton, which is west. What was she doing near a pharmacy in Dorchester? I sense a trap, one that's about to snap its metal jaws around my ankle.

A torso appears behind Kim on my phone screen, and arms lift the plate of cookies off the counter. The person disappears for a moment and then reappears, or at least part of her face does.

My heart sinks.

Ada. Kim is in Ada Jackson's home.

Even though my camera is flipped around, I imagine Kim can read my stunned expression. I must have told her how much Ada means to me. She rotates the phone toward a smiling Ada, who's just taken a seat at the round table, a yellow place mat in front of her.

The sweet woman with gray-black hair and kind eyes gives me a little wave and laughs. "I can't see you, Dr. Sullivan, but hello."

I try to speak. My stutter makes a return performance for

the second time in ten years. "Hi, Ada. S-s-sorry. The call caught me by surprise. I'm not presentable." I try to keep my voice calm to avoid alarming her. "I'd f-forgotten you and Dr. Lombardi knew each other."

"Oh yes," Ada says. "She took care of my Otis before he got transferred to the ICU for his sepsis."

At this, a shadow of sadness crosses Ada's face. The camera remains focused on her, nice and steady. No tremor at all in Kim's hand. That alone seems suspicious.

"He needed the ventilator," Ada continues. She dabs her pinky finger at the corner of her eye. "His pneumonia got so bad he couldn't breathe. Then the rest of his organs gave out too."

"He was a good man," I say, hating to see Ada have to rehash these painful memories.

She gives a little shake of her head, as if clearing the images away. After a beat, her smile returns. "Anyway, I was leaving the pharmacy with my digoxin when I ran into Dr. Lombardi. She had some time to spare before her dental appointment, so I invited her up. I'm always happy for a little company. It's too quiet around here without Otis in the study, grumbling at his newspaper or singing his made-up songs." She smiles wistfully, and Kim's hand squeezes her shoulder. My colleague's sympathies are no doubt as fake as the EMR note she wrote in my name.

If I thought I couldn't feel worse than I did with my hangover, I was wrong, because now not only do I want to puke again, I feel like I might explode too.

Ada peers through the phone's camera, her face growing larger as she shifts closer. "Would you believe Dr. Lombardi takes digoxin too? She had heart problems as a little girl and still takes it. So see? I'm not the only one on the dinosaur pill."

Ada tilts her head playfully at me. She's referring to the fact that I keep trying to switch her to a newer cardiac drug with fewer side effects. She insists she doesn't want to fix what isn't broken.

I respond to her joke now with a forced laugh. There is no way this meeting was a coincidence. Kim has no reason to visit a dentist in Dorchester when they are a dime a dozen in Brighton.

"Would you like some more coffee, dear?" Ada asks Kim.

"That would be lovely." Kim's tone is syrupy sweet and faker than my drawer full of disguises.

When Ada disappears to fetch more coffee, Kim shifts the phone back to herself. She stares hard into the camera, her eyes flashing a rare spark of energy. After a furtive glance in Ada's direction, she lowers the camera. A blur of beige fabric clouds the lens. Then Kim's free hand comes into view. She has pulled something out of her pocket, and when I see what it is, I jerk upright on my bed.

A syringe.

Why is Kim holding a syringe? And, dear God, what's in it? A fatal dose of narcotic? Potassium chloride? Intravenous digoxin, aka digitalis?

The syringe returns to Kim's pocket, and the camera does a wild swing back to her face. After a wink—another gesture I have never seen from her before—her coffee cup reappears, along with Ada's arm.

When Ada sits down, Kim's pretend smile is back in place. The irony of how pretty and sweet it makes her look fills me with a cold dread.

"Well, it was great to chat with you," Kim says to me. "Why don't we meet for a late lunch to talk about that *patient* of yours we share. I have some information you'll want to hear before deciding your…treatment plan." The way she stressed the word *patient* suggests she could mean Michael or any of the others I believe she's killed. "We'll discuss where to go from here. I'll text you, okay? Then I'll be out of Ada's way."

"Oh, you're not bothering me. I enjoy the company." Ada chuckles. "Two doctors in my kitchen. I should take advantage of that."

"I'd be happy to pay you another visit." Although Kim is speaking to Ada, she looks my way through the phone's camera, her lips pursed in superiority.

"What a kind offer," Ada says, oblivious to Kim's treachery.

But I'm not oblivious to it. While Kim's words may be cleverly cryptic, I know exactly what she is saying: She has something on me, and if I don't meet with her, if I go to the police or do anything that doesn't comply with her veiled demand, she'll return to Ada's home.

And she'll slip that injection into my favorite patient's vein.

35

K im's text said to meet her in the Faneuil Hall Marketplace of Quincy Market. In other words, a very public place. This at least ensures she won't kill me. Not yet anyway. Nor I her.

I sit at a scratched-up table for two against a brick wall and wait for her. The din of voices and steady foot traffic in the massive room makes for lulling white noise, and despite my edgy state, I fight to keep my eyes open. My bottle of diet soda remains untouched. I could use the caffeine, but my hungover stomach fights it. Food is an even more unpleasant thought. Just the smell of the burgers and pizzas surrounding me makes my insides swirl.

Through the window on my left, throngs of people in shorts and tank tops stroll the outdoor pedestrian mall. They duck in and out of shops and restaurants, no doubt appreciating the air-conditioned relief from the sticky July heat.

A few minutes later, Kim approaches my table carrying a large cup of tea, its string swishing outside the container as she walks. Dressed in beige Bermuda shorts that fall above her knees and the same white blouse from our FaceTime call an hour ago, she takes a seat across from me. Her expressionless face reveals nothing.

My muscles are tense and my nerves jittery, but although I'm dying to know what she thinks she has on me, I remain quiet and let her take the lead. I don't even greet her. She seems to enjoy keeping me in suspense because she takes her sweet time removing her cup's plastic lid and dunking her tea bag several times. Up down. Up down. Up down.

Finally, I can't take it anymore. She wins. "What do you want, Kim?"

Her gaze wanders away from her beverage and up to my face. Her complexion is smooth, her eyebrows thick, and her amber eyes quite striking. Despite this, her perpetual facial laxity makes her appear overall plain. There's a spark of pink in her cheeks this afternoon, though, and likely not from the heat.

"Hope," she says my name in her flat tone, "I'm *hoping* we can come to an understanding." A hint of a smile lifts the corner of her mouth, as if she finds her pun funny, a pun I've heard in one variation or another many times over the years.

"Yeah, how so? You threatened to kill Ada Jackson. That pretty much proves I'm right about you and gives me the upper hand."

"Does it?" Kim dunks her tea bag twice more and then replaces the lid. "But I suppose you're right. No sense in me denying everything. We both know you're too smart for that." She sighs. "You've always been smarter than me. Made me feel so inferior as a resident, you know that? All I ever wanted was to be your friend."

"That's news to me, but I'm sorry you felt that way. I *was* your senior resident, though, so maybe you're mistaking tutelage for criticism."

She shrugs, as if it's not worth debating. "My point is, if you say you can prove something about me to the police, then you probably can."

She has misinterpreted my words from my drunken phone call last night, at least from what I can remember, which, truthfully, isn't much. I don't believe I said anything about having proof of her killing Michael—or anyone else, for that matter—but if she believes I have proof, so be it. It only strengthens my hand.

So why doesn't she look scared? Mildly concerned, even?

"Let's not waste each other's time," she says. "Instead, let's set some ground rules."

I snort out a laugh. A child making a French fry fort at a nearby table gawks at me. I lower my voice. "Ground rules? Here's a ground rule for you: I call the police right now. Tell them what you've done. You can't go back and hurt Ada with the cops on your back."

"Hmm." Kim taps her chin. "No, I'm thinking a ground rule along the lines of: You say nothing about me, and I'll say nothing about you torturing a man in a barn."

Her words stun me. *How does she know?* I reach for my soda bottle and uncap it, fizz spraying my fingers. I hope she can't read my distress.

"Oh yes," she says. "Michael Yerli had a very interesting video on his phone, a phone that's since disappeared, by the way." She lifts an eyebrow. "That was fun trying to explain to his father. The best I could come up with was that it got swept up in the bedding and carted away, but we both know where it's really at, don't we?"

Yes, locked away in my home safe, reset to its factory settings.

If Kim has seen the video, why hasn't she said anything about it until now? Saving it for leverage, I suppose. Maybe she heard me tell Michael I planned on looking into her.

"But don't worry." Kim takes a sip of her tea. "I AirDropped a copy to myself. Grabbed some screenshots from it too." She digs into her Fossil purse and pulls out her phone. After a few flicks of her finger, she turns it toward me. "Here's a nice one of you smacking the man in the face." Another flick of the finger. "And here's one of you squeezing his chest with pliers. Maybe we should show that one to Ada. I'm sure she'd love it."

So Kim Lombardi can make a joke, even in her monotone. Who would've thought it? But it's not funny. Not funny at all. The thought of Ada, or any of my patients, seeing that video makes me sicker than the wine I guzzled last night.

I point to the screenshot on her phone, trying to play it cool. "I don't know what you're talking about. That woman isn't me. We don't even look alike."

Kim gives me the same look a parent might give a child who has been caught lying. "We both know it's you. Well, at first I didn't, but then I recognized that red wig. You wore it during the faculty roast skits, remember? Back in residency."

Shit.

"The audio is muffled, but it still sounds like you. The police probably have fancy tools to confirm it, and that's clearly your build beneath those cargo pants and hoodie."

I say nothing. Simply work my jaw back and forth. I don't always wear the padded suit for my tune-ups. I like to change things up. But oh how I wish I would have worn it that night with the wife beater. Of course, he wouldn't have left the bar willingly with me if I had. Not a guy like that.

Kim moves on, flipping to another photo in her collection. "This one with the knife is my favorite." She swings the phone back to me again. "See here? You've just stabbed his thigh. Michael did a great job with this recording. The police could probably ID your victim through face recognition." She lowers the phone to her lap. "Bet he'd have some interesting things to say about you."

My ballet flats tap the brick flooring. "So, what are you proposing? That I ignore the fact you're killing patients if you ignore what you think I did there?" I point to the phone that's no longer visible. "Not that you can prove it was me."

"If you replay our conversation here, you'll realize I

haven't admitted to anything, but yes, that's exactly what I'm proposing."

"How do you know I'm not recording us right now?" I bluff.

"Because you'll incriminate yourself as much as me."

"Me teaching some guy a lesson is a lot different than"—mindful of the French fry architect less than four feet away, I lower my voice again—"killing a patient. I might get arrested for assault, but it's nothing compared to what you would get."

Kim brushes the air with a flick of her hand. "I know you, Hope. You're Miss Perfect. The last thing you'd want is for your precious Ada and all your other precious patients to know what you do in your spare time, not to mention the horrible publicity it would rain down on your clinic colleagues."

I squeeze the soda cap still clenched in my hand, its ridges digging into my palm. Kim is not wrong about that. I'd rather be fed to a woodchipper than have that be my legacy. The only thing Kim *has* been wrong about is her saying she's not as smart as me. From my end of the table, she's looking sharper than a diamond blade. Having my patients and colleagues remember me as a deranged vigilante who squeezed a man's nipple and stabbed his thigh is definitely not the way I want to go out.

"Besides," she says, "you have no real proof on me. Not really. Sure, you can make accusations, and maybe the police will start digging, but then again, maybe they won't. I'd paint you as a mentally unhinged stalker who never recovered from her parents' or boyfriend's deaths."

My cheeks flame hotter than the outside pavement. "Don't you dare bring them up."

She ignores me. "Then the police will start looking into *you.* I bet your victims will start coming out of the woodwork. Tell their stories about a crazy doctor who did terrible things to them—assuming there are others." Her gaze bores into me.

"But of course there are, right? Hope Sullivan doesn't do anything half-assed."

I quietly clap my hands. "Well, well, well, look who's had us all fooled. Dull little boring Kim. Pretty but bland. Can't keep a man." I work to keep my voice steady, but the dread in my stomach grows. "Is that why you do it? Can't stand people having more than you? Being happier than you? Being better than you?"

A flush creeps up her neck, and her jaw muscle contracts. I feel momentarily victorious for having gotten to her. I was only guessing at her motives, but it appears I whacked the right mole on the head.

"How would you like living in everyone's shadow?" she asks. "Your parents'? Your siblings'? Your husband's, a man who ignores you and has an affair less than two months into your marriage?"

"You kill him too?"

The two of us are speaking low but aggressively, our bodies pitched forward over the table and our heads close enough that I can smell the Earl Grey on her breath. She doesn't answer my question about killing her husband, which for me is answer enough.

How long has she been a murderer? Was her spouse her first? Was it Jasmine Bonnet, Michael's wife? Some patient all the way back in med school?

"Some people don't deserve to live." The flush has now reached her cheeks. "Spoiled, unappreciative, dismissive of others."

"But aside from your husband, what did they ever do to you?" Although my question stems from shock and disbelief, I'm genuinely curious too. "How could Jasmine Bonnet have wronged you? Or Ted Orenson, for that matter? They were your patients."

Kim leans back, her face relaxing, as if her emotional stores have been spent. "You were a fool to fall for Orenson's nice-guy act. He was making shady deals with that lottery money he won. I caught him scrolling through an escort service on his laptop too. A little something-something on the side for when he got out of the hospital. And believe you me, those women looked barely legal. Think his wife and family deserved that?"

I open my mouth. Close it again. If that's true, Orenson did indeed have me fooled, but that doesn't mean he deserved death. "And Jasmine Bonnet?" I say.

"Successful lawyer, married to a man who adored her, twin babies on the way."

"So? How is that any concern of yours?"

"They weren't Michael's, you know."

"What weren't?" Then I understand. "The babies?"

"Yep. She screwed some guy at a conference. Let Michael believe they were his. I found out because she was worried a blood transfusion—should she need one—would harm the fetuses."

I slouch on the bench. Poor Michael. Jasmine and those twins were all he cared about. He lost his whole livelihood when the three of them died. "Please tell me you didn't let him know the truth."

"Oh, I did. He needed to learn that the princess he'd been worshiping was really an evil witch."

My heart breaks all over again for Michael. It doesn't matter that he stalked and abducted me. I don't think he was ever going to hurt me. He just wanted answers. Knowing that the last thing he heard was that the babies weren't his makes me want to smash my soda bottle into Kim's face.

She must see my fury because she says, "That's enough talk. If we both stay quiet, we both win."

"And what? I'm supposed to let you go on killing patients? Let you keep pulling syringes out of your pockets?"

"I never admitted to any such thing." She winks at me again. "Nor can I help it if you mistook my pen for a syringe."

Pen, my ass.

Her brazenness, her absolute lack of empathy or sense of humanity astounds me. She is the very type of person I target for a tune-up. Maybe even the pinnacle.

"By the way," she adds, as if reading my mind, "if you decide to…deal with me yourself, I've got a copy of your little torture video on a thumb drive, along with a letter saying I suspect you've been killing your patients, and if something happens to me, it must be because you knew I was on to you."

"You can't prove anything of the sort," I bite back. "Because it never happened."

"Can't I? After all, it's your name on Jasmine Bonnet's chart. Throw in the trouble you've been in with the Medical Board and that video, and, well…"

I stare at her. That part about my name being in Jasmine's chart is true—Kim made sure of that—and so are my problems with the Board. How Kim found out about the complaints, I don't know. Someone gossiped. Maybe the allergic patient himself since she took care of him in the hospital. Or maybe his wife, who probably felt guilty over her own role in the man's drug reaction, not recognizing the trade name of the drug.

Kim breaks my thoughts. "Even though you think you're better than me, I—"

"I've never thought such a thing."

"Haven't you? Is that why you never offer anything but polite—well, more like *bored*—conversation when I'm around, always looking around for someone more interesting to talk to?"

"I've never done that." *Have I?*

"Or why you sometimes ask other hospitalists about patients of yours I'm caring for, as if you don't trust my judgment?"

I haven't done that either. Not intentionally. But as the

adage goes, perception is everything, and apparently that holds especially true when it comes to Kim's delusions.

"If I did," I say, "it's only because I didn't realize who the doctor was. I've always trusted your clinical skills."

"Tell yourself whatever makes you feel better, but the two of us aren't that different."

"Yeah, right. How's that?"

"We both do things we feel are morally justified."

I start to object but realize I can't. Murder is far worse than what I've done, of course, but how close am I to that line? Kim might have been the one to stop Michael's heart, but I was the one who put him in the hospital. That makes me responsible too.

God help me, maybe I *am* like Kim. Different agendas but on the same spectrum.

"Truce?" she says. "Because if one of us brings the other one down, we both go down." She crosses her arms. "And in case that's not incentive enough for you to make this little pact, I'll see to it that Ada Jackson joins her dead husband."

Kim has me. She has me bound more tightly than the plastic ties Michael used around my wrists and ankles.

Slowly, I nod. What else can I do? I refuse to let Ada get hurt, or anyone else for that matter. And while I'm not yet sure how to stop her, and I don't yet know how this will end, there's one thing I know for certain: If I voluntarily choose to check out of this cesspool of a world, I am taking Kim Lombardi with me.

36

———

The following day I lay on my duvet, one hand petting Diva and the other gripping my phone to my ear. Martin Hernandez has taken my Friday afternoon call, but gone are his previous reassurances from the earlier bogus Board complaint. Now, in a serious voice that suggests we're no longer casual allies, he tells me he will be conducting a deeper investigation of my conduct and skills, and that I should not discuss the case with anyone until he has finished.

"According to the complainant," Mr. Hernandez says— (he's no longer *Martin* in my mind, not with that somber tone) —"he reported all his drug allergies to you, but you prescribed the wrong medication anyway."

"I was…"

"Distracted," he finishes for me. "Or so the patient claims."

The patient claims correctly.

"Will you have to interview my colleagues again?"

Mr. Hernandez hesitates. "I can't disclose any more to you. I've probably said too much already, but I assure you, we will be detailed in reviewing the medical records, among other things. We want the best outcome for everyone."

So, in other words, yes, he will be talking to my colleagues again. Will his inquisition go beyond the doctors and medical staff at Congress Medical? Will he reach out to hospital staff too? Will he question Kim Lombardi?

I squeeze my phone more tightly. "Medical mistakes happen, right? Doctors don't lose their licenses over them."

"Of course not, but we still need to investigate whether there's a…pattern."

I sit up on the bed, disturbing Diva at my side. "There's no pattern, I promise you. This is the first time something like this has happened to me, and it will be the last time too. I'm very conscientious when it comes to my patients. Besides, the man is fine now. He has complex medical issues to begin with."

I realize I sound like a whiny child. That is not going to help my case.

"I'm sorry," I try again. "I'm just stressed out. Medicine is all I have."

Now I sound pathetic. So be it. The statement is true. Even these few days away from the clinic, as ordered by my paternalistic but sweet senior partner, have left me feeling marooned.

"Try to be patient," Mr. Hernandez says. "It will get sorted out."

This appears to be the best reassurance I'm going to get from the man, so I thank him for his time and say goodbye.

After tossing the phone on the bed, I catch a glimpse of myself in the mirror above the dresser. I stare at my reflection. My hair is matted on one side, my face ashen, maybe even thinner too. As someone who values fitness over thinness, this weight loss doesn't please me. One whiff of my pajama top reveals a woman in need of a shower. Poor Diva. Her human reeks of desolation and self-pity.

Opening my nightstand drawer, I pluck out my mother's silk scarf, a multi-colored wrap with geometric shapes outlined in gold threading. Its posh look jibes with its exorbitant cost. As a senior partner at her investment banking firm, my mother made loads of money, and she enjoyed a luxury here and there, but she also gave lots to charity. Boston General, homeless shelters, a college scholarship every year to a disadvantaged student wanting to pursue the world of finance, a world that might otherwise be closed to them. She donated her time too.

Contrary to popular belief, not all rich people are assholes. Some rich people do wonderful, selfless things, and my mother was among them. She used the money she made from rich people to help others who had little of their own. Ironic that one of her charities was a rehab center (where she helped cover the cost for those who couldn't) when it was an alcoholic who snuffed out her life.

Since our heated exchange in my kitchen two nights ago, Bo has left me several voice messages—well, my heated exchange, his horrific confession. In his last message, he said if he hasn't heard from me by Monday, he's going to turn himself in to the police. He is finally going to own up to his tragic mistake. Pay the piper, serve the time, clank the ol' jail bars. He claims he has a prior commitment to the youth shelter this weekend and can't let them down, so that's why he's choosing Monday as the day he finally gets what he deserves.

Refusing to let thoughts of Bo taint the memories of my mother, I push him away. There will be time for him later. Instead, I close my eyes and run my mom's silky scarf over my cheek. Inhale its lingering spiced scent. Try to remember her when she was all smiles and laughter instead of a corpse.

"I miss you, Mom. More than you could know."

At my soft words, Diva snuggles closer to me, as if sensing my grief, a grief tempered by time but not even close to being extinguished. My mother should be going wine tasting with me, discussing politics, shopping for the latest hiking gear. She shouldn't be silent in the ground.

I return the scarf to the drawer and pull out my dad's reading glasses. Even though they distort my vision, I slip them on. I picture him in front of his college students, scribbling on the interactive whiteboard, teaching a chemical equation. I long to bounce one last idea or problem off him. Such a wonderfully pragmatic mind he had.

Next I grab *How to Be the Husband Your Wife Needs* from the drawer, the last book Manuel was reading. It was a needless read on his part because he was already a perfect fiancé. At least in my opinion, and isn't that the only opinion a fiancé needs?

I remove my dad's reading glasses and scan the book's silly pages. I think about all the dinners Manny made for me, his pathology residency less time-intensive than my internal medicine one. Or the way he would take my car in to be serviced when I had neither the time nor the thought to do so. Or how he would console me with anecdotes or quotes (he was a quotes guy) whenever I had a day too frustrating to endure.

The book's words grow blurry, and I close the pages before the rain of tears begins. I return the book, along with my dad's glasses, to the drawer, next to my mom's scarf. Also inside is my engagement ring, tucked inside a velvet box. I wore it for a while after Manny died, but the constant reminder of his absence hurt so much I finally removed it.

My hand falls to my belly. I have nothing tangible to remember from that loss. Not even an ultrasound. It was too early to need one. And yet my memory of the life inside me is as clear as if I had just miscarried yesterday. It feels like I lost *all* of my loved ones yesterday. After two years of Manny being gone and over three without my parents, how is that still possible?

The last thing I pull out of the nightstand drawer, the only other thing in it, is my bottle of exit-door pills. The name on the bottle's label is Manuel Torres. It was one of Manny's opioid prescriptions during his final weeks of pain, and almost two dozen pills remain. Expiration-related side effects are not a problem for me when permanent sleep is the desired outcome.

I rub my hands over my face, my fingertips caked with cat dander. I can't take the pills. Not yet. There are things left to do.

I return the prescription bottle to the drawer and close everything back up. Then I plant my hands on my thighs and rise from the bed. My time of wallowing is over. It's time to act.

After giving a quick face nuzzle to Diva, I head to the bathroom to get cleaned up. I've got two last tune-ups to perform.

The first with Bo. The second with Kim.

Then I can take the pills.

37

Once I'm smelling of honey-almond soap, primped in makeup, and dressed in a summer jumpsuit that ties at the waist, I take an Uber to the Brenton Youth Shelter. How it got its name, I don't know, but I do know Bo is there today, at least according to our clinic receptionist. I called earlier to ask if he was seeing patients, and she informed me he'd been in this morning but left a few hours ago for a prior commitment at the shelter. So it appears he wasn't lying about that.

Our receptionist then lowered her voice and asked how I was doing. From her breathy tone, I deduced I've been quite the topic of conversation at the clinic.

I assured her all was well—*it isn't*—and that everything would be sorted out shortly. Whether she thought I meant the second Board complaint against me or my getting back to work at the clinic, I'm not sure. Even I don't know the answer to that, especially with those pills calling me.

At only a little over a mile away from my loft, the shelter is walkable, but the late-afternoon heat is oppressive, even with an overcast sky, and I didn't want to be a drenched rat by the time I arrive. The last time Bo saw me I was two steps past deranged. Best to put on a prettier display this time around. I also didn't want to worry about having to find parking.

The shelter is sandwiched in the middle of a long confluence of brick buildings near Boston Common. Stepping out of the Uber, I can just make out a section of the park. My dad and I used to walk around it during coordinated work breaks. Sometimes my mom was able to join us, and the three of us would enjoy a picnic lunch.

I push the painful memory away.

My plan of what to say to Bo is still not formulated. I only know I need to bring this nightmare chapter of the Book of Hope to a conclusion. I'd like to act like an adult this time around, but we all know what happens to best-laid plans. No telling what will froth out of me the moment I see Bo's killing face. That's why I chose to meet him in a public place. My kitchen, which houses too many knives and a variety of heavy cookware, is best avoided, at least until I have a solid strategy.

I twist my paracord bracelet around my wrist and think of my parents again. Then I try not to imagine the tiny blade slicing open Bo's neck.

When I approach the building, I find a security panel mounted near the center's door, but the door itself is unlocked. Inside the entryway, a scent of cabbage and sweat greets me. A front desk—or, rather, a sturdy folding table—welcomes visitors, but it is currently unattended. A short hallway extends behind it, and after a few minutes of waiting, I wander down the corridor. I spot two administrative offices to the left and a room with a sofa and a chair to the right.

One of the offices is occupied by a woman with pink bangs and purple eyeglasses. She's in the middle of an impassioned phone call, flipping through a calendar book on her desk, so I keep walking. Clearly there are other people around because muffled laughter and shouting reaches me from somewhere in the complex.

At the end of the hallway, just to the left, a large room

opens up. About twenty cots with thin mattresses but clean bedding (or at least it looks clean) dot the wood flooring. Decorative murals cover the walls, maybe painted by the kids themselves. In the far corner, a teenage boy sleeps with his back to me. No one else is around. Apart from the murals, the space isn't particularly attractive, but I imagine hungry—and in the winter, freezing—homeless teenagers care little about that.

To the right of the hallway lie a dining room and kitchen, which explains why the cabbage smell is now so strong. The laughter and cheering grow louder, too, and I'm still not sure where those voices are coming from. The dining hall with its long, mismatched tables is empty, save for three women working behind a chrome counter in the rear kitchen. Chopping, stirring, pouring. They chatter away, but none look at me.

I'm about to step out of the dining hall when I notice a door on the right near the back. Figuring I've come this far uninvited, I might as well keep going. Once there, I find another hallway that opens up into a recreation room. Inside the large space, teens play foosball and pool. Others lounge on colorful beanbag chairs scattered in front of a flatscreen TV, and beyond them a girl relaxes on a sofa, reading a novel. Shelves of books flank her on either side.

In the other half of the room, where the laughter and cheering is coming from, guys play basketball on a mock court, its flooring made of the same wood tiling as the rest of the shelter's floors. Strips of yellow duct tape mark out the center line and out-of-bound borders.

One of the players is Bo. Given his recent head injury, I'm not sure basketball should be on his agenda yet, but there he is all the same. As a blond, middle-aged guy, he stands out in a sea of black, brown, and white teenage faces. A couple of the kids surpass him in height, but as he sidesteps an opponent and sinks a lay-up—a grin on his face—it appears he can hold his own.

Something shifts inside me when I see his joy, along with that of the kids he is mentoring. Suddenly, I'm less sure about what I want to say—and do—to him.

Most of the teens watching TV or playing arcade games have noticed me by now, and a few of the older boys eye me up and down. Given the abundance of T-shirts and nylon shorts in the room, I'm overdressed in my blue jumpsuit, even though it came off the rack from Target.

I have never been shy, but I feel as out of place as a zebra at a horse race. I consider backing out, pretending I was never here, but before I can, Bo spots me. A kid eight inches shorter than him has stolen the ball, and when Bo pauses to catch his breath, hands pinching his sides, he locks eyes with me.

For a moment, he stands frozen. Maybe he wonders if I'm a hallucination. Then he says something to another player and trots my way. Wordlessly, he motions for us to exit the rec room, and as we depart through the door a few whistles and whoops follow us.

He walks me back through the dining room and into the hallway that leads to the entrance foyer. I start to wonder if he is literally showing me the door, but instead he veers off into the room with the couch that I spotted earlier. Inside that room, he unlocks another door. I would have assumed it to be a closet, but it is actually a small exam room, or at least it has been converted to one.

He drops the keys back into his athletic shorts and waves me all the way in. As I walk past him, I catch a whiff of his sweaty scent and feel the heat of his exercised body.

An exam table, a few decades old by the looks of it, sits against one wall. A small table with a laptop fronts another. Two folding chairs sit near it. Although no medical equipment hangs on the walls, a crash cart is littered with an otoscope, stethoscope, tongue blades, and other medical supplies.

Bo nods toward one of the folding chairs. So far, neither

of us has spoken. As he sits down on the other seat, he wipes his brow and tugs at his T-shirt.

Simultaneously we break the silence.

"Is this your office?" I say. "Welcome to my pseudo exam room," he says.

I let him continue.

"Sometimes the teens or young adults who come here need medical aid, so I take care of that," he says. "We've got a pretty steady revolving door. I do some counseling too—not psychotherapy, of course; I'm not trained for that—but, you know, I offer a listening ear, sprinkle in my own experience with addiction, that kind of thing." He points to the crash cart. "That's more a storage bin than a crash cart. A few gowns, lab collection kits, gauze."

"Medication?" I ask, genuinely curious.

"Some. Top drawer." He pats the keys in his shorts. "I keep it locked, of course—not that there's anything more powerful in it than asthma inhalers and epinephrine injectors."

"How often do you come here?" I try not to sound impressed. I don't owe him my admiration.

He shrugs. "Every weekend. Tuesday and Thursday nights too. But they can call me anytime if something comes up."

"Do they pay you?"

"No. Not in money, anyway." Despite his obvious nervousness—scratching his neck until it blotches, jingling the keys in his pocket—a smile curls his lips. "The payment I get is hanging out with the kids. Getting them to trust me and the staff. Helping them prep for a job interview. Seeing them get that job. Helping them graduate."

I don't know what I expected from my visit here, but it wasn't this. It wasn't to see Bo's humanity, his satisfaction over his work here, his sense of charity. And yet, it's as plain as the pride in his face as he tells me about the center's art sale this weekend—creative projects the troubled youth have made. The proceeds will benefit the kids and the shelter.

"Is that why you mentioned Monday as your deadline?" The words are out of my mouth before I can stop them.

Bo rolls a pen on the table underneath his palm. "That and Jeremiah. He's one of our frequent fliers. Runs away from his foster homes all the time. Fifteen years old and smart enough for college level classes, just a run of bad luck, you know? He's been set up with a new family. Meets them on Sunday, and I told him I'd go with him. Can't let him down."

Bo frees the pen and faces me head on in his folding chair. "But you didn't come to hear about that. Honestly, I can't believe you came at all. I'm glad you did though." He pauses. "I'll turn myself in, I promise, but I'd hoped to get your"—the red splotch on his neck grows—"forgiveness first. Well, not your forgiveness per se. I don't deserve that. But…well… maybe some closure, I guess."

"You mean something other than me screeching at you like a demon and charging you with a kitchen knife?" My ability to joke surprises me, and even more so when I laugh.

Bo laughs too, but it's a quick one. He struggles to make eye contact with me. "You need to know how sorry I am. That counts for nothing, I know. I feel stupid for even saying such trite words, but what words could possibly convey my profound sorrow? My continuous self-hatred. My horror every single day over what I took from you."

I fidget with my paracord bracelet and struggle to maintain eye contact myself. Soon I'm looking at his Nikes, the heels worn and the white mesh torn, as if he feels himself unworthy of even new shoes.

I search for my rage, but it's slipping through my fingers like powder. Where did my urge to cut him up into bloody bits go? Where is my desire to rip his head from his body like he nearly tore my mother's from hers?

No matter how hard I grind my teeth, I can't reconcile

that drunken Bo Linton with the altruistic doctor in front of me. A doctor who could be making big bucks at a fancy clinic but instead works only enough locum-tenens jobs to allow him to give the rest of his services away for free.

He's a walker, my mother would say. *Not just a pretty talker.* Her way of differentiating those who made pretty-but-empty statements about helping the less fortunate from those who actually did.

Bo is indeed a walker. A self-flagellating, heavy-hearted, tattered-shoed walker.

My mom would forgive him. My dad probably too. His pragmatism would recognize that Bo's penance benefits a whole lot of people, and that putting an end to his good deeds would make little mathematical sense.

"Hope?" Bo says, breaking my thoughts. "Can I just be sure you've heard me? Not to forgive me, of course, but maybe just to…I don't know, maybe to help yourself find a little peace? I'll spend ten, twenty years in prison, I don't care, but I *do* care that you find some peace." He bites his lower lip. "There's only one person in this room who deserves to carry this anguish, and it's me, not you. It never should have been you."

We sit quietly for five minutes. Maybe it's fifty, I'm not sure. Me twirling my paracord bracelet, him leaning forward on his chair, elbows on his knees, head between his hands. At some point during our silence, my soul—not just my brain because when it comes to my parents' deaths, the two are not always one and the same—realizes Bo is right. This is his burden to carry, not mine. I can grieve my parents, but that doesn't mean I have to be consumed by hatred too.

Ironically, as I sit here next to the man who killed them, the choking rage that has been a constant parasite on my grief starts to release its pincers. My sorrow remains, of course, and it's heartbreaking I'll never see my mom and dad again, but for the first time since they died, I feel a beauty in knowing they were in my life at all.

I release my paracord bracelet. I fold my hands in my lap. "Don't turn yourself in."

Bo lifts his head, his face a cabbage patch doll of shame, his eyes moist. "No. I have to. It's only right."

"What's right is you continuing to do what you do." My voice grows stronger. "The best way for you to honor my mom and dad is to keep helping others. Every day. Every week. Every year of your life."

He wipes his face on the sleeve of his T-shirt. "No...I..."

"Yes." It comes out a command. "That's what I want." I rise from the folding chair. "And you need to do what I want, right? You need my forgiveness."

"Well, yes, sure, but I can help people in prison too. I can—"

"No." I wave my arm in the direction of the rec room. "You make a difference in these kids' lives. You show them how to make the right choices, choices like not getting drunk and killing people with your car." I close my eyes but again feel sorrow, not rage. "I want you to help these kids before it's too late to change them. Got it?"

He nods, slowly at first and then more convincingly. "Yes, I can do that. I *want* to do that."

"Good." I cross to the door before I can change my mind. Pausing, I turn to face him. "And Bo?"

"Yes?"

"This little pact is between us. Our knowing each other stops here. I don't ever want to see you again. Not on the street. Not at the clinic. Not anywhere."

"But—"

"No, that's the deal. I *can't* see you again, don't you get it? Tell Frank whatever you need to, but your days at Congress Medical Clinic are over. There are tons of other locum jobs for internists around Boston." I'm not sure why I'm demanding this, seeing as how I probably won't be around much longer, and yet I feel the need to have him out of my orbit completely.

I wait for a confirmatory nod from him. A few seconds later I get it.

Then I leave the Brenton Youth Shelter, vowing never to let Bo Linton or what he did to my parents hold me hostage again.

38

———

After I leave Bo at the youth shelter, I stroll past Boston Common and enter a sandwich shop a few blocks away. Hungry for the first time in days, I order a turkey and Swiss on wheat and sit at a rickety table outside. It's well past five, but the air is still heavy and hot, and the sky has darkened even more.

Pedestrians parade past me, some quickly, maybe eager to get home from work or meet up with a dinner companion, others leisurely, voices animated, phones open. A small child presses her face between the wrought-iron pickets that separate my table from the sidewalk and crosses her eyes at me. When I return the funny face, she laughs and rejoins her mother a few paces ahead.

I hold my hand out in front of me. No shaking. Good. Maybe the subject of Bo Linton can finally be closed. I worried that as soon as I left the shelter, I would regret my decision to let things go, but it's actually the opposite. A hundred pounds of concrete have been chiseled off my chest. Bo has retreated to the recesses of my brain, and I allow him no more space in there than I allow the crushed potato chips at my feet or the pigeon droppings on the fence.

Dr. Kim Lombardi, on the other hand, hogs the spotlight one hundred percent. Bland, dull, boring Kim, a master of deception.

While I chew my sandwich, I distract myself from my obsessive Kim thoughts by scrolling through my phone and tending to a few mundane tasks, starting with today's affirmation. I wonder why I even bother to open the app, but when I read today's words of wisdom I do a doubletake. Its message is so on point it's as if it were written specifically for me: *I will appreciate the freedom in letting things go.*

I close my eyes and allow myself to savor that freedom. For the briefest of moments, my perpetual cloud lifts.

After a long beat, I return to my phone and move on to my email. My inbox shows the usual spam, newsletters, and journal alerts. There is also a message from the hospital IT department in response to my "stolen" laptop. They sent the email yesterday morning, but I haven't checked in until now.

Beth from IT tells me I need to set up a new password the next time I log in to the hospital system, and she gives me a link to do so. No mention is made of any chart snooping done in my name, so maybe my probing didn't get flagged. That means I might have overreacted and was too hasty in reporting my computer stolen, but it's better to be safe than sorry, which is why I need to dispose of Michael's laptop too. I already have a plan for that.

Next, I scan an article forwarded from Terrence about a drug trial for a new sickle cell polymerization inhibitor. This is followed by a perusal of my credit card apps. In light of my upcoming plans, these activities seem pointless, and yet my routine is harder to brush off than Diva's cat hair.

Finally, when it's past six thirty, I toss my sandwich wrapper, recycle my water bottle, and head toward Congress Medical, my purse slung over my shoulder. It's a dozen blocks away, but that's okay. My jumpsuit is a lightweight fabric, my ballet flats are comfortable, and now that my encounter with Bo is over, I no longer care about getting sweaty or wilted.

The clinic staff should be gone by now, including the physicians. Everyone likes to escape by five on Fridays, even if it means completing charts at home. Unlike me, they all have families to see, lives to enjoy.

When I arrive at the clinic, I slip in the back door and lock it behind me. The corridors are dark, and everyone is gone for the day. To confirm, I stroll through the maze of hallways to the waiting room, using the lingering daylight from exam room windows to guide me. When I return to my workstation, I flip on the light and log in to my clinic laptop's EMR with a new password. Then I pull up my list of Monday patients. That way, if any of the doctors return for whatever reason, I'll have a legitimate excuse for my presence—I am simply reviewing next week's patients. Frank said to take this week off. He said nothing about the next one.

Once Monday's schedule is on the screen, I grab my purse and meander a hallway away to the treatment room. Lined by laminate countertops, its cupboards house everything needed for minor procedures, including suturing, lancing, and sigmoidoscopies, which all of us still perform save Irene.

The treatment room also contains a patient bed, a controlled-substance cabinet for which the nurse and physicians know the security code, and a supply cabinet filled with IV catheters, fluid bags, and tubing. Routine medications are stored in there too. Occasionally, we have severely ill patients show up, either because they don't want to deal with the ER or they don't realize how sick they are. For them, we have a crash cart and more critical medications like antiseizure drugs, cardiac meds, insulin, injectable steroids, and so on.

What I'm most interested in tonight hides in the crash cart, not the controlled-substance cabinet, although I've nipped from that in the past. Tonight I'm interested in a cardiac drug.

When I find the ampules I'm looking for in the second drawer, I hesitate for only a second before snatching them up. Just because I take some doesn't mean I will use them. I simply need Kim to be aware I have the drug. *A taste of your own medicine, right?* Just as Michael said to me before he learned I wasn't the target after all.

I tuck the ampules into my purse and close the crash cart drawer. Next month's inventory check by Alice will reveal their absence, but it's possible it could be written off as human error. Why would any of the staff take ampules of digoxin?

Why indeed.

Next I grab a syringe from a drawer by the sink. Then I turn off the light and exit the treatment room. My heartbeat is steady. No adrenaline rush. No second thoughts. No worries I'll be caught. It's liberating when you know you won't be around for the consequences.

Back at my workstation, I power off my laptop, grab my purse, and head out the same way I came in.

It is now 7:40 p.m.

In less than twelve hours, Kim will get her tune-up.

39

———

At six the next morning, the physician parking ramp of Boston General buzzes from nearby street traffic and stinks of gas fumes. Although the sun is rising and light streams through the concrete openings, nothing but dark shadows hover in the corner where I wait for Kim Lombardi.

She should be leaving soon. The hospitalists pass off their patients at 6:00 a.m. to avoid the bustle of the nursing staff change at seven. According to the hospital operator I spoke to last night, Kim was on shift during the night.

One row over a door clicks open, and an engine starts. Soon a Prius rounds my way. It's doubtful the driver can see me since I'm pressed against the wall in the shadows behind a pillar, but I make myself smaller all the same.

Kim's Nissan Altima is close by. Finding her car took a few minutes of wandering the deck, but at least I knew what to look for. Back in residency when she was dating Dan Knudson and hunting for a new car, the two of them debated whether she should go with an Accord or an Altima. She decided on the latter, probably because Dan preferred the former. Once it was registered, he teased her about the license plate. Its first three letters spell MUF. To this day, he calls it the Muffmobile.

Does that bother Kim? With her, you never know, but I do know that her license plate made the Muffmobile easy to find.

My clothing is dark—dark shoes, dark jeans, dark hoodie cinched around my face to reveal little of my features—but that's the extent of my disguise. Kim knows me. She also knows it was me in Michael's sneaky video. No sense pretending otherwise. A security camera hangs near the hospital access door, but it can't capture me here against the wall behind the pillar. It might spot me once I approach Kim, but it will catch nothing more sinister than two women huddling near a car.

Inside my right hoodie pocket, my gloved hand clenches my stun gun. In the other pocket, a syringe contains the last of my sedative reserve. Roofies won't work. No way can I get Kim to take them.

The duffel bag over my shoulder holds the rest of what I need. Duct tape, a few sharp tools for incentive, and—as a last resort—my syringe of pilfered digoxin. I can't imagine it will come to that. Hopefully, I'll extract the information I need from her—the names of the patients whose lives she has stolen—before the digoxin ever comes into play. Then I'll turn her over to the police.

But if plan A fails and I have to use plan B, I will be forced to leave this world shortly after because I will become no different than Kim. I will no longer be worthy to breathe.

So far, only one physician has exited the building during my wait, although two have entered. The early-morning hour helps ensure an unpopulated deck. Still, the tension in my neck and shoulders won't ease until both Kim and I are in her car, me driving, her slumped in the back seat.

At six ten, my palms start to tingle inside my medical gloves. At six fifteen my mouth tastes the sting of adrenaline. She'll be here soon.

As if conjuring her with my thoughts, Kim exits the hospital stairwell. Even from across the parking ramp her understated form is recognizable despite the rest of her being forgettable. She wears a shapeless linen dress and pointed-toe loafers that tap softly on the concrete deck. Her highlighted hair with its darker roots is pulled back in a ponytail.

I shrink farther into the shadowed corner of the wall. I can't act until she clicks open her car. My pulse ratchets up, and this is how I know I've done the right thing with Bo. The thought of hurting him sparked nothing inside me but regret. Stopping Kim sparks the opposite.

My gaze travels from her advancing form to the hospital door she just exited. No one else has exited behind her. When she is less than fifteen feet away, she clicks her key fob and unlocks the door. She returns her keys to her purse. When she is five feet away, she pulls her phone from her dress pocket, pauses, and reads what is likely a text.

I hold my breath. If she's called back to the hospital, my plan will be ruined. By the time she comes out again, it will be too close to the seven o'clock shift change, and abducting her will be far too risky. Someone would notice something.

There's always tomorrow, I suppose, but I have no idea whether she works tonight. Showing up at her house today is an option, too, but as soon as she sees it's me, I'll lose the element of surprise which might give her time to act first.

Now my heart is in my throat. I haven't made a plan C.

But no need. She types a return message and then crosses the last few feet to her car, her gaze still on her phone. When she reaches for the door handle, I noiselessly leave my shadowed corner, pull out my stun gun, and slink up next to her.

In one smooth motion, I press the weapon against the side of her neck and zap. A breathy cry escapes her, and at first she struggles, but I hold firm, pressing her body against the car with my own. I administer a good four seconds of voltage. When her body weakens and no longer resists me, I hold her tightly in an embrace, as if we are merely friends having a good hug.

As a unit, we step back to the rear door, my feet moving, hers dragging. She is a couple of inches shorter than me and maybe ten pounds heavier, which makes the movements awkward, especially with her purse poking me in the chest, but within seconds I ease her into the car and close the door. Only when I'm seated in the driver's seat in front of her do I scan the parking deck to see if anyone saw us.

No one. Only a guy in scrubs who is just now exiting the hospital door across the ramp. He turns right instead of continuing straight and soon disappears down the next row of cars. When he does, I pull the syringe from my pocket, uncap it, and turn around.

From the back seat, a temporarily disabled but twitchy Kim stares blankly at me. It's not much different from her usual expression, so it's difficult to know how much of her vacancy is from electrical stupor. Shocking her for as long as I did should net me at least five to ten minutes of incapacitation, maybe even more. Still, I don't dare drive until she is sedated because it's not like I can duct tape her to the inside of the car without someone noticing on the road, and I certainly can't drag her out to the trunk. I took enough risk as it is.

Leaning over the seat, I inject the sedative into the crook of her elbow. Thanks to her lack of resistance, I manage to slip the needle into a vein for quicker onset of action, even without using the tourniquet in my pocket.

"I'm not going to hurt you," I say as I depress the plunger. "Well, any more than this. Unless…" I narrow my eyes and, in a much crisper tone, add, "you don't cooperate."

When I finish, I snatch the ID badge still attached to her dress pocket and leave it up front with me. Then I return to a seated position behind the wheel and watch her in the rearview mirror, lowering it so I can get a view of her lying down. In my gloves, I'll leave no fingerprints. When her eyes close and her breathing deepens, I put on my seatbelt and push the car's start button. The keys in her purse are close enough to allow it.

Then I pull out of the spot, work my way down the ramp, and exit through the gate with her ID card, as if this were simply any other day.

40

A conked-out Kim sits strapped to the chair in the middle of my barn. Her head hangs low, and her chin hovers above her chest. Duct tape encircles her body, pinning her arms to her side and tethering her ankles to the wooden legs.

It is barely past eight in the morning, and already the air hangs like a sodden coat. Overcast daylight slips through the slats of the barn's walls, and some crows have made the roof their home. It's been *Caw! Caw! Caw!* ever since I got here, and it's starting to grate on my nerves.

The scattered straw on the dirt floor smells pungent, made worse by the urine-soaked stain at the crotch of Kim's taupe dress. Being on the receiving end of a stun gun can do that, especially when followed by a sedative chaser. Her humiliation brings me no joy. My goal is to make her stop killing people, not to debase her.

Seeing her tied up like that, I'm reminded of the wife beater nearly seven weeks ago. His was the last tune-up that brought me satisfaction. Gave me a reason to live. Made me feel like I was doing my small part for humanity. After that, everything got smeared with crap. I took too much sick plea-sure with the dog abuser (although I did free Shelly—now known as Maggie—so that should justify it), and with the barista, I lost control and went overboard.

I stare at Kim from my cross-legged position on the ground. She'll sleep for a while still, which is good because I need to pay a visit to her house in Brighton. First though, I need to finish snooping through her phone. Luckily for me, she has made her face-recognition setting less secure. Doesn't require a direct, open-eyed gaze. My own phone's setting is similarly disabled, but I'm rethinking that now. It's ironic, the very thing meant to make a phone secure—face recognition to unlock it—makes it wonderfully helpful to those of us who cross questionable boundaries.

I already deleted Michael's video of me, along with the screenshots she took from it. Although she claims to have another file of it on a thumb drive somewhere, I find nothing else ominous on her phone. Not that I expected her Notes app to have a bulleted list of the patients she's killed, but her phone is as featureless as she is. Medical apps, shopping apps, a meal-delivery one too. Even her contact list is thin, mostly other physicians and hospital personnel she needs to connect with on a professional level. Very few names seem personal.

Her text messages are similarly job-related, save for one from her transplant-surgeon sister who sent no less than seven photos of herself posing with her recent award, and another one from her father asking if Kim has finally considered doing a fellowship program instead of remaining "just a generalist."

I glance up at her sleeping form. "Jeez, you're not kidding. What a bunch of assholes."

After finding no other personal items on her phone, no pictures with boyfriends or girlfriends or even any pets, sympathy swells within me. Not enough to stop what I'm going to do, but enough to at least help me understand the woman's motive. Even the sickest minds have a motive. It doesn't matter if it's illogical to us. Kim is a sociopath. She hates "perfect" people who don't appreciate what they have.

Or worse, they screw it all up. In her mind, that's what Jasmine did. Got pregnant with another man's babies and then lied to Michael about it, letting him believe he was the father.

"But that doesn't make it right," I say to her.

I'm not so dimwitted as to not realize someone could say the same to me. The wife beater certainly would. The dog abuser and the barista too.

Returning to Kim's phone, I spot what I was hoping for: a home security app. I stand, my knees cracking, and gently pull her head back. Using her face once again, I unlock the app. From there I disarm her home security alarm.

I release her head, tear off a piece of duct tape, and press it against her mouth.

"Sorry, Kim," I say, and I am, but I don't want her screaming if she wakes up before I get back. Not that anyone but the crows would hear her.

After putting the roll of tape and Kim's phone in my duffel bag, I check her pockets for any items that might help her escape. My fingers brush the wet patch on her linen dress, and I again feel bad she wet herself. When I find nothing beyond two tissues and a wrapped butterscotch candy, I put my gloves back on and return to her car, ducking the light rain that has begun. The keys are still in her purse, which I placed on the front seat earlier.

I pull out a wadded T-shirt dress from my bag and change clothes in the driver's seat. The tan color and lack of a waist should help me pass as Kim. A shoulder-length wig comes next. It's blonder than Kim's highlights, but it's the closest one I have to match her.

After a glance in the rearview mirror to make sure everything is in place, I pull out onto the dirt road next to my barn and drive to Brighton.

Even in the hammering rain, I can tell Kim's neighborhood is older but pretty, with closely spaced homes and small yards. I approach her house, a sage split-level with a single-car garage and a narrow driveway.

The garage-door opener is attached to the passenger side visor. I press it open and drive inside, closing the door behind me. With this much privacy, I might not have had to dress like her. Things are working in my favor. I wonder what my neighbor Nathan would say about those odds.

Exiting Kim's car with my duffel bag, I clutch her purse under my arm, adjust my wig, and straighten my Kim-ish dress. Then, with my gloves still on, I dig in her purse for the house keys and let myself into the side entrance, which dumps into a laundry room. Thanks to my foresight and her phone app, the security system is already disarmed.

Inside the laundry room, I slip off my shoes and wander into the home, taking in the surroundings. The living room beyond the kitchen and dining room is a study of neutrals, not that I'm surprised. The kitchen, too, is awash in beige tones, but both are neat and tidy, and the open space is cozy. I wonder if she or the owner before her knocked out a wall. The home seems too midcentury for such an open design.

A jigsaw puzzle spans the oval table, the box displaying two girls blowing bubbles while puppies prance around them. I imagine Kim fitting its pieces together, reruns of ER or Law & Order on the TV in the background. For some reason this rekindles my sympathy.

Knowing I don't have all morning, I get to snooping. I'm not sure how long she will stay asleep, and I'm not such a monster that I want her waking up in the barn and being terrified for her safety.

The fact I feel this empathy reassures me I haven't completely lost my way yet. Even so, I rummage through kitchen drawers and cabinets guilt-free. Her laptop on the sofa is next, but it is password-protected, and unless I find a cheat-sheet like Michael's, I doubt I would be able to guess the code. I close it back up and move on to the bathroom vanities, followed by a spare bedroom that is furnished with a faux-distressed bedroom set and a treadmill. I end with her bedroom.

As a hospitalist, Kim makes decent money—although nowhere near as much as her transplant-surgeon sister and CEO brother—and she has no dependents, yet her bedding and furniture seem more Big Lots than Ethan Allen. Nothing wrong with being frugal, of course.

Unless you're trying to blend in.

Because you do dirty deeds.

So far, I have found nothing to incriminate her. What did I expect? A dead body under the bed?

The walk-in closet is what I search next. Its racks of clothing show so few hues that I wonder if I've gone color blind.

I flick through her dresses. So much similarity between them. As I pull out one for a closer look, something catches my eye on the wall behind it. A small gap, as if a panel is crooked.

Why would there be a panel on a closet wall, a poorly cut one at that? The answer is an easy one. It's the perfect place to hide something.

I spread the dresses apart and wedge my fingers through the gap in the drywall. I remove the makeshift panel.

And blink at what I find.

41

A collection of five-by-seven photographs stands up in the closet's cut-out gap, behind which insulation and wood frame are visible. I remove the stack from the shallow hole. All my senses tingle—and not in a good way.

The top picture is a selfie of Kim with a patient. It appears to have been created by a home printer, the quality a bit off. The patient lies supine in a hospital bed, Kim's face close to his, a slight smile on her lips. His eyes are open, but he's not smiling. In fact, he doesn't look right at all.

A quick flip through the other photos reveals similar selfies, all with a patient in a hospital bed, all of them wearing the same vacant expression.

It takes a moment for my brain to catch up with my eyes.

These patients are dead!

My body recoils in horror. Are these the people she's killed? Are the selfies her…her trophies?

I do a quick tally of them, nine in all. In some, Kim looks younger—face thinner, hair cut short by her ears. Was this back in medical school?

I can hardly believe what I'm seeing. What I'm holding. It's proof of her killings. At least it's all the proof *I* need.

My palms sweat inside my gloves. I leave the closet for the better lighting of the bedroom and study each photograph more thoroughly. Men, women, younger, older. Kim did not discriminate. All wear a death mask, eyes open or closed, mouths slack or grimacing. Kim squats next to them, her face close in for the shot, her arm extended to capture it.

I stare hard at a picture of one of the women. Her onyx hair lies matted against the pillow, angst on her pretty but clearly deceased face. This must be Jasmine, Michael's wife. The woman whose death tormented him so much he made it his mission to end me, not realizing until too late I wasn't the killer.

A noise escapes me, and I struggle to swallow my emotion. I have spent the past couple of years feeling nothing but anger or apathy, but during this past month almost every emotion in the dictionary has exploded inside me. Every emotion but peace.

I notice something else. Jasmine's photograph is the thickness of two pictures. I free it from the eight other images and flip it over.

My heart sinks.

It's Michael, Kim squatting next to him, taking a shocking, twisted, morbid selfie with the man one week ago.

I lower the picture and close my eyes. I was right. She killed him. He didn't suffer a fatal arrhythmia as she claimed. Well, he *did*, but only because she injected him with an untraceable heart-stopper. What better victim than a critically ill one? Who would think to question his death? It doesn't matter he didn't fit her MO. He was on to her, and that was all the motive she needed.

Feeling sick to my stomach, I sort through the other pictures again, this time studying the faces more closely. When I come to a middle-aged man, recognition slaps me. It's Ted Orenson, my former patient. Thin from his recent bout with pancreatitis and head turned sideways a bit, but it's him. A man Kim claims was a phony, sleazy conman and for that he deserved to die.

"Oh, Ted," I whisper. "What—"

A thump against the bedroom wall makes me jump. I'm terrified it's Kim. Terrified not because I fear her, but because she will do whatever she can to destroy the evidence I have just found.

But no, that's impossible. I'm not thinking clearly. She is duct taped to a chair in my barn.

Thunder cracks the sky. The rain pummels harder now, and outside the window a gust of wind sweeps a tree's branches back and forth. With another strong blast, the limb thumps the window, the same sound I heard moments earlier.

I exhale. My muscles relax. A tree, I can handle.

Still, I get moving. I need to put these pictures back. Leave everything in place for when I tip off the police—anonymously, of course. But first, I lay the disgusting photographs on Kim's quilted bed and take a picture of them as a group. It makes me cringe to have their death masks on my phone, but I need them as proof in case something goes wrong and she destroys the pictures before I can stop her.

When I finish, I return the horrifying images to the carved-out cubby. In doing so, I'm startled to see I have missed a few more photographs, these ones wedged deeper.

With an acidy dread, I pull them out. What depravity am I going to find this time?

When I see what they are, I'm stunned all over again.

They are pictures of me.

In the top one, I'm in Michael's hospital room, standing next to his dead body, my medical mask on, my hand clutching his. I hadn't even noticed Kim took the picture. It must have been after Polly, the nurse, left the room.

But why? To incriminate me somehow? I'm not the one posing with dead patients like the Grim Reaper.

The other pictures in this second collection are equally

surprising. They are shots of Kim and me back in residency: sitting next to each other at Grand Rounds, standing at a patient's bedside, listening to a lecture at a resident lunch. Who the hell took them? It's not like Kim and I hung out together, although the accusation she lobbed at me in Quincy Market—that I ignore and dismiss her—made it clear she held more interest in being friends than I did. What was it she said? That I always made her feel inferior? That she only wanted to be my friend? It's as if we're back in grade school.

Maybe Dan Knudson snapped the photos. Forwarded them to Kim when they were dating, hoping his perverted wish for a threesome might actually come true.

The thought makes me gag, but the final picture in this second stack of photos makes me freeze. It's me kissing Kim. Not in a romantic way, but during a skit at our faculty roast. I was playing the role of one of our attendings, a woman with long red locks and an infectious smile who everyone was gaga for. I can't remember the exact details, but I think Kim, whose acting skills were about as good as one might expect from a blank surface, assumed the role of a female patient who was infatuated with our attending. It had played well for laughs but, in retrospect, was probably in poor taste.

Regardless, who took the picture? Dan again?

It's not just the kiss in the photo that makes sweat break out on my forehead. It's what I'm wearing in the picture that does. A long auburn wig. The same one I'm wearing in Michael's video of me assaulting a wife beater in my barn.

Shit.

Is this Kim's way of framing me? She clearly has some reason for keeping these photos. If it's not to frame me, then she is far more obsessed with me than I knew.

I need to call the police, make sure they search her closet and find the pictures of her dead patients. The ones of me, however, I set aside on a shelf in the closet while I fish around the wall's makeshift storage compartment for anything else.

My fingers find a thumb drive at the bottom. It's probably the one that holds the backup copy of Michael's video and the letter she supposedly wrote that implicates me. With relief, I slip it into my pocket.

One last search of the hole in the closet wall reveals nothing else. If only she had kept vials of potassium chloride or other drugs inside it, but she is evidently not that stupid.

I picture the injectable sedative I keep at home, the last bit used to get Kim into my barn. Then I picture my more ample supply of roofies in an old tin can, as well as my stun gun, my Krav Maga certificates, and my pending online order for a new Taser cartridge. If anyone is stupid, it's me.

Still, I need the police to find these photographs. To look deeper into the patients who have died under Kim's watch. Once I've dealt with her and she is out of my barn, I'll place an anonymous call to 911. I'll tell them what I found in her house and that she is currently attacking me there. When no one answers her door, that will hopefully be enough of an exigent circumstance to allow the cops to barge in without a search warrant. Unfortunately, her laptop on the living room sofa could hold copies of the photographs of me, not to mention Michael's video, but stealing her computer would be too suspicious. Best I can do if the police make the connection is to prove her guilt and my innocence.

To help with that proof, I return to my duffel bag which I left on one of Kim's dining room chairs. The sad-looking jigsaw puzzle cluttering the table elicits no pity from me this time around, not after seeing those horrific selfies.

After stuffing the photos of me in a side pocket, I pull out Michael's laptop, the one I stole from his basement apartment. I was planning to leave it in Kim's bedroom, but after what I discovered in the closet, I decide to hide it in her secret space instead. Seems like something she would want hidden away with the pictures.

It takes a bit of elbow grease to wedge the computer into

the makeshift cubby, but after a little cramming, it fits. I stand the disgusting selfies upright in front of it and then replace the drywall panel, leaving the cover off-kilter so it will be obvious to the police. I then toss the place up a bit to make it look like a struggle took place. My plan is weak, but it's the best I can come up with on the spur of the moment.

I collect my duffel bag and Kim's purse, but before I leave, I unlock the front door to make it easier for the police to get in. Then I exit her beige world through the side garage door and climb into her car to drive back to my barn.

My initial plan was to have a little "chat" with her. A persuasive one, using the tools in my bag to get her to change her behavior or turn herself in. Foolish, I realize now. People like her (*and like you, Hope?*) don't change. If I couldn't convince her, then I figured I would cross that barn when I got to it.

But now, after finding that sickening and damning evidence in her closet, I want to sedate her again, get her back into her Altima, and dump the car—with her in it—someplace where she can sleep it off. By the time she wakes up, hopefully the police will be raiding her place.

And when she stumbles back home, they will arrest her ass.

42

My barn is a good hour's drive from Brighton, so it's nearly 11:00 a.m. by the time I arrive back with Kim's car. Rain pelted the windshield the entire way. The Altima's wipers barely kept up, and with as dark as the thunderstorm clouds are, it could just as easily be evening.

The only thing I feel like doing is curling up with Diva in my loft and forgetting I ever saw those awful images in Kim's closet. Unfortunately, that's not an option. The only option is stopping her.

Before I leave her car, I take off the wig and dress and change back to my cargo pants, T-shirt, and hoodie. After covering my head, I dart out with my duffel bag and race to the barn. Thunder cracks in the distance, followed by a burst of lightening, and by the time I release the huge padlock that secures the barn door, my clothes and the canvas of my duffel bag are soaked.

Once inside, I'm relieved to find Kim is still sitting there. Still sleeping, head lolled over. Still duct taped, thick pieces encircling her dress as well as her bare ankles. The acrid urine scent is stronger, perhaps from a second accident.

No empathy this time around. She took her patients' dignity. It's only right I take hers.

I remove the stun gun from my hoodie and tuck it into one of my many pants pockets. The syringe I leave in the duffel bag. With its lethal dose of digoxin, drawn from all the ampules I snatched from the clinic's treatment room, I don't want to risk sitting on it or doing something else stupid that sends me to an earlier grave than planned. I can't hardly check out before Kim, can I? Not after what I found in her house.

An accidental lethal injection with digoxin is unlikely. To cause a quick and deadly overdose, the drug should be injected intravenously. But I still don't want to take the chance of getting poked. Potassium chloride would be a better pharmaceutical weapon to have on hand—just ask Kim—but we don't stock that in our clinic. Not that I want to use either drug. Hopefully, things will not get that far.

I remove my drenched hoodie and drop it on the ground by my duffel bag. The air in the barn is still muggy, but the storm has lowered the temperature several degrees. Aside from the chair that holds Kim, the outbuilding contains only the green plastic tarp I dragged her in on earlier. It remains spread open on the dirt floor. All over, tiny puddles pool on the ground where the ceiling has leaked. When the wind hits right, rain sprays through the gaps in the wall as well.

"Kim," I say sharply from a few feet away.

No response.

I move closer, sidestepping a puddle, and raise her head. Her skull is a boulder in my still-gloved hand.

Is she really asleep? It has been four and a half hours since I abducted her. Maybe I shocked her too long or overshot the sedative dose. Red marks from the stun gun blemish her neck.

I squat and slap her face gently, and then more forcefully. "Kim, wake up. We've got some interesting photos to discuss."

Nothing.

"You're quite photogenic when you're posing with corpses. Seems you're obsessed with me too."

Again, nothing. Worried now, I check her carotid pulse. Its thrum is strong beneath my fingertips. Maybe she really is still out cold.

Thunder claps outside, and a gust of wind rattles the loose sideboards. Lightening electrifies the barn's interior, but a second later the daytime darkness returns.

What if she's faking? I need to drag her back out and abandon her in her car someplace while the police search her house, assuming they will come that quickly after I call them. I can't risk her waking up and fighting me while I do that. I had planned to dose her with a bottle of roofie-infused water, which I figured she would gobble up in her thirst, unaware of its alteration, but how can she drink it if she's conked out? My well of IV sedative runneth dry, and I need more reassurance of her compliance than simply another round with the stun gun.

I stand and pull her head back again, this time yanking it up by her hair. She is as lax as a newborn colt. I pluck up one of her eyelids. Her pupil is still small from sedation, but that tells me nothing.

Back-stepping to my bag, I retrieve the scissors. After a brief hesitation, I start cutting away the tape around her ankles. I'm almost disappointed. I had hoped to interrogate her. Of course, it's a moot point now that I've found those pictures, and good God those pictures are worth a million words.

Once Kim's feet are free, I work on the tape that binds her torso and pins her arms to her side. Before I release her, I pull the stun gun from my pocket just in case.

Once her body is free, she flops over. I reach under her shoulders from behind and heft her off the chair. The chair falls, and I nearly do too, but soon I'm dragging her back to the tarp, my stun gun awkwardly gripped in my right hand should I need to zap her.

And that's when it happens.

The woman I convinced myself was still asleep—because she is too crummy of an actress to be otherwise, right?—suddenly comes alive. With a grunt, she uses the force of her legs to press her loafered feet against the dirt ground and propel herself sideways. Before I can even react, she grabs the stun gun in my hand and zaps me through my V-neck tee, just below the shoulder.

My muscles cramp and I fall down on my side, toppled more from the force of her sudden movement than the short zap itself.

It happened so quickly, so startling fast, and yet I wonder how I could be so clueless. Why do I keep underestimating her? She has had everyone fooled for years, killing people right under our noses, all while fading into the background like the taupe dress she wears. Of *course* a sociopath like that could fake sleep.

As she stares down at me, her face an unreadable slate but her breaths heavy, I understand I have at least outsmarted her in something: the use of a stun gun. While I had zapped her for a good four seconds directly on her neck, she blasted me for less than one second through clothing. It will take little time for me to recover.

Then she outsmarts me again. She bends over, places the prongs against my bare neck, and electrifies me once more. Luckily, the contact is no longer than before. She must not be aware that the quicker the zap, the shorter the incapacitation.

Regardless, with this one my bladder empties.

Fucking irony.

Slowly, Kim steps back and rights the fallen chair. She drags it closer to me and sits. The upper half of my rain-soaked body lies on the plastic tarp, the lower half on the dirt.

Water drips on my face from a leak in the roof. As it does, I try to clear the voltage-triggered fog in my brain.

She shakes her head and sighs. "Did you really think you could beat me at this? Everything else in life, sure, but this?" Her impassive voice shifts to a bizarre and disturbing girlish tone. "Oh, look, I'm Hope Sullivan. So perfect and smart. Solving diagnostic puzzles. Getting picked as chief resident." She pokes a finger in her cheek as if carving out a dimple. "Everybody loves me. Everybody feels sorry for me. Mommy dead, Daddy dead, boyfriend dead. Boo hoo, sob sob. Poor little broken Hope." Her voice returns to its normal pitch. "You think you're the only one to suffer personal pain?"

I strain to speak. To blink. To do anything.

I can't.

Kim leans back in the chair and studies the stun gun. "So you found my pictures. I suppose you think you're going to turn me in now."

Apparently, Kim is more perceptive than I gave her credit for.

"But what proof do you really have? The only thing those pictures prove is that I get my kicks from posing with dead patients." She makes a weird chortle. "That's my favorite time with them, you know. That quiet lull before the orderly fetches their bodies and wheels them to the morgue. Plenty of time to pose for pictures. Sick, sure, and I'll probably lose my job, but it's not a crime. Not that I know of, anyway. You?"

She stares at me as if expecting an answer. A trickle of drool slides down my cheek.

"For you, on the other hand, questions will be raised. For starters, there's that red wig. If you think the police can't prove you're the star of Michael Yerli's video then you're not as smart as I thought you were." She flips the stun gun to her other hand. "And suppose they do think I'm guilty? Snoop through some of my patients' charts maybe. Find the loosest thread that might point to a suspicious death. Well, then, I'll tell them we're in it together." Her expressionless face now puckers at the lips, and she blows me a kiss.

My toes move inside my sneakers.

"You kissed me, remember?" she says. "I have a picture of it. Lots of pictures of you and me together. I found them at Dan's place back when he and I were dating. Gross, right? So I took them from him. You probably found them too." She sniffs. "He was the one obsessed with you, not me. Well, okay, maybe me a little bit too. Maybe Dan thought I'd be so desperate for a boyfriend he could use me as a stepping-stone to you."

The tiniest wiggle of my finger. My muscles are coming back.

"He probably jerked off to that picture of us kissing—skit or not." She grunts a laugh, and it's frightening in its flatness.

My tongue sweeps my mouth. I'm pretty sure I could bite my lip if I tried.

"So my point is, if it comes to that, I'll tell the police we were in it together, that you got off on that kind of thing. Miss Angel of Death, you know? After all, some of the patient notes are in your name. I made sure of it. My insurance policy, so to speak."

As if prearranged by the gods to time with her wickedness, a round of thunder booms outside, and wind shakes the rickety barn.

"When the police watch the video of you torturing a man, they'll know how deranged you are. You took pliers to his nipple, for crying out loud. So yeah, Miss Perfect, you'll be the one to go down." She leans forward in the chair, her shapeless dress bunched at the waist. "Imagine poor Ada Jackson. She'll find out her favorite doctor is a psychopath and a serial killer."

Kim is right, of course. It could play out exactly as she says. Even if I check myself out of this universe, she will ruin any legacy I leave behind.

"Who knows?" Kim says. "Maybe I'll even pay Ada another visit. No telling what might happen if I do."

It's at this moment I know I have to kill her. No police. No carting her off to jail. She needs to die. If she doesn't, at best we will both go to prison. At worst, she will go free and keep killing.

I can't let that happen.

She rises and tests the stun gun on the air, as if debating whether to make it a part of her future arsenal. Using her momentary distraction, I allow my limbs the tiniest motion, just to make sure I can move them as a unit.

I can.

She squats down next to me. "All that being said, I can't have the police involved. Even if I get off scot-free, I would be on their radar, and I'm not ready to be done yet. So I think you can understand why I have to end this between us right now. I wish there was a more humane way. Suffocation is an awful way to go, but it's all I have at my disposal." She shrugs, as if that's an apology, and stares at the plastic tarp that contains half of me.

She reaches out with the stun gun, but before she can zap me again, before she can roll me up in the tarp and turn me into a smothered sausage, I punch the weapon away with as much force as I can muster. It's not my best delivery, but it's enough to make the stun gun fly from her hand and send her staggering on her haunches.

Using that window, I roll out of her reach. She hurries toward the stun gun.

As swiftly as my quaking limbs will allow, I stand, and just as she reaches for the weapon, I kick the top of her hand with my heel, axe stomping the soft tissue there.

She grunts in pain but doesn't release the stun gun.

Using her crouched position to my advantage, I drop down and elbow punch the base of her skull. It's one of Krav Maga's dirty moves, and even with my weaker muscles, she's no physical match for me. She murders with needles and IV ports, not eye gouges and throat kicks.

My elbow punch sprawls her flat, her dress twisting up by her thighs, but she quickly rolls over on the wet ground. When she does, I land another axe stomp, this time to her solar plexus. Air whooshes out of her, and the expression her face makes is almost comical.

I am about to kick her again but hold back. I shouldn't leave too many bruises. Her death needs to look like an accident.

After a final elbow to her throat, not as hard as with Michael but with enough juice to subdue her, I pry the stun gun from her hand and plant it against her neck near the mark that's already there.

I zap for three seconds. Once again she's mine. This time though, I can't let her live.

With her eyes pinned on me, I drag her onto the tarp. By now, the barn floor is full of incriminating evidence, but I'll deal with that later. I'll bleach away and hose down whatever the scattered waterfalls don't.

Once she is on the tarp, I shuffle back to my duffel bag. A headache from the stun gun's voltage rips through my brain, each thunderclap outside amplifying it, but at least all my muscles are fully under my command. I grab the digoxin from the bag and return to Kim.

She eyes the syringe. Thanks to her own electrical charge, she is unable to show any fear, but I can smell it.

I crouch down next to her. "Looks like the tables have turned."

As soon as I speak, a different voice surfaces inside me. The voice of Hope Past, I suspect. Or maybe it's Manuel or my parents. Regardless, it tells me I shouldn't do this. That if I do, I will cross a line that can never be uncrossed. But it's a very short line, isn't it? One that will end tonight with those pills in my nightstand.

"I'm sorry," I say, as much to the voice as to Kim, "but I can't let you go on killing." I choose my words carefully. "You and me, we both take our resentments out on the world, so maybe that makes us alike. But I only give terrible people their due. You? You take from decent people what you don't have. What you will never have."

I pull the tourniquet out of one of my many pockets and wrap it around the short sleeve of her dress to avoid leaving a mark on her skin. Then I uncap the syringe and place my finger in the crook of her elbow, locating the needle mark from my earlier injection of sedative. Nathan's words about injecting someone in the eye to avoid autopsy detection come back to me. If I could, I would dose her there, just for some poetic symmetry, but the drug needs to go in a vein. Besides, I'm not sure Nathan is right about that.

With one last pause, I weigh my options again. If Kim goes free, she will keep killing innocent patients, and she will take my reputation with her. She might even go after the people in my life. Ada, Terrence, Frank, Nathan.

I press my thumb against the syringe's plunger and bring the needle toward the plump vein in her antecubital fossa. What I'm doing is for the greater good. Isn't that one of the ethical principles they teach us in med school? Of course, they also teach us about beneficence and to first do no harm so…

I shake the philosophical arguments away. In my opinion, to save the future lives of anyone Kim plans to snuff out, it is the right thing to do. Maybe not the legal thing. Maybe not the moral thing, but in my mind, the *right* thing.

Before my brain can counterargue again, before the old me surfaces and releases Kim out of guilt or morality, allowing her to become an even more twisted and murderous Kim Lombardi 2.0, I slip the needle into her juicy antecubital vein and inject the lethal dose of digoxin until the syringe is empty.

I am now a killer.

43

Later that evening, after the deed is done, I return to my condo, shower, and put on leggings and an oversized top. With a cup of chamomile tea warming my hands, I sit near my massive windows and stare out at the harbor beyond. The thunderstorm passed shortly after Kim did. There must be some meaning in that. Although a gentle rain continues, it carries a cleansing energy, beading off Massachusetts Bay in a steady, hypnotic fashion.

Diva purrs in my lap. She seems particularly attentive tonight, as if aware I won't be here much longer. A lump forms in my throat. Is this truly what I want?

Funny, now that I have made the decision to end my life, the tea bursts with flavor like never before, the harbor shines more luminously than I've ever seen, and Diva's devotion comforts me more than I ever thought possible. Even today's affirmation bucks my decision: *I am strong enough to conquer life's punches.*

But it has to be this way. I am a killer now. Whether Kim deserved to die or not is up for debate, but the fact I was the one who silenced her is not. Now I am the monster who needs to be put down.

The world doesn't need me. Not really. Sure, my skills as a doctor might be missed, but there will always be other doctors. My clinical work is not saving the world. Besides, my license might get suspended. At least now I'll never have to know. Martin Hernandez will have one less case to deal with. And my will stipulates that all my money goes to charity, so in that sense, Boston is better off without me.

Despite what I like to tell myself, my vigilante work isn't saving the world either. Whether one fewer bully or ten, there are a million more to take their place. I liked to think I was helping people, changing the course of their lives, both the brutes and their victims, but maybe it was all spin. Maybe my seeking justice for others was simply a failed means to get justice for my parents. Each miscreant brought down was one step closer to justice for Mom and Dad. For Manuel, too, I suppose, because cancer is just a beast in a different form.

But my parents are still gone. Manuel is still gone. My unborn baby is still gone. The person who needed to pay for my parents' deaths has already been paying in full. Bo's daily acts of goodwill, his deprivation of the material gifts his profession could bring, his constant shame and sorrow over what his addiction wrought is more payback than anything I could deliver with my own hands. More than anything ten years in prison could do.

"I understand this now," I say to Diva, treasuring the steady heartbeat of her body, the gentle nudges of her nose against my palm. "But it's too late."

And it *is* too late. As Kim said, I am broken. Living in such a dark world for the past couple of years has leached the color from my soul. I have hurt people. For the greater good, I told myself, but I hurt them nonetheless. Their comeuppance fed me. Sustained me. Turned me into something wicked and tarnished. It's one thing to torture a wife beater or dog abuser, but it's another thing entirely to kill. Now that I have jumped over that line, how could I be sure I would never jump it again?

"So yes," I say out loud, swallowing the last sip of tea and placing the mug on the window ledge near my feet. "It's *me* I need to protect the world from now."

It's ironic, too, in a *that-figures* sort of way, because I don't think anyone will suspect me in Kim's death. I'm not sure the medical examiner will even label it a homicide. I was careful to cover my tracks. Maybe he or she will simply believe Kim took too much digoxin, a drug she was already on. Its therapeutic levels are not that far from its toxic ones, which is why we switch patients over to newer medications nowadays, but as in Ada's case, Kim must have thought, *Why fix what isn't broken?*

After I injected her with the digoxin and her heart stopped, I wrapped her up in the tarp like a mummy, just as she had planned to do to me, and dragged and hefted her into the trunk of her car.

I made sure no visible traces of either of us remained in the barn. No lost earring, no drop of blood, no puddle of urine I hadn't already smoothed over with dirt. I even considered burning the place down, but I've read enough about forensics to know that finding biologic traces outdoors after Mother Nature has done her thing is unlikely. The inside of my barn, with its leaking roof, mud-caked floor, and frequent animal visitors who burrow under the loose boards is about as outdoors as an interior can get.

Besides, opaque LLC or not, a fire could draw attention to me. No need to do that when nothing about Kim's death should point anyone my way. Michael's video is gone from her photos app and her cloud account, and her backup thumb drive has been smashed by my hammer. If a file of the video exists on her laptop, I'm at risk, but it would be difficult to definitively prove the attacker was me.

And who is to say the wife beater would even come forward? Should the police track him down, he would likely deny that was him in the video. Guys like him would rather have their nipples wrenched than have the world see a woman take them down. With no victim to complain, how much effort would be spent in investigating? I feel pretty safe on that count. The only tie Kim will have to me is as the hospitalist taking care of my patients. The hospital notes she submitted under my name cast doubt her way, not mine.

Not that the police will need more doubt when they find the death pictures and Michael's stolen laptop in her closet.

Once she was in the Altima's trunk outside my barn, I changed back to my Kim outfit in the front seat of her car. Then I drove the hour back to her place. Carefully, so as not to draw any state-patrol eyes my way. The last thing I needed was a cop asking me to open the trunk. *Surprise!*

Inside Kim's garage, with my gloves still on, I gripped her purse under my arm and opened the side house door. Getting her out of the trunk and up three steps into the house was the tricky part. I had already removed her body from the tarp, not wanting to drag barn debris into the house, and I was exhausted from the day's events, my fatigue making her seem heavier.

Once inside, I slipped off my shoes and made sure all the home's blinds were closed. I also relocked the front door. No need for the police to barge in now, unlike with my initial plan.

Lifting Kim under the arms, I dragged her through the kitchen, past the sad jigsaw puzzle on the dining room table, through the living room, and into the spare bedroom with the antique dresser set and treadmill.

After catching my breath, I returned to the primary bedroom and retrieved Michael's laptop from the makeshift cubby in the closet. Doing that meant having to see those awful death selfies again, but I knew it would be best to have Kim's prints on his laptop.

After placing her dead fingertips all over it, I returned the laptop and pictures to the hole in the closet drywall. Once I sealed it back up, haphazardly to make it more obvious, I rummaged through Kim's dresser drawers and closet for workout clothes. Shorts, sports bra, wicking T-shirt, gym socks, and sneakers. Back in the spare bedroom, I changed her clothes. Twice, the realization of what I was doing made me pause in shame, but I couldn't let emotion rule me now. After each hesitation, I slipped back into clinical mode and completed the costume change, returning her stained dress along with her shoes to the laundry room, where I ran the dress through the washer with a load of clothes.

Inside a kitchen cabinet, I found a water bottle and filled it halfway. In the spare bedroom, I placed the cup on her lips and in her hand to leave evidence behind of its use. After putting it in the cup holder on her treadmill, I dragged her body close to the exercise machine and turned her prone. Then—and this part made me hate myself even more—I pulled her head up and slammed it onto the side of the tread-mill, after which I positioned her body in an awkward position with her head and neck at the base of the machine and the arm I injected over her head. When I powered the treadmill on, I set it to a brisk walking pace of 4.5.

I stood back and surveyed my work, watching the belt *thwump thwump* beneath her cheek, neck, and arm, leaving nasty burns in its wake and a cannonball of shame in my gut.

My hope was that eventually someone would realize she wasn't returning calls or messages, likely someone from the hospital since her personal connections were sparse, and send the police to check on her. Once there, the police—and later the pathologist doing the autopsy—might assume she fell and hit her head, probably after a sudden cardiac arrest. Given her history of congenital heart disease and surgical scars from childhood operations (I saw them when I undressed her but already knew about her condition), the pathologist may very well attribute a faulty ticker as the cause.

He or she will probably check a digoxin level, along with a general tox screen. Although digoxin would be expected in Kim's system, my overdose will push the level high. That could raise questions. I will have to hope they assume she was either taking too much of the drug or not metabolizing it properly. Working in my favor is its narrow therapeutic window.

I will also have to hope the bruises she sustained during our tussle and the stun-gun burns I gave her, not to mention the injection mark in the crook of her elbow, will be written off as damage from the fall on the treadmill. If I'm lucky, the treadmill belt will grind them off, hiding the fact they were premortem should anyone look that thoroughly.

That is a lot of hoping, I know. A deeper forensic examination could grind all those hopes into dust. But if foul play isn't initially expected—and with her cardiac history there is a good chance it won't be—then an autopsy examination might be less intense. Either way, it's unlikely to be traced back to me, and when those sick pictures in her closet are found, along with Michael's laptop, all focus will be on what *she* did, not on what someone *might* have done to her.

At least this is what I have been telling myself all day, between bouts of stomach cramps and throat tightness brought on by my monstrous behavior.

I cleaned up any last traces of me from her car and house, including removing the tarp from her trunk and stuffing it into my duffel bag. Then I left her purse on the kitchen counter, both her keys and her phone inside it. That meant I couldn't lock the door, but leaving a side garage door unlocked isn't suspicious. Even if my hair and skin cells were found in her car, I would say she's given me a ride or two in the past. Similar story if traces of me remain in the house.

Then I removed my still-wet cargo pants and hoodie from my duffel bag and changed out of my Kim outfit into my own clothes, cinching the hoodie around my face. After stuffing my dress and wig into the duffel bag, I slipped out the back door of the garage into her backyard. With the rain, no neighbors were outside to see me. They probably wouldn't have spotted me over her privacy fence anyway. After walking four miles, jittery and soggy, I deemed myself far enough away to power on my phone and call an Uber. I always turn my phone off during trips to my barn. No need to leave a GPS footprint.

Now I sit here, an empty mug of tea on the window ledge, drizzle pattering the glass and the bay below, Diva purring on my lap.

Diva.

She is the one I have to focus on now.

I raise her to my face and nuzzle my nose into her fur. "You're the only one I can't bear to leave."

It's as if she understands because her tiny tongue nips the side of my cheek.

After a few more seconds of soaking her in, I sigh and lower her to the floor. With a heavy heart, I head across the hallway and knock on Nathan's door. He is quick to answer, and, as has been the case ever since he consoled me after my freakout on Bo, his face folds in concern. I have tried to reassure him I'm fine, but it's obvious he doesn't believe me. For a numbers guy, he is surprisingly perceptive.

"Hey, Nathan." I try to sound nonchalant. "Can I ask you a favor?"

"Of course."

His unconditional response warms my heart. I think I'm going to miss him.

"You like Diva, right?"

"I do," he says, "and I realized I might already have antibodies to toxoplasmosis because my aunt had cats when I was a boy. As for the actual percentage of people who do, it's maybe around—" He cuts himself off and narrows his eyes. "Why?"

Damn. Maybe he is *too* perceptive.

I shrug. "You know, in case I need someone to keep her if I go on a trip, that kind of thing."

The muscles in his face relax. "Oh, yeah, sure. You planning on traveling somewhere? You still have to worry about Covid. It's never going away. In fact"—he rubs the front of his neck—"I was wondering if I could be catching a new strain of it. My throat is a little scratchy."

The next thing I know I'm looking in the back of Nathan's throat with his phone's flashlight and palpating his lymph nodes. It actually feels good to taste this bite of normality.

Back inside my own loft, the momentary lightness fades, and the darkness returns. My body resists every step I take. Toward my bedroom, toward the nightstand, toward my exit-door pills inside the drawer.

I realize I might not want this. I'm not sure I *ever* wanted it. Not really, anyway.

I also know I don't have a choice. I justified my killing of Kim by the fact she could no longer kill anyone else. Shouldn't the same apply to me? How can I be sure I will never do it again?

I sit on the edge of my bed, its duvet neat and fluffy. I open the nightstand drawer and remove my mother's scarf, my father's glasses, and Manuel's book about how to be a good husband. A tear falls down my cheek. I swipe it away with the back of my hand and pull out the bottle of pills. Manny's name on it brings me some comfort. I have never been a religious person, but I would like to believe our souls will reconnect. Folly, no doubt, but a folly I need to cling to if I'm going to make this happen.

I uncap the bottle. As soon as I do, Diva pounces up on the bed. She sits at the end and stares unwaveringly at me. My guilt is immense.

"Don't worry," I tell her, my voice cracking. "Nathan is a really nice man. The kind humanity needs more of. I left the door unlocked for him. He'll be the first to come looking when no one hears from me—of that I've no doubt. He'll buy you the good food, too, I bet."

Realizing I'm stalling, I reach out to stroke her neck but pull my hand back before I can. It will make it too difficult.

Instead, I pour all the pills into my cupped palm, ignoring as best I can that nugget of uncertainty in my mind. Just as I am about to toss the tablets into my mouth and chase them down with the glass of water on my nightstand, a loud knock on the door makes me jump.

Several tablets spill onto my duvet. I sit there, perfectly still, waiting. Another knock follows.

Nathan. It must be Nathan. Who else could it be?

44

A third knock on the door now. Clearly, whoever it is isn't going away.

Tony didn't ring to inform me I had a visitor, so unless the doorman was using the facilities, it has to be Nathan. Plus, no one could get into the building without being buzzed in.

But what if the doorman *was* using the restroom? What if another tenant let the person in? Wouldn't be the first time. That means it could be Bo again. Anyone else would have texted first.

I scoop the fallen pills off my duvet and pour them, along with the ones still in my hand, back into the bottle. If it is Nathan and I don't answer, he'll get worried, especially given my agitation of late. That will risk him calling 911, which will bring an intervention for me too soon, one that could result in my survival.

I stuff the bottle back into the drawer and rise from the bed. Diva is at my heels. Together we leave the bedroom and cross the short distance to my door. When I open it, any words I was about to say die in my mouth.

It's not Nathan.

Or Bo.

It's Polly. The nurse on the internal medicine ward.

I couldn't be more stunned if Kim's corpse itself appeared. Why in the world is Polly here? We know each other from the ward, sure, but only on the most basic level. She was hired shortly before I finished residency, and we only worked a few shifts together before I moved on to the clinic.

Oh God. Has someone been to Kim's house? Has her body already been found? This soon?

Before, I felt only angst and guilt for what I had done to Kim. Anxiety took a backseat. I figured I wouldn't be around for any consequences. But now? Now panic swells within me like a mushroom cloud.

My shocked muteness must creep Polly out.

"Um, I'm sorry," she says. "I can leave."

"H-h-how…?"

She must think I'm about to ask how she got in the building—and honestly, I'm not sure what I was going to ask —because she says, "I slipped in when someone left to go walk their dog. There was no one at the front desk, so I thought it would be okay to come up, but I'll go if—"

My intelligible speech finally returns. "No, of course not." I hold the door wide, glancing over at Nathan's unit. No doubt he's peeking through his peephole, making sure it's not Bo again. "Come in."

The petite nurse enters. Her dark hair is parted down the side and tucked behind her ears. Her linen pants fit loose with a drawstring around the waist, and her sleeveless top is modest with a high neck. She fidgets with its hem, and I wait for the worst. Someone must have found Kim and thinks I had something to do with it, but why Polly is delivering the news, I have no freaking idea.

"Again, I'm sorry to bother you. I got your address from Dr. Knudson."

I flash back to a hospital meeting where Dan weaseled my building's location out of me. He wanted to know if a waterview loft was worth the investment. *Maybe he can buy my place when I die. He would probably get off on having my ghost haunt him.*

"I hope that's okay." Polly hugs her bare arms close to her torso.

"Please, sit." I direct her to my kitchen island. "Tea? Water?" I take in her skittish demeanor. "Maybe we should make it wine instead?"

Her gaze covets the bottle of Pinot Grigio I pull from the fridge, and I can tell she wants it, but as I reach for a glass in my cabinet, she says, "No. I better not. He…well…he might smell it on my breath. I'll take some water though."

He? Who is he?

Polly has my full attention now.

I pour us both a glass of strawberry-infused water and join her at the island.

"Who's he?" I ask calmly, almost professionally, as if I am interviewing a patient in clinic.

"My…" Polly takes a sip of water, her fingers trembling around the glass. "My husband. He's…um…he's why I'm here."

Well, this is interesting.

For the first time, I notice the bruises on her arms. A faded yellow one on the inside of her left wrist. A green one shaped like the state of Florida on her right forearm. An angry purple one on her upper inner arm just below her armpit.

That one is fresh.

I glance at her neck. A faded linear bruise peeks out above her shirt there too.

"Your husband beats you," I say in a soft but matter-of-fact tone. The beating part is obvious. The part that isn't is why she's here telling me.

She hesitates and then nods. "Yes, I found…" She shakes her head and starts to rise off the stool. "I'm sorry, I don't even know how to say this. Maybe I better—"

I reach out and place a hand on her forearm. "Just say it. That's the easiest way. Nothing surprises me, believe me."

She lowers herself again and takes a deep breath. "Remember that patient, Michael Yerli? I went through his phone the day after he woke up from his coma."

Okay. Consider me surprised.

"I wasn't trying to snoop," she says. "Really. I was just trying to see if there was someone we could call. A family member or something. Until you came, no one had visited, and, well…"

"I was too late."

"Yes, but that's not why I'm here. When I was going through his phone, I opened his photos. Thought I might find someone in there." She looks at me and adds quickly, "It was wrong, I know, but I just felt so bad for him, especially after he woke up. No one to make him feel better."

She pauses, as if not sure whether to continue, so I nod with calm encouragement, but on the inside my heart thumps behind my ribs. I prepare myself for what she's about to say. She saw the video of me, and now I'm going down.

"Well, I…I found a strange video." She lowers her eyes. "It was a woman. Hurting a man. A man who, from what I could tell, deserved it."

I try to play it cool, but my chest rises and falls too visibly for her not to notice my unease. Is she here to blackmail me? Is that it? Now I understand why she seemed so shy around me the night Michael died.

"But while I was watching the video," she says, "Michael woke up. I jumped when I saw him staring at me and apologized for invading his privacy, but he just kept looking at me. He seemed focused on my arm, a bruise I had there." She glances down at the faded bruise near her wrist. "This one. My scrub jacket had ridden up. And then he noticed the slap mark on my cheek. I thought I'd hid it with makeup, but maybe not so well, I guess."

"And?" I prompt, beginning to see where this is going. My unease morphs into a feeling I can't yet articulate, but a tiny flame alights inside me.

"While I was apologizing, Michael pointed to his bedside table for his paper and pen. He couldn't talk well. His vocal cords were injured."

I nod. *That's because of me.* If only I could take that kick back. Rewind it all. He and I could have brought down Kim together.

"I wheeled his bedside table closer," Polly says, "and he wrote something down. When I read it, I could hardly believe it."

The flame in me burns a little higher.

"He wrote that it was you in the video. That I should call you. That you would help me."

Higher. Hotter.

"Could you, Dr. Sullivan? I mean, would you? I won't tell anyone, I promise. But I…"

She starts crying and rubbing her arms, her fingers caressing bruises in different stages of healing. I now understand why she wore a sleeveless shirt to come see me.

"I can't take it anymore," she says. "I tried to get a restraining order once. Or at least I told him I would. He said if I even dared think about that he would kill me, and then he beat me so bad I believed him. He even pulled out his gun."

"Do you have kids?" The flame of vengeance leaps so high now it's licking my throat.

"No, thank God, no. He doesn't want them."

"Do you?"

Her eyes tear up more, and she nods. "Yes, very much, but I don't dare have them with him around. I'm too scared he'd hurt them. He controls everything. My money. My phone. Our credit cards. Where I am every minute of the day. The only reason I'm here now is because I convinced him another nurse needed me to cover her for a couple hours. I parked at the hospital and walked over here. Left my phone in the glove box because he tracks my location."

"Have you considered going to a shelter?"

She wipes her eyes. "I made it as far as the front door once, but then I realized even if I tried to run away, he would hunt all over the country for me, and I would never feel safe. He'd find me, and he'd kill me. They always do, don't they?"

Even though it might make her feel better, I don't dispute her because she is probably right. Some women get away, sure. Others end up dead from trying. Far too many.

Polly does not deserve to be one of them.

"So will you?" she asks. "Will you help me?"

"You want me to make him stop, is that it?"

"Yes."

I could tell her she has made a mistake. I could say Michael was high on morphine when he told her the woman in the video was me. It was only his imagination. But not only would that fail Polly and put her at risk, it would betray Michael. He told Polly I would help her for a reason. He had seen what I could do. Seen what I *would* do. And he trusted me enough to do it for Polly, to keep going after the monsters of this world, just like I went after the monster who killed his wife and then him. Honoring his trust in me would be one more step I could take to atone for the injuries I caused him.

"Will you?" Polly asks again.

I twist my water glass around on the granite island. I picture the pills in my nightstand. If I don't take them, I'll face another chat with Martin Hernandez from the Medical Board. As Frank suggested, I'll need to hire legal counsel. I'll also face possible disciplinary actions for dipping into unauthorized medical charts should someone finally take notice and my stolen-laptop story doesn't fly. And, the big granddaddy of them all, I could face murder charges if someone connects me to Kim's death, no matter how unlikely that is.

Diva weaves around Polly's feet. My heart squeezes with

affection for the cat. I'll miss her so much if I leave this world. I think about my friend and colleague, Terrence. I picture his skull ties and his spy novel that I'll never get to read (or see Idris Elba star in). And what about Nathan? Won't I miss him too? And Frank, Irene, Rishi, Alice. All these people have touched my life. Even Bo manages to worm his way into my sentimental montage.

Then I imagine all the other Pollys out there, people who have been abused, swindled, neglected, wronged.

If there was ever a sign from the universe, surely Polly showing up at my door is it. Maybe my tune-ups don't have to save the world. Maybe they only need to save one person at a time.

The fire ignites my entire body now. Its glow practically lights up the loft.

The pills can wait. Maybe even be discarded forever.

As if to say *I told you so*, an affirmation from my phone app pops into my mind: *I will accept who I am, and I will make peace with it.*

That peace envelops me. I lock eyes with Polly.

"Yes," I say. "Yes, I will help you."

THE END

AUTHOR'S NOTE

The characters, storylines, and medical institutions in *Broken Hope*, including Boston General and Congress Medical Clinic, are fictional, created by me, and without the use of AI. As always, I tried to be as accurate as possible in my world-building, but some liberties were taken. For example, although Hope has to work around the restrictions of HIPAA, in real life she might have faced even more roadblocks in her chart-snooping. Electronic medical record systems are always evolving. I also took some liberties with the Medical Board investigative process to move the story along. The actual procedures vary from state to state. Furthermore, I made minimal references to Covid. I think we're all tired of reading about that.

I'm not exactly known for light fiction, but *Broken Hope* is even darker than my usual fare. This probably reflects my mood during the challenges of Covid, followed by some family heartbreaks we've suffered. But writing is an escape, and I think book lovers *read* to escape, so I sincerely hope I have helped you do that. If so, maybe you would consider leaving a review on your book site of choice. Reviews help

other readers decide if they, too, might like to give it a go, and
your support means the world to me.

ACKNOWLEDGMENTS

Thank you so much, dear reader, for your interest in *Broken Hope*. From books to TV to the internet, entertainment options abound, so the fact you chose my book to settle in with brightens my day. Thank you as well to Mike, Susan, and author Kevin Brennan for your early reads and suggestions. I appreciate the feedback a great deal. I'm also grateful to Tea Jagodic for her wonderful cover art. As always, thank you to my online friends, both writers and readers alike. It's a joy to interact with you! And finally, a thank you to my husband for his (weirdly eager…) willingness to act out scenes of physical struggle with me. For *Broken Hope*, that meant pulling him across the floor on a tarp to see if it's possible a woman my size could do that.

It is.

ABOUT THE AUTHOR

Carrie Rubin is a physician turned novelist who writes medical-themed thrillers. She enjoys exploring other genres as well, so she has a novel of magical realism published under the pen name Dannie Boyd and a cozy mystery under the pen name Morgan Mayer. She is a member of the International Thriller Writers association and lives in Northeast Ohio.

For more information, visit:

www.carrierubin.com

ALSO BY CARRIE RUBIN

The Liza Larkin Series:

Fatal Rounds

Malignant Assumptions

The Benjamin Oris Series:

The Bone Elixir

The Bone Hunger

The Bone Curse

Other Medical Thrillers:

Eating Bull

The Seneca Scourge

Pen Name Dannie Boyd:

Fractured Oak

Pen Name Morgan Mayer:

The Cruise Ship Lost My Daughter

9 781958 160077